WHERE BEAUTY NEVER FADES

WHERE BEAUTY NEVER FADES

A Destined Encounters Novel

Nikota Brault

For You...you know who you are 💛

Chapter One

The departure boards blink at me, the destinations all begging for me to pick them to be my escape.

"Boarding for train nine eighteen New York to Chicago!" The voice crackles through the loudspeaker overhead.

I adjust the strap of the bag digging into my shoulder. It's weighed down with as many of my belongings as I could fit inside. The suitcase at my feet has the rest. The things I left behind didn't hold enough meaning for me to worry about bringing with me. I shift my focus from the board to the station around me. Even at this time of night, Grand Central Station is a bustling hub. People rush around me, hurrying to and from their trains. A mom tugs on the hand of a sleepy pajama-clad child while a man and woman embrace in a corner, tears streaming down her face.

"Last call for train one eleven New York to Philadelphia!"

The ticket clutched in my hand could be for any of these trains that are waiting to whisk people away. I'd asked the woman at the ticket booth to give me a one-way ticket to anywhere—I didn't care where. She'd hesitated, searching my face before nodding and printing the ticket. Something about me must have been enough to convince her. Sadness? Desperation? Whatever it was, it had been enough to keep her from asking all of the personal questions that I could tell were on the tip of her tongue. She didn't tell me where I was headed, and I haven't had the nerve to look yet. The possibilities that this tiny piece of paper could bring me are both terrifying and exhilarating.

I feel a brush against my shoulder as someone joins me at the boards. I can hear him mumbling to himself under his breath, and I try to sneak a glance sideways at him. From the corner of my eye, I can see that he's anxiously scanning the boards.

"Bloody hell, where is it?" he mutters to himself, still searching the boards.

I keep my eyes forward and try to focus on my situation.

"S'cuse me? Miss?"

I turn and am forced to tilt my head up to meet the steady blue-eyed gaze of the man next to me. His voice is deep, and the accent I thought I'd detected is thick but smooth, capturing me to my core. Dirty blonde shaggy hair falls into his eyes, and the stubble on his chin gives away the fact that he hasn't shaved in a couple of days.

"S'cuse me, but, um, I'm trying to find my train. It's the uh"—he pulls out his ticket—"The 9-1-8. I'm afraid I've gone and missed it."

I don't answer right away, and he bends to try and meet my eyes.

"Miss? Are you alright?"

"Oh, shit, sorry." I blink, shaking my head a little, embarrassed for just gawking. "Yes, I'm fine. You're trying to find your train. What was the number again?"

"The 9-1-8. Says platform twenty-two."

"I think that's the one on the other end of the boarding area. It hasn't left yet though. They just called to start boarding."

"Whew! Good. Thanks so much." Relief washes over him, and he smiles, revealing an uneven front tooth and dimples.

My stomach dips at the sight of those dimples, and I have to look away before more gawking ensues. He turns to leave, and I split my attention between his retreating back and the departure boards. I catch that there are words on the back of his shirt. 'It might not be easy, but it'll be worth it.' The words hit me in the gut, and before I realize what I'm doing, I call after him.

"Hey, hold on a second." I have no idea what I'm doing.

He turns back to me, a brow raised. "Everything alright?"

I clench my fists, and I feel the ticket still clutched in my hand. "Can I ask you a favor?"

"I don't know, can you?" He winks at me, obviously joking. "Go on then, ask away."

"I..." I hesitate, not sure how to ask without sounding completely insane. "I don't know where I'm going."

His head cocks to the side, and his face scrunches in confusion. "Like what platform? Love, clearly I don't know my way around this place."

My cheeks burn, and I rub the spot between my eyebrows—my nervous tick. "No, like I don't know where my ticket is for."

He smiles. "It says it right on the stub there." He points at his ticket.

I bite my lip because I don't know how to explain it. "I asked the lady to print me a ticket to anywhere in the United States. She didn't tell me where it's for, and I haven't looked."

"I'm confused. What exactly do you need from me?" He checks his watch and glances over his shoulder.

I feel ridiculous for having bothered him at all. "You know what, never mind. I'm sorry I wasted your time. I'm keeping you from your train. Ignore the crazy lady in front of you." I give him a halfhearted wave and turn back to the departure boards. I can still feel his eyes on me, watching me. I glance sideways to find him staring at me, a look of amused curiosity on his face. I glance back at the boards and then back at him. He chuckles.

"You've piqued my interest. Can't turn away and ignore the so-called crazy lady."

I shake my head. "No, really, it's ok. I'll be fine."

"Nope, invested." He takes a step forward. "You're telling me you have no idea where you're supposed to be going? Is this part of a stunt? Or one of those crazy TikTok challenges? Are there hidden cameras somewhere?" He scans the train station as though he believes he's being secretly filmed.

"No, it's not a stunt or a challenge. No hidden cameras. I just need to get away, and I didn't care where I was going." I drop my eyes to the floor, and when he doesn't respond, I look back up to find him staring at me still, a small smile playing at the corners of his mouth.

He holds his hand out. "Can I see your ticket?" He waits patiently for me to hand it over.

I place my ticket in his outstretched hand and notice a scar running up the center of his hand that wraps around to the back. He takes the ticket, and I watch his face. I don't know what I'm looking for in his reaction, but he gives nothing away.

"Right, I have an idea; it's a bit unconventional, but so is the situation."

I narrow my eyes at him. "Ok?"

"You're going to close your eyes, and I'm going to walk you to your train, help you aboard, and then I'll be on my way. This way your destination remains a mystery for now."

I shift my bag to my other shoulder. "But won't you miss your train?"

"I'll be fine." He waves me off.

"So I'm supposed to close my eyes and let a stranger lead me through the train station? What could go wrong?"

He holds out his hand again, dimples returning as he grins at me. "I'm Oliver Adley, from London. The accent might've given me away." He shrugs. "Now we're not strangers. Besides, it's a very crowded train station. What's the worst that can happen?" He continues to hold his hand out to me, waiting for me to return the introduction.

I laugh, but I think it's more from exhaustion from the day and confusion over this whole situation. I shake his hand, and it's strong but soft and oddly comforting. "I'm Rem—"

"Let me guess," he says, cutting me off. "Remy Montgomery."

I shouldn't be surprised he knows who I am. My name and picture have been in the gossip columns for weeks now.

"It's on your ticket, love." He waves my ticket around.

I feel a strange sense of relief that he doesn't know me from elsewhere. He looks at his watch again.

"So, are we doing this?"

I survey the departure boards once more. My ticket is for any one of those places. Any of those locations will get me away from here and away from this fucked up life. I gaze around again at the people hurrying past. I wonder how many risks they've taken in their lifetimes. I've never been a risk-taker. Everything I do is by the book or with someone else in mind. I never do anything for myself. Oliver is right. It's a crowded train station, and, after all, I asked him for help. What did I expect would happen? It's time I start doing something for myself.

"Remy?"

The way my name rolls off his tongue—like he's been saying it his whole life—tugs my eyes back to him like a magnet. He's looking at me expectantly. I search his face for malice or deceit and find none.

"Listen," he says, "I'm not going to force you to do something you're uncomfortable with. I just wanted to try and help, like you asked. I can walk away right now if that's what you want." Oliver takes a step backward. "But, what have you got to lose?"

I take a deep breath and nod. He smiles, holding his hand out, and I take it.

"This is probably the craziest thing I've ever done."

"Eh, probably ranks in the top ten for me, but not the craziest." He smirks, and I can't tell if he's joking or not. "Alright, close your eyes. Don't worry, I've got your bag."

I pause and then let my eyes slide shut. He tugs me close to his side and starts guiding me through the station. The loudspeaker is still yelling out departure times and boarding calls. A moment later we stop, and he lets go of my hand, placing his hand on my shoulder.

"Don't move, and don't you dare open your peepers."

"Wait, what? Are we there?"

"Just wait here."

His hand disappears from my shoulder, and I start to panic. I almost open my eyes but stop myself. "Oliver?"

He doesn't respond, but I can hear his voice faintly in the distance. I can't make out what he's saying, though. I keep my eyes closed as the crowd surges around me. I hear a few grumbles over the fact that I'm just standing here, not bothering to get out of the way.

"Ok then, here we are." Oliver's hand is back on my shoulder. "Put these in your ears." He presses something into my hand.

"What is it?" I try to feel the packaging and feel something squishy between my fingertips.

"Earplugs. We've got to keep the mystery alive, haven't we? If you hear the train number, you're likely to know where you're going with as much as you studied those boards. Now, once I've got you in your seat, keep your eyes closed and the plugs in until you can really feel that the train has gotten going. No spoilers here. I've already given your ticket to the gentleman on the train. So, go on then, put them in."

My heart races as I fumble to get the earplugs out of the package. I press them into my ears, and the station quiets to a faint hum. Oliver places a hand on my lower back and gently pushes me forward. He guides me up the steps onto the train and finally into a seat. Oliver squeezes my shoulder and pulls one of the earplugs out. I can feel his warm breath against my ear, sending shivers down my spine.

"Good luck, Remy."

He tries to put the plug back but fumbles it, so I reach up to push it back in. His hand leaves my shoulder, and I know that means he's leaving the train. I resist the urge to open my eyes. The thrill of this crazy, reckless adventure thrums through me. I feel the seat next to me shift as someone sits down. At last the train jerks into motion and begins the slow departure from the station. Finally, I'm leaving this life—this nightmare, this prison—behind.

Chapter Two

Three Months Ago

"Hey, babe, where's my Armani jacket?" Gage calls to me from the bedroom.

I'm snuggled under a blanket on the couch. There's a glass of wine to my right and a bowl of popcorn on my left. My latest read sits perched against my knees. I'm so close to finishing this book and then I can get the review up on all my socials. I hear the closet door bang against the wall, and I look up, waiting for the tantrum I know he's about to throw. I catch a glimpse of my diploma on the bookshelf next to the fireplace. A lot of good the degree is doing me. The original goal had been to get into publishing, maybe as an agent or editor. However, my bookstagrammer and booktok accounts are as close to a literary career as I'll ever get. Gage thinks it's best if I focus on the charities that my time has already been promised to—instead of getting a job. In reality, it's my mother who promised my time to those charities. I'm not selfish; I truly don't mind helping them. In fact, I'm all for philanthropy, but I crave a career so badly.

Gage storms into the living room, shirt untucked and unbuttoned, and stands in front of me. "Remy? Are you even listening to me?" He snaps his fingers in my face. "My Armani jacket, where is it?"

I stare at him because it always pisses him off more when I don't answer right away. His black hair is pulled back into a bun, and his beard is trimmed close. I watch as his brown eyes flash with annoyance, and I smile inside because I know exactly where that jacket is.

"I sent it to the cleaners this morning." I calmly sip my wine and pop a piece of popcorn in my mouth before turning my attention back to my book.

I had planned to take it to the cleaners earlier this week so that he could have it back for tonight. He'd been reminding me all weekend. That was the plan until I found not one but two pairs of panties that most certainly were not mine in the jacket's pocket. I let it conveniently slip my mind until this morning.

"Dammit, Remy! You knew I wanted that jacket for tonight. I reminded you all weekend. Why the hell didn't you get your shit together and get it cleaned earlier this week?"

I don't look up from my book. The doorbell chimes and that means the 'D Squad' is here. That's what Gage's friends have been calling themselves since they met freshman year of college. Gage pulls the book from my lap and tosses it across the room where it lands with a thump on the carpet.

"What the fuck, Gage?"

"They're here. Can you make yourself useful and get the damn door? I have to try and find something else to wear, thanks to you."

He stalks back into the bedroom, leaving me annoyed on the couch. I get up lazily from my cozy corner and shuffle to the front door. The doorbell chimes again and loud voices permeate through. I swing it open and am greeted by the overpowering stench of after-shave from six former frat guys on the other side of the threshold.

"Remy! What's happening, beautiful? Where's Gage?" Trey asks, swooping in to plant an unwanted kiss on my cheek. They move around me and into the apartment.

"Yes, please, won't you come in?" I mutter sarcastically to myself as I shut the door behind them.

"Yo, Gage! Hurry the hell up, man. No amount of time in there will make you prettier than me," Trey yells. They all laugh. "We've got another wild night of clubs, booze, and babes planned."

They don't even try to hide what they're doing anymore. I know Gage cheats on me weekly, if not daily—hence the panties in the jacket. He's even been bold enough to try and include me in his extracurriculars. I don't know what he's told the squad, but they don't bat an eye to any of it.

Our relationship is one of those complicated Upper East Side ones. Being from the world we are, our parents always ran in the same social circle, and our moms always found ways to throw us together hoping one day we'd fall in love and get married. Despite Gage's mom's attempts to make him a sweet and caring boy, he developed the privileged, rich-boy attitude. I couldn't stand him. Around puberty he started showing interest in me—but only because I was there and he thought I'd be an easy way to get his first lay. During freshman year of high school his mom passed away, and his dad was forced to bring him home from boarding school when he got kicked out for drugs and drinking. Gage was threatened with the loss of his inheritance if he didn't straighten up. Mr. Donovan started taking Gage along to company events and parties to groom him for taking over the company one day.

Gage emerges from the bedroom, his arms spread out, and does a spin, showing himself off. "Sorry to make you wait, boys.

Had to make sure I looked good." The guys high-five him, and he turns to Trey. "I will always be prettier than you." Gage pats his cheek before turning to pull a couple of bottles of whiskey and seven shot glasses from the cabinet. "A little pre-game drink?"

"Hell, yeah!" they chorus back.

"So, Gage, how's the company? I heard through the grapevine that Remy's dad was supposed to be working on the account from Sweden?" Josh asks. He used to work for the company, and is one of the least dickish friends Gage has.

My father's business had been dying, and Gage's father thought it was a sound investment to merge their companies together. It was at the merger party that Gage and I first connected, despite all those playdates. We hadn't seen each other in a few years, and he told me I'd grown up well as his eyes lingered on every part of my body a moment longer than necessary. We talked for a while, and it seemed like he was trying to grow up, to be more mature than the guy I had known before. He told me he really wanted to make his father proud by taking over the company one day. We talked for hours about our dreams for the future, and by the end of the night, he wasn't the Gage I remembered—but someone I could actually see myself being with.

It was a whirlwind romance. We couldn't keep our hands off each other and were always finding ways to sneak off and be together. It never seemed like we could get enough time together. Two years into the relationship I found out he'd been cheating on me the entire time. The memory of that night floods my mind as if it was just yesterday.

⟫ ⋯ ✦ ⋯ ⟪

I slam the door, the front hall blurred through my tear-filled eyes.

"Remy, must you be so loud?" My mother's voice drifts from the sofa in the living room.

I see her draped over it, a hand dramatically resting against her forehead. She opens an eye to look at me. One look at my red, blotchy, tear-soaked face makes her roll that one eye and sigh.

"Why are you crying? Your face is all puffy. Really not your best look."

I hesitate and resist the urge to roll my eyes at her dig at my appearance. My mother and I have never had a relationship where I can share personal stuff with her, but right now I'm hurting and could use a mom.

"I broke up with Gage tonight."

Two seconds and she's off the couch and standing in front of me, panicked wide eyes on me. "What do you mean?" Her voice is shrill and loud.

Dad comes into the room. "What's going on?" He sees me and rushes over. "Honey, what's wrong?"

"Don't coddle her, Charles. She's fine."

"Clearly, Sylvia, she's not fine. Remy, what happened?"

"I broke up with Gage," I repeat, but this time, my voice shakes.

Dad steps forward and wraps me in a hug, letting me stain his shirt with tears.

"No," Sylvia says, shaking her head. "Absolutely not."

I pull back from Dad and wipe my eyes. "I went over to meet him so we could go to dinner, and he..." I swallow another lump in my throat. "He and Sarah were together."

"So?" my mother prompts.

"They were having sex, Mother."

"Oh, please. Gage wouldn't cheat on you. He has the whole package with you."

Anger flares in me. "Funny. I must have totally misinterpreted his dick inside of her as sex. Maybe they were just wrestling, naked."

Mother rolls her eyes, and Dad flinches at my blunt, harsh words.

"Apparently he's been cheating on me the entire two years we've been together." Fresh tears spill out as I think about how stupid and naïve I've been.

Dad wraps an arm around me as Mother starts to pace around the room.

"You need to fix this, Remy." Mother points at me, still pacing.

"Sylvia," Dad warns. "that's enough."

"Charles, she has to fix this. It's going to be an embarrassment to me, our family—and it could jeopardize the merger."

Dad laughs. "How could the love lives of two teenagers have any effect on a company's business?"

"What would you know, Charles? After all, if you'd run the company a bit better we wouldn't need this merger."

Dad falls quiet beside me, and his shoulders slump. Mother steps in front of me, leaning close.

"Now, you're going to fix this. Think of the life you would have. Think of the beautiful babies you would have, Remy."

"Because that's what's important!" I explode. "You can't be serious."

"Oh, I'm serious, and don't you dare raise your voice to me. Fix it!" She jabs her finger in my face.

"I'm not staying with him. You're batshit crazy! Why don't you lay off the pills, Mother?"

A hand across my cheek leaves it burning.

"Sylvia!" Dad shouts. "What the fuck is wrong with you?"

Sylvia doesn't answer immediately, but first turns toward him, a wicked glint in her eyes. "Quiet, Charles." She turns back to me.

"And you, Remy—you want to go to college, yes? Stay with Gage to make sure this merger isn't in jeopardy, and we'll pay for it. Every penny. No loans looming over your head."

"Sylvia, we can pay for it anyways. She's our daughter, for crying out loud. She doesn't need to stay with him."

"I'm sorry, is it your family's money that's in our bank account? Is it your family's company?"

Again, Dad goes quiet, his cheeks brightening.

"Stay with Gage, through college, and I'll pay your way."

"I have scholarships, you know?" I offer. "I don't need you to pay."

"Oh right, so you'll have scholarships to cover part of it, and then you'll enter the world with a mountain of debt on your shoulders?"

"A mountain of debt sounds a hell of a lot better than this fucked up plan."

"Just take the deal, Remy. Take the deal, and I'll leave you alone and let you live your life."

At the time, college was my ticket to some form of freedom from this twisted world. My mother didn't ever think I needed college. Marry well and I'd be taken care of. I wanted out. So, I stayed with Gage. I figured four more years, long enough to get through college and my mother would let go of this fantasy, let go of me, and I could leave for good. Gage wasn't going to turn me down when I came back. He had the best of both worlds: a respectable girl to have on his arm at all the events and plenty of other girls to have in his bed.

***

"Remy?" Gage pulls me out of my thoughts. "What's with you tonight? I asked if you wanted a shot."

I shake my head.

"Suit yourself. No business talk tonight, boys. Now, drink."

They all toss back their shots and slam the shot glasses back down on the table.

Gage turns to me. "You know the drill. No need to wait up. I'll be back late."

"Or early," one of the guys throws out.

"Or not at all." Trey wiggles his eyebrows.

"Shut up, Trey," Gage shakes his head, kissing me on the cheek and herding the D Squad out of the apartment.

I sigh as the place falls into a comfortable silence. Just think, Remy—in three painfully short months, you'll be the lucky girl to become Mrs. Gage Donovan.

Chapter Three

I wait until the train is gliding smoothly across the rails at full speed before taking the earplugs out and opening my eyes. Blackness rushes past the window outside, the lights of the city skyline fading in the distance, and the gentle hum of voices fills the train car. A bag crinkles beside me followed by a loud crunch. I glance over to see who I'll be next to for the ride, and I think my jaw may bruise as fast as it drops.

"I much prefer the potato crisps back home, but 'spose these will have to do in a pinch." Oliver offers me a smile and the bag as he pops another chip into his mouth. I sit staring, my mouth still hanging open. "Would you like one?" He moves the bag closer to me.

"How...why?" I twist in my seat and look up and down the train. "You're on my train," I say, leaning my back against the cool glass of the window.

"Your train? You mean you own this train? That's bloody brilliant! How does one go about owning a train?"

I see the laughter in his eyes when he looks over at me. "Ha ha," I say. "Are you following me?" I ask, shifting again in my seat.

Oliver pulls the bag of chips back to himself and reaches in for another, popping it in his mouth before turning to look at me. He pulls a leg up under himself. "Do you believe in fate?"

"Fate?" I ask, raising an eyebrow.

"Right, you know, fate. Something that happens and is un-avoidable, but it's meant to happen to you for a reason. Or what about destiny? Kismet?" He talks with his hands, gesturing around, the chip bag crinkling with each motion.

"Um, I don't know. Fate, destiny, all that stuff just seems like it's for the books and movies. It's something for fairytales. I feel like people can use them as an excuse to avoid making decisions. That whole 'what happens, happens' saying."

Oliver frowns at me, pulling a soda from his other side. He opens the bottle, and it hisses as he takes a sip. Setting it down, he resumes looking at me, frowning. "Sorry, but who pissed in your Cheerios?"

"Excuse me?"

"You are very pessimistic about fate."

I shrug. "People look at a situation, and instead of choosing to act in the moment, they use fate or destiny as an excuse for whatever happens. It's a good way to avoid taking respon-sibility for your life."

"Ouch! Not a hopeless romantic then? So, it wasn't fate or destiny that led to us meeting in the train station then? Or to you asking for help? Because you made a decision to act in the moment?"

"Right." I nod my head.

"If you don't believe in fate or kismet, what do you believe in, Remy? What's left?"

"Reality."

Oliver rests his head on the headrest, brow furrowed. I turn forward in my seat and watch the darkness outside again. "You never answered my question." I glance at him, his brow still furrowed. "Why are you on this train?"

"You wouldn't like my answer." He gives a sheepish smile.

I narrow my eyes. Did I get myself mixed up with some sort of psychopath? "What's your answer?"

"My ticket was for this train."

"So you're telling me that we just happened to have tickets to the same train?"

"Fate." Oliver coughs the word into his fist, smirking at me.

"Show me your ticket." I hold out my hand. Oliver digs in his jeans pockets, extracting a crumpled stub.

Oliver Adley, Train 918, Platform 22. New York City, New York to Chicago, Illinois. Departure time 11:00 pm, Arrival time 8:00 am.

I hand it back to him but don't say anything. It registers in my head that I finally know where I'm going: Chicago. A small wave of excitement goes through me.

"Satisfied?" Oliver asks. "I'm not a crazy person. In fact, if you remember correctly, I asked you about this train before I ever knew your train number."

I look away, trying to not let myself get lost in those eyes. "Ok, so we happened to end up on the same train together, just like all the rest of these people. Not fate, or destiny, just coincidence."

Oliver smirks but doesn't say anything. He takes another sip of soda and I watch him watching the people around us. His jaw clenches and unclenches, and he keeps biting his lip. Is he nervous? He catches me looking at him and smiles.

"So, Remy, what brings you to train 9-1-8 on this lovely evening?"

My mind instantly flashes to earlier this evening—to the look on my dad's face as I walked out—and my stomach lurches. I reach for his chips so Oliver can't see the look on my face. "Just needed a change of scenery I guess." I'm happy my voice doesn't betray me. "What about you?"

He clears his throat and shifts in his seat. "I'm going to see my mum." Oliver fidgets with a loose thread on the seat, not looking at me.

"Wouldn't it have made more sense to fly?"

Oliver starts to turn a light shade of green before replying. "Can't stand flying. The trip across the pond 'bout did me in." He swallows hard. "Try to avoid it whenever possible." He blows out a breath and nods. "I can ask the same of you. Train travel isn't necessarily a common thing in the States these days. Why aren't you flying?"

"A change of scenery calls for a change of transportation. What scenery can I get from the sky?"

"Point," he says. "So you get a ticket to a random location that you don't want to know the destination of."

"Mhmm."

"And all of this just for a change of scenery. Have I got that right?"

I look at him and lean in. "Wanna know the truth?" I ask, whispering.

He leans in, and I can see the dark gray ring that encircles his blue eyes. "Lay it on me," he says.

"I'm on the run for murder. Killed a man, just to watch him die." I give Oliver my best serious scowl. "Oh, and I robbed a bank." I nod my head and lean away, trying hard not to smile.

"You're a complete mystery, Remy."

"Maybe that's what I'm going for," I reply.

"Well, it's a mystery I want to solve." A determined look fills his eyes.

My phone rings, and I pull my gaze away from Oliver to look at the screen. My mother's face flashes across the screen, and I want to puke. Her words from tonight are ringing in my head. I press 'ignore' and turn it off before tossing it in my bag. I lay my head against the seat, wrapping my arms around myself.

"Remy? You ok?" Oliver asks.

I can see his face reflected in the glass, and when I don't answer, he turns in his seat, facing forward, and lays his head back. I focus on the endless void rushing past and let it consume me.

Chapter Four

I watch as my mother pops two aspirin and washes them down with her mimosa. She holds the bridge of her nose, something she always does when I'm stressing her out, which is most of the time. Poor Sylvia. To have such a burden of a daughter must be so hard!

"Remy, I don't understand what's so damn hard about it. We go, try some cake, pick the one we like the most, and we're done. We're already behind on so much for the wedding. We should have had the cake picked out months ago. Your stubbornness, however, has put us behind. I've had to pay a great deal more for such a short-notice cake at the bakery we want." She pauses, taking another swig of mimosa. "You didn't put up this much of a fight with the invitation."

"A bakery you want, and you did the invitations, Mother. Remember? You made the guest list, picked out the flowers, and have chosen every other detail about this wedding. I'm honestly surprised you haven't picked out the dress, too."

Sylvia purses her lips and looks down, examining her nails.

"What?" I ask, narrowing my eyes at her skeptically. "What did you do?"

"We have an appointment after lunch at the bridal salon."

I groan. If I'm being honest, I've been stalling on the wedding dress for as long as I could. I don't want to see myself in a wedding gown. At least not one for a wedding I don't even want to be a part of. "Why, Mother? What if I have plans after this?"

"You don't. I checked with Gage."

I snort. "Why the hell would Gage know my schedule?"

"He's your fiancé," she says simply.

I just shake my head and pick at my brunch with my fork, tearing and shredding it to pieces.

"I don't understand why you put off the dress this long. We should have gotten it at least six months ago. Your options are going to be limited. You might have to get off the rack, and I'll have to pay so much money to get it rushed through alterations."

"God forbid we get from the rack like normal people."

Sylvia stares at me. "We aren't normal people, Remy. We're better than normal people."

"You're so fucking ridiculous, Mother."

"Watch yourself." Sylvia leans forward, pointing a finger in my face. She sits back again and taps her fingers on the table. "You know, Gage's father and I were thinking—"

"Don't talk to me about Gage's father." I cut her off. "I don't want to hear what you guys have to say."

"With Gage's mother gone, his father is who I have to discuss wedding plans with. I don't understand what's going on with you, Remy."

"I'm sorry, Mother. Am I not being enthusiastic enough for you? Am I not living up to the dream you've always had of planning your little girl's wedding? Oh wait. That's not something you've dreamed of. It can't possibly be. Not the woman who has made it her life mission to remind me what an unwanted inconvenience I've always been."

"I don't appreciate your bad attitude or the sarcasm. You're getting married. It's going to be the happiest day of your life. Start acting like it."

"Was it the happiest day of your life, Mother?"

Sylvia gives me a long, cold, hard stare before upending her mimosa glass and emptying it into her mouth. She leans forward once more, placing a firm grip on my elbow, pulling me towards her. "You're about to marry Gage Donovan and start a life that any other girl could only dream of. You will be living a fairytale. You need to start being a little more grateful."

My phone buzzes and I look down to find a message from Gage.

Gage

I won't be home tonight, business meeting.

I roll my eyes. The last "business meeting" he'd had sent him home with panties in his jacket. "Yup, a real fucking fairytale, Mother." I raise my glass to her, finishing it in one gulp. "I get my so-called Prince Charming, and you finally get to be rid of the daughter you never wanted."

"Always the dramatics with you." Sylvia sighs, rubbing her forehead. "Are you finished? We have an appointment to keep."

"I'll need you to pull all of these dresses in her size. Don't deviate from the list, and bring us more champagne. We are celebrating after all." Sylvia waves off the bridal shop attendant.

"Bridezilla much, Sylvia?" I ask. "I thought that was my job."

"You know I hate when you call me by my name."

"Yeah, well, you don't seem to like it when I call you Mom either," I mumble. I check my phone. The dress appointment is an hour long. Only fifty-seven minutes to go. "I don't see why Celia couldn't come with us," I say, casually thumbing through some of the dresses next to me.

Celia, my rock, my defender, my best friend. We met at an author signing during our freshman year of college. Her main motive was the ultimate level of hotness this guy possessed and mine was because I couldn't put his book down and had devoured it in about eight hours. I wanted to have coffee with him and grill him on his work but was too chicken to ask. Celia, always bold and brave, fearlessly invited him to coffee with us and he miraculously said yes and that sealed the deal on her being my new best friend.

"We've been over this." Sylvia sighs. "I wanted a special day, just the two of us. We never do anything, just the two of us."

I wonder why that is, I think to myself. The attendant returns with a nervous smile and I instantly feel bad for whatever is about to come out of my mother's mouth.

"I'm very sorry, Mrs. Montgomery, but we don't have three of the ten you've selected in the store."

"Does calling ahead do nothing anymore?"

"I'm so sorry. Those dresses left yesterday for a trunk show."

"They left, did they? Just grew legs and walked themselves out of here? I specifically called ahead to hold these ten dresses. This is unacceptable. Now our options are even more limited."

"Aren't I supposed to be the one picking the dresses?" I jump in, trying to save this poor girl from any more of Sylvia's wrath. "Here, this one looks decent." I regret saying it as soon as I see the look of disgust on my mother's face.

"Decent? That's how you want to look on the most important day of your life? Decent? Honestly, Remy. Gage will look handsome in a tux, and you just want to look decent?"

"Gage would probably show up in jeans if he had the choice."

"Oh, please, his father would never allow that."

"Because you know so well what his father would and wouldn't allow," I shoot back. The shop attendant looks nervously between the two of us, unsure of what to do.

Sylvia rolls her eyes dramatically. "Pull the dresses you do have, and we—"

"You know what?" I say, cutting her off again, and turn to the shop attendant. "Can you give us a moment, please? I need a word with my mother."

The woman nods and hurries away, probably glad to be out from under Sylvia's withering stare.

"Remy, we don't have all day. We have a cake tasting next. Why did you send her away?"

I pace back and forth, my hands on my hips, as I try to breathe deeply. "You know, Mother, I can't do this."

"Do what, Remy? You know, you really are exhausting when you don't explain yourself." Sylvia pinches the bridge of her nose and takes another swig of champagne.

"Any of this." I motion around the shop. "The dress or the cake or any of it."

"You're being so dramatic. I hate when you're like this."

"You're the reason I'm in this mess." I continue pacing back and forth, anger continuing to build inside of me.

Sylvia narrows her eyes, giving me a calculating stare. "What makes you say that?"

"Have you seen Mr. Donovan recently?" I ask, watching her carefully.

She brings a hand up to fiddle with her necklace. "Here and there, at various events, maybe a business dinner or two."

I stop pacing and stare her down. I watch as she leans back a fraction of an inch. "I know what you've been doing, Mother," I hiss.

She rolls her eyes and tries to wave me off. "I have no idea what you're talking about."

"You know exactly what I'm talking about. Gage told me all about it."

"If you're not going to try on dresses today then I'm ready to leave. This was pointless and a waste of time." Sylvia tries to walk around me.

I move over and block the entrance to the shop. "Why are you doing it?"

"I'm not having this discussion with you, Remy."

"Oh, but you are. What would Dad say? He's done everything for this family."

Sylvia snorts. "You've always thought the sun shined out of that man's ass." She pauses. "I don't understand how any of this relates to your engagement."

"It has everything to do with it. Gage will screw us all over if I don't marry him."

Sylvia looks down and huffs. "I still don't see what the big deal is. You get to marry a prominent man and have everything you could ever want."

"Except freedom and to be truly happy. Except a husband who doesn't cheat on me every night of the week."

Sylvia takes a step towards me, smirk on her face. "If you're going to live in this world, Remy, you've got to learn that infidelity is just part of survival. You'll see, Gage won't be the only one doing it soon enough."

"You're sick." I stare at her in disgust. "Don't you understand? I don't want to live in this world. I never have. I want you to know I'm only doing this to protect Dad."

"Well, aren't you the hero?" Sylvia rolls her eyes again.

"Let's get one thing straight, Mother. I might be doing this to protect Dad, but you're going to be the one to tell him why we're all in this fucked up mess."

"Well," she scoffs, "that's certainly not happening."

"You have until the rehearsal dinner. If you can't bring yourself to tell him by then—well, let's just say you're not going to want to find out what happens if you don't." I turn to walk out of the shop, pausing to look back. "Pick whatever damn dress and cake you want. I don't fucking care." I walk out, leaving my mother open-mouthed and speechless for once.

Chapter Five

My eyes flutter open as something brushes against my face. I squeeze them closed again as the harsh light of the sun attempts to burn my retinas.

"You looked so peaceful, I was trying to close this so the light didn't wake you." Oliver pulls the blind down, dimming the red glow. "Sorry 'bout that."

I sit up a little straighter, massaging my neck. I'm not sure at what point I fell asleep, but there's a twinge in my neck from being in an awkward position for too long. I wipe the sleep from my eyes as a yawn escapes me.

"What time is it?" I yawn again, searching for a hair tie in my bag.

"Round quarter to eight. We should be getting close." Oliver watches me as I pull my hair into a messy bun. "Your hair looks like fire when the sun hits it."

I roll my eyes because I've heard all of the insults about being a redhead. "I don't need your mockery about my red hair, pale skin, or my freckles. All of which I happen to like. I've heard them all before."

"Why would anyone want to insult it? It's beautiful."

I look at him—expecting to see a smirk on his face—but instead find that he's blushing, and my own cheeks flush unexpectedly.

"Well, I mean..." Oliver clears his throat and looks around the train, shifting in his seat. "Coffee? Tea? I could grab some from the food trolley."

"Oh, um, yeah. Coffee would be amazing, actually."

"Cream or sugar?"

"Black is fine, thanks."

Oliver scrunches his nose but tips an imaginary hat toward me before climbing over the sprawled legs of some of the still-sleeping passengers. I stare after him until he disappears through the door into the next compartment. There's something about him that intrigues me. He's so sure of himself—but not in the cocky asshole way that Gage is. And sure, he's attractive—but not in an overly obvious way. His eyes are gentle, but a fierceness shines out from deep inside him. When he looks at me, it's as though he actually sees me. And he doesn't speak at me or through me, but to me. I lift the shade and watch out of the window as the scenery passes us by. Fields have shifted to more of an urban setting as we get closer to Chicago.

I hear the compartment door slide open, and Oliver squeezes past a man going in the opposite direction. He struggles through the aisle and finally makes it to his seat holding the two steaming cups. He passes one to me as he settles in.

"Thank you." I take a careful sip. "Not bad for train coffee."

"You mean sludge," Oliver says, wrinkling his nose again.

"Excuse me?" I ask.

"Black coffee? No cream or sugar." Oliver makes a face showing his disgust. "Don't know how you do it."

I trace the hole in the lid of my cup. "My dad drinks black coffee. It's something I picked up from him," I shrug.

"I'm your typical Brit and love my tea." He smiles and shrugs. "So, Remy, I'm curious..." Oliver stops to sip his tea.

"Haven't you heard?" I ask. "Curiosity killed the cat."

"Lucky I'm not a bloody cat then," he chuckles. "Don't you know? I have no special talent; I am only passionately curious."

I stare at him, an eyebrow raised in question.

"Well, ok. That was Albert Einstein. But I, too, am passionately curious."

"Mmm, I see. And what exactly are you so passionately curious about, Oliver?"

He turns in his seat, a serious expression settling on his face as he leans closer to me. "You see, I'm passionately curious about..." Oliver reaches out to brush a piece of hair from my face that has come loose from my ponytail, but I lean away. He looks embarrassed. "Sorry, I..." He doesn't finish his sentence.

"It's fine," I say.

"No, that was forward of me." Oliver won't meet my eyes.

"You were saying?" I prod. "About being curiously passionate?"

"So, then." He clears his throat and seems to regain a little of his composure. "As you have no actual destination in mind, and you're just looking for a change of scenery, what is it you plan to do once we get to Chicago?"

"I..." My mind goes blank. I haven't thought about it. I never really thought beyond getting my things, the ticket, and getting the hell out of there. I didn't even know I was headed to Chicago until I was already on the train. "Maybe I'll do the whole tourist thing?" I say, uncertainly.

"So, you're staying in Chicago then? After the whole tourist bit?"

I narrow my eyes at him. Why does he care?

"Passionately curious. Remember?"

"Riiight..." I drag the word out. "In case you haven't realized it yet, I don't exactly have a plan."

"Ah, I see." Oliver turns back around in his seat and chews on his lip while he watches the other passengers start to wake up.

I watch out the window once more. The skyscrapers of Chicago are steadily growing larger as the train chugs closer and closer to the station. I've only been to Chicago once. It was right after Gage and I had gotten engaged. Our parents had a gala to attend and wanted us to come along and publicly announce our happy news. When I found out we were going to Chicago, I was excited at the idea of spending a day in the Windy City and seeing all of the places I'd only ever read about. In reality, all I ever saw was the tarmac as we exited the private jet to climb into our waiting limo, followed by the buildings as we drove past them, and, finally, the closed and private courtyard of the gala.

The static from the speaker overhead crackles to life. "Train 918, New York to Chicago will arrive in approximately five minutes' time. Please remain seated until the train comes to a complete stop at the station. Thank you for choosing Amtrak."

Despite the captain's orders, passengers stand, stretching their arms over their heads, and begin messing with the luggage in the compartments above. The train gradually slows, and I see the station just ahead. Laughter fills the air from a group of college girls a few rows up, while restless children begin to whine at their parents. The train enters the tunnel, and the lights inside flicker on. Finally, the train comes to a full stop, and we are forced to wait as the mass of people push through the aisle to the exits.

Oliver stands to pull our bags down. "I've got this for now, until we're out of the crowd." He slings his bag over his shoulder and hoists my suitcase into his arms before stepping into the aisle, holding off the people behind him so I can slip into the line ahead of him.

Our feet shuffle forward little by little until we're finally off the train and standing on the platform. The pungent smell of the warm station air instantly fills my nose.

"Thanks for grabbing my bag," I say, taking it from him.

"Not a problem. It's what a gentleman should do."

"And thanks for helping keep the mystery alive and not being too much of a creep. I realize that could have gone wrong."

"Too much? So, I was a little creepy?"

I pause before I answer. "Well, there were a lot of questions. And, speaking of, why were you so curious about my plans for the city and after?"

"Maybe I wanted to buy you a cup of coffee." He shrugs.

"But you bought me one on the train."

"Or dinner?" he says. "Regardless, this has been, oddly enough, the most fun and amusement I've had in some time."

"I see. Well, raincheck on the dinner."

"Raincheck? Does that mean I'll be seeing you again?"

"If you believe in fate and all of that, then, yeah, maybe." I say, smirking at him. "It was nice meeting you, Oliver. I'm, uh, going to see if I can catch a ride." I point a thumb over my shoulder at the station.

"It was an unexpected pleasure meeting you, Remy." He smiles warmly at me.

I return the smile and turn towards the exit, the last few people on the platform heading for the doors.

"So, I guess I'll see you around," Oliver calls out.

I turn around, continuing to walk backward. I should know better with how clumsy I can be. "Yeah?"

"Like you said, fate and destiny." He winks at me.

I feel myself blush as my face stretches into a grin, and I shake my head. I turn around and force myself to continue walking through the doors.

I've been standing in line for twenty minutes trying to get a taxi. Beads of sweat slip down the back of my neck. I realize I could easily get an Uber or Lyft, but that requires me to turn on my phone. I don't really want to deal with the barrage of missed calls and texts that will blow up my phone the second I turn it on. A hot gust of wind brushes past me bringing me no relief from the heat.

"This is ridiculous." I shake my head, exasperated. "I'll just walk. I don't even know where I'm going anyways."

"Do you always talk to yourself on crowded sidewalks?"

I turn and see Oliver standing beside me, grinning his lopsided smile.

"Following me again?" I narrow my eyes in mock suspicion, although I'm a little confused as to why he's still here.

"I told you I'd see you around." He adjusts the straps of his backpack. "I honestly thought you'd have been whisked away in a car by now. Troubles?"

I gesture at the line in front of me full of middle-aged couples bickering and waiting for a taxi. "The line doesn't seem to be moving."

"What century are you living in? Why not just get an Uber or a Lyft?"

I look down at my feet and adjust the strap of my own bag. I rented a locker for my suitcase so I didn't have to lug it around. "My phone is dead?"

Oliver doesn't reply at first, instead just looks at me. "Ah, right. Of course," he finally says, clearly knowing I'm lying. "Didn't I see you switch if off on the train?"

I sigh. "Ok, fine, it's not dead. You caught me."

"Liar liar," he teases.

"If it's so easy, why are you still here?" I ask, crossing my arms. When he doesn't answer right away I shake my head. "Maybe we should both just be honest?" I let out a sigh. "I don't want to turn on my phone and deal with any of the missed calls and texts."

He nods. "I left, on foot, but was worried about you, so I came back to make sure you got on your way ok."

"So now you actually are following me? I don't need you to worry for me, Oliver. I'm a big girl and can worry about myself."

Oliver turns red, and his brow shoots up. "Look, I was just concerned. I have a sister so it comes naturally for me to worry about the women around me."

"Right, well, fine," I don't have a good response for him.

"Look, let me get you that cup of coffee."

"Was that your plan the whole time?" I ask, raising an eyebrow.

"No, I swear." He holds his hands up.

I stare him down and can see the sincerity on his face. I roll my eyes because I'm annoyed, hot, and way over standing on this sidewalk. "One cup. That's it. And only because I'm tired of standing in the heat." Oliver smiles but doesn't move. "Why are we still standing here?" I ask.

"Well I can be quite daft sometimes." He pulls his phone out, still grinning. "I'll get us a ride."

Chapter Six

I struggle through the front door, a box full of gift bags waiting to be stuffed with swag in my arms. I can't even remember how I got roped into helping with this museum charity event. Was it my mother? Or did I agree to this one on my own? There've been too many recently, and I can't keep them all straight. I set the box on the table just inside the door and toss my keys in the bowl. A low snore rumbles from the couch, and I peer over the back of it to find Gage sprawled on his back, a leg hanging over the edge and an arm draped over his eyes. His shirt is untucked and wrinkled, and his belt is halfway out of the loops. He burps in his sleep, and the smell of whiskey wafts up to make me gag.

Rolling my eyes, I make my way to the bathroom, splashing cold water on my face before lathering it with soap and finally rinsing it with warm water. I finish washing up and go into the bedroom, stripping down to my bra and panties, ready to be in some cozy jammies. I hear a thud behind me and turn around to see Gage leaning against the door frame, rubbing his face and swaying. He looks at me through bleary, bloodshot eyes that roam hungrily over the curves of my body.

"Hey, baby, I didn't hear you come in." His words are slurred, and he stumbles forward a few steps.

"How could you when you were passed out drunk...again," I say, pulling on my sleep shorts.

His hand slips onto my waist, and I feel the stubble from his five-o-clock shadow rub against my shoulder as he leans in to kiss my neck. I shrug him off and try to make for the closet. Gage reaches for me and catches my wrist, trying to tug me towards him. In his drunken state, my resistance throws him off balance, and he stumbles again but manages to keep his fingers wrapped around my wrist.

"Why aren't you out with the guys?" I manage to pull my wrist free and step back, crossing my arms over my chest. I watch as his eyes dip to the tops of my boobs, distracted. "Gage?"

His eyes move sluggishly back up to mine. "I had to work late, so I pounded back a few drinks at the bar down the street. I guess I fell asleep waiting for you. Where were you?"

I laugh. "Yeah, right. You were waiting for me. That'll be the day. I was working on the museum charity gala. And I'd say you had more than a few. It smells like you bathed in it."

Gage takes another step towards me, clearly not listening, and runs a hand down my arm. "You're looking sexy tonight. C'mere."

I push his hand off my arm, but he manages to grab my wrist again and tugs harder this time. I'm against his chest and the stench of whiskey pours out of every inch of him. I turn my head away to keep from gagging in his face, but he grips my chin, bringing my face up to his.

"That lace bra and those curves, mmm, baby they're really doing it for me tonight, Remy." He lowers his hand from my chin and runs a thumb across the front of my bra. "Whatcha say, huh?"

"Oh I don't know how I can refuse that sexy pick-up line." I say flatly.

"Don't be like that." He says, wrapping a hand around the back of my neck and pulling me even closer.

I try to pull away. "You're drunk, Gage. Go to bed." I tug my wrist trying to free it, but he squeezes his fingers tighter around it.

Gage steps forward, backing me into the door frame and pressing his body against mine. "I haven't had you in a while, Remy. I miss you." He presses his lips to mine and I turn my head away laughing.

"What?" He asks, leaning back just enough to get a clear view of my face. "Why are you laughing?"

"You can't be serious." I say, still laughing.

"About what?" He asks.

"We both know your 'business meetings' are just an excuse for you to go fuck whatever girl you want. The only time you want me is when you're drunk or when we're at some stuffy event and you're bored looking for a distraction. The last time you wanted me was six months ago at your dad's birthday dinner, and afterwards you told me I needed to drop a few pounds because I was getting more than just curvy." I push against his chest, but he doesn't budge. Where the hell did his drunken stumble go? "Gage, move." I shove again, but he still doesn't move.

"Baby, I'm sorry. You're not fat." He runs a hand over my hair, resting it on the back of my head. "I still care about you."

"Whatever, Gage. You stopped caring for me right after I first let you in my pants. It was only ever a game for you, and the second you scored you didn't give two shits about me. It wasn't even a week later, and you were off hooking up with my supposed best friend."

He rolls his eyes and finally steps back. "Are you still going on about that? We're past all that shit now, Remy."

"Are we really past it? I'm sure as hell not past it."

Gage runs his hands through his hair in frustration, and I take the opportunity to try to move past him. He grabs me by the shoulders and pushes me against the door frame again. "You're my fiancé, and soon you'll be my wife."

"Lucky me." I mutter.

His grip tightens. "My wife has a duty to make her husband happy and to make sure he's taken care of no matter how many business meetings he has. So, you should start acting like my wife." He presses his lips firmly to mine, gripping my arm with one hand and yanking my head back with the other, giving him more room to deepen the kiss. I cry out in pain and push hard against his chest. He's still off balance just enough in the moment that I knee him in the thigh, duck under his arm, and dart across the bedroom.

"Dammit, Gage!" I wipe my face with the back of my hand, my mouth filled with the taste of whiskey, and tears pricking the corners of my eyes. "You're such a prick!"

"You're a fucking bitch, Remy!" Gage is holding his thigh, grimacing.

"Why do I bother staying anymore?" I say, more to myself than him.

I grab a shirt from the hamper and turn to see him advancing on me once more, this time with a slight limp in his gait. He grabs me by the arms and gives me a slight shake, the anger in his eyes boring into me. "Do you need a reminder of why you stay with me? Need I lay it all out for you? Or show you the video?"

"Let me go, Gage." Anger and anxiety course through me.

"You know if you were to ever leave your whole world would come crumbling down and you'd have nowhere left to go." He smiles a cocky smile, pulling my face up to his once more. "You know that your only option is to stay and play the game. As you said, I do like a good game. Now, play the fucking game, Remy." Gage rips the shirt from my hands and tosses it aside. "You won't be needing that." He chuckles to himself.

"Gage..." I don't like how unsteady my voice is. "Gage, you're drunk."

His eyes roam over my body again and his hands follow suit. He slips the straps of my bra off my shoulders and I try to shove his hands away but he's sobering up and isn't as unsteady as he was. He grabs my face in his hands and kisses me hard, waiting for me to return the kiss. He pulls back and my stomach is churning. I look up at him and he's smirking at me. "Act like the wife." He whispers.

"I'll start acting like a wife when you start acting like a man. You're a pathetic excuse for one and you disgust me." Taking advantage of his shock, I tear out of his grip and this time he lets me go. I storm over to the bedroom door and hold it open, gesturing for him to leave. When he doesn't move, I grab the book sitting on the dresser and throw it at him. "Get the hell out!" The words explode out of me.

Gage throws his arms up to protect himself and the book bounces off them. He comes towards me, stopping inches from me and stares down. "Pathetic and disgusting? I've never heard any complaints before."

"Probably because you were too busy listening to your narcissistic self talking to hear what they had to say."

His jaw clenches and his fists tighten. He's never hit me before, but he's also never been this out of control before. I swallow and pull the door open further.

"Actually, Remy, I was too busy enjoying a better fuck than your chubby ass has ever been able to give me." Gage pushes past me, grabs his keys, and slams the front door behind him.

Chapter Seven

The cold from the cup in my hand is a relief against my hot skin. There's a gentle hum in the cafe as people have quiet conversations around us. Others have their noses buried in books or computer screens. Oliver takes the seat across from me, rubbing his hands together, his eyes bright with excitement as he stares down at the muffin on his plate.

"Sorry to make you wait. But nothing beats a warm blueberry muffin. I love blueberries. Quite literally anything that has blueberries, I will eat." He peels the paper away and takes a huge bite, crumbs scattering on the table and his shirt.

"Anything with blueberries?" I ask, sipping my cold brew.

"Mmm, yeah, anyfing." His mouth is full of muffin as he tries to speak.

I laugh as he attempts to swallow a huge bite. There are now crumbs on his chin and a smudge of blueberry on his lip. "You have…—" I point to my own face, trying to indicate the muffin on his face—"muffin on you."

Oliver grabs a napkin, wiping his face. He takes a swig of tea and finally manages to swallow the muffin. "Sorry 'bout that. That's a damn good muffin, though."

"You know, I read somewhere once that there are blueberry farms in Michigan." I watch as his eyes grow wide in excitement.

"You're joking."

"Nope. I think it was in a travel blog? Somewhere in Michigan there are miles and miles of blueberries."

"I've got to see that someday," Oliver says, tapping his head. "Mental note about blueberry farms."

I smile and take another sip of my coffee.

"You sure you don't want anything to eat?" Oliver asks, gesturing towards the counter. "My treat,"

I shake my head. "I'm fine. Thanks, though."

"Right then, suit yourself. A game of twenty questions, then."

"Wait, what?" I ask, looking at him quizzically.

"We've traveled together, Remy, but I feel like I barely know you. Hence the game."

"There's a reason you barely know me: we just met."

"Right, but we've traveled together, we're having tea and coffee together—aren't you just a little bit curious about me?"

"We may have traveled together, but I slept most of the way. Another reason you barely know me."

"You didn't answer my question, though. Aren't you curious about me?"

Of course I'm a little curious about him, but I'm not giving him the satisfaction of hearing me say it. "Didn't you ask enough questions on the train?"

"Nope." He grins. "Come on then. Who knows how much time we'll spend together—and you intrigue me," he says it so matter-of-factly, like this is just how it is, and shrugs.

I roll my eyes and smile, my hand darting across the table and snatching a piece of his muffin, popping it in my mouth. "You're right, this is good."

He laughs, and I'm surprised by the flutter in my stomach when I hear it. I take a deep breath and lean forward. "Alright, ask away."

"Excellent!" Oliver responds. He leans forward. "Where did you grow up?"

"Born and raised in good old NYC. Upper East Side with my mother and my dad."

"I've seen *Gossip Girl* and—"

Oliver isn't able to finish his sentence because I spray coffee all over the table and his face as I laugh at his confession. I cover my mouth and look up at him, my eyes wide with shock. His face is scrunched up and his eyes are closed. He opens them just enough to grab some napkins and wipes off his face. I notice the person at the next table giving me a disgusted look.

"Thanks for that," Oliver says, coffee dripping off the end of his nose. "I've always seen that happen in the movies, the drink-sprayed-in-the-face bit, but never in real life. It's always the bloke that gets it, too."

"Sorry." I'm still laughing as I hand him more napkins. "But you said you've watched *Gossip Girl*. I thought that show was for, like, binge-watching sixteen-year-old girls swooning over Chuck Bass."

"I have a sister, you know. It was she who watched it. Obsessively. I could probably recite episodes, she watched the show so bloody much. You've seen it, then?"

"I was sixteen at one point. I saw the show, but it wasn't really my thing." I shrug.

"I just don't see it." Oliver shakes his head. "You could never pull off being a character on that show."

"Well, good. Now, time for my first question. You mentioned a sister. How many siblings do you have?"

"Two. I've got a younger sister, Sophie, and an older brother, Jack."

"Middle child." I nod. "They say the middle child is always the troublemaker." I lean forward, a serious expression settling on my face. "Are you a troublemaker, Oliver?"

Oliver leans closer, a smile playing at the corners of his mouth. "Is that your second question, Remy?"

My eyes widen. "Shit, no. I take it back. That one doesn't count." We're both laughing, and the person behind me shushes us, making us laugh more.

"Ok, ok," Oliver says. "I'll answer it anyway. Your freebie question. I wasn't too much of a troublemaker, actually. Jack was always loud and rambunctious, and Sophie was a clone of Mum. I was just the quiet one." he sips his tea, a faraway look in his eye.

"Sounds like a pretty busy house." Our house was never busy with just the three of us. The busiest ones were the housekeepers.

"It could be overwhelming at times, and other times all the chaos was exactly what a person needed." Oliver looks as though he gets lost somewhere in time before shaking his head and returning to the present. "Right, my turn. Where do you work? Or what do you do for a living?"

"Um...well, that's a complicated one. I don't work, not exactly."

"Well, what exactly do you do?"

"I help a lot with charity events at different organizations. I go to some corporate functions." I bite my lip, trying to think of other things to mention.

"Do you get a lot of satisfaction helping with the charity events and such?" Oliver asks, picking at the crumbs of his muffin.

I tilt my head to the side, thinking about his question, and I feel my nose scrunch.

Oliver chuckles. "That nose scrunch doesn't exactly scream 'yes.'"

"I do enjoy helping out, I really do. There are so many people and organizations out there that need the help, and I can give it. But..." I trail off.

"Your heart isn't truly in it?" Oliver asks.

I shake my head. "I like keeping up with my bookstagrammer and Tiktok accounts."

"Wait, you read for a living?"

"No, I just do it for fun. But the perks are cool. I get sent free books to read and review on my accounts. Plus, I feel like I'm connecting readers with some pretty amazing books, and giving authors a boost, too."

"That sounds fascinating."

"I can't tell if you're being sarcastic or not." I eye him suspiciously.

"No, not at all! It's cool as hell. Plus, you get paid in one of the best currencies...books."

I smile, excited that someone is taking such a strong interest in what I love to do. "Book mail is the best. Seeing those packages waiting for me is so exciting. I've started writing reviews that I actually get paid for, so that's cool too."

"What kind of books do you read and review?" Oliver is leaning forward now, as though at any moment he might start taking notes on what I have to say.

"All kinds." I say. "Fiction, nonfiction, romance, mystery, horror. I'm not generally a picky reader."

"Any favorites?"

"That's like asking a kid what their favorite ice cream flavor is."

"Ah, but they can all give you one."

"Fine, ok. Um..." I think about it for a minute. "I'm going to sound like a typical girl with this one, but I truly love a good romance novel."

"Well, isn't that interesting." Oliver remarks.

"What?"

"The skeptic on fate and destiny loves a romance novel."

I roll my eyes. "Meghan Quinn is the queen of romance novels, in my opinion. But so is Emily Henry, Colleen Hoover, Sylvia Day, and Sara Cate."

Oliver cocks his head to the side and smirks.

"Yes?" I ask. "Have something to say?"

"You read smut?"

I blush, knowing the authors I threw out, but never expected him to recognize them. I lift my chin and own it. "So, what if I do?"

"Getting more interesting by the minute." Oliver smiles, flashing his dimples at me.

"How do you know any of those authors are smut?"

"I don't live under a rock, Remy. Plus, I read, too."

I narrow my eyes at him, unsure if this means he's read Sara Cate, too—or just that he reads in general. He interrupts my chance to ask him by asking another question.

"If you could do anything, be anything you want...when you grow up,"—he chuckles—"what would you do?"

"Is this your freebie question?" I ask, smirking at him.

"Yup." His lips pop on the 'p' as he nods.

"Well...it's kind of ridiculous, actually," I say, picking apart a napkin.

"No dream is ridiculous, Remy. What is it?"

I take a deep breath and shake my head before blowing the breath back out. "I've always wanted to own my own bookstore/coffee shop combo." The words tumble out in a rush.

"That doesn't sound so ridiculous."

"It is. For me, it's ridiculous."

"Why?" he asks, shrugging a shoulder.

"Because…" I don't know how to answer without giving away too much about my life. A conversation I definitely don't want to have. "Because I have a degree in English Literature not Business. It seems silly to do something I'm not trained to do."

"Nah"—he shakes his head—"Loads of people do stuff they're not trained to do and succeed every day. Why should you be any different? If you want to own a bookstore/coffee shop combo then do it. But, please, for me, serve hot tea."

I laugh. "Well, even if I wanted to jump into that, now is not the time. My question." Time to change the subject before things get too deep into my world. "What do you do for a living?"

"I work in an art gallery doing various tasks. Sometimes I help with art installation, sometimes I help work the openings, and occasionally I get to help bring in new artists."

I raise my eyebrows in surprise. "Wow, that's impressive. I can't imagine some of the talent you get to see."

"Eh, it certainly has perks. But, I wouldn't call it impressive. Although, I could be helping discover the next Monet."

"Does your business card read, 'Oliver Adley, Artist Hunter'?"

Oliver's eyes go wide. "No, but it bloody well will now! That's brilliant."

I laugh. "You're welcome." I take a bow in my seat.

Oliver chuckles. "What else do you do? For fun, I mean."

"Put me in front of Netflix, and you won't see me for days," I say, taking another drink of coffee. "Bad habit of binging."

"Typical American." He winks. "Nah, I'm only joking. I too, love binging shows. Just last week I went through the first three seasons of *The Office*."

"British or American?" I ask.

He looks at me as though I've lost my mind and deeply offended him. "You can't be serious?" he asks.

"It's a valid question! You're obviously British, but the American version is the superior one."

"This coming from the not-at-all-biased American." He chuckles. "It was the American one. Can't get enough of Pam and Jim's story. I'm a hopeless romantic and a sucker for a good love story. But I think you've figured that out about me already."

"Of course the charming British guy is a hopeless romantic." The words slip out before I realize what I'm saying.

"Oh"—a grin spreads across Oliver's face—"so, you think I'm charming."

"I..."

Shit. I called him charming.

I hurry to take a drink of my coffee and choke on it, spluttering and coughing.

"You said 'charming British guy'. Which means you think I'm charming."

I huff. "Well, I'm still here, aren't I?" I offer.

Oliver smiles and clears his throat, waving a hand toward me. "I believe it's your turn again."

"Same question, what do you do for fun?"

Oliver shifts in his seat. "I like art, obviously. I dabble in photography, but I love the classics and spending time in museums and other art galleries."

"There is something so peaceful about art museums. Just sitting and staring at the artwork and almost watching it come to life." I take another sip of my coffee, and when I look back up he's staring at me in bewilderment. "What?" I ask, confused by this sudden shift.

"That is exactly what going to museums is like for me. It's like you crawled inside my mind and fished that out."

I smile sheepishly at him and shrug. "The probability of me being a mind reader is fairly low. If I were one, then I'd already know your next question. Alas, I do not. So, what is it?"

"Hmm"—Oliver ponders a moment before asking—"What's your family like?"

I groan. "Pass."

"What? You can't pass."

"Assholes. They're absolute assholes. Except for my dad. He's the only one I give a damn about." My tone is sharper than I intended, and I think Oliver can tell he's hit a nerve, because he doesn't push me further.

"Your turn," he says, his voice quieter.

I take a deep breath and let it go, trying to blow out some of the annoyance from the last question. "Right, um, what part of England are you from?"

"Liverpool originally. That's where my parents met and where I was born. When I was 'round seven, they moved us to London for my dad's job."

"What's it like there?"

"Not as glamorous as all the travel magazines make it out to be, but still pretty cool. Lots of history and old buildings and dead guys who did something heroic."

"Oh, well, in that case, book me a ticket right now. You make it sound so appealing."

He laughs. "It truly is worth seeing. I just feel like once you've lived there the magic wears off from a place. I mean, it's probably the same with New York, right?"

I think about it: Times Square, the Empire State Building, the Statue of Liberty. I used to find them exciting and wanted to go see them every weekend when I was little. The older I got, the more they became just a part of the city to me. "Yeah, I guess you're right. But, I mean, there has to be somewhere that you can live where the magic stays alive. A place where beauty never fades."

"I believe it exists." Oliver nods. "We just have to find it."

It's not lost on me that he just said that *we* have to find it. I sit back in my chair and try to think of where that place might be. Will I find it on this adventure? I shake my head and look to find Oliver lost somewhere else, too. "I believe it's your turn to ask a question," I say.

Oliver sits up, scratching his chin. "Favorite animal?"

"Like favorite animal of all time or what animal I'd like to own?"

"Both."

"All-time favorite would have to be the penguin."

"I definitely could have called that one."

"Are you saying I'm predictable?"

"Far from it. But you do have a penguin vibe about you."

"What the hell is a penguin vibe?" I ask, laughing.

"Just means I can totally picture you at a zoo fawning over the little tuxedoed creatures as they waddle about."

"Right." I shake my head. "For the record, I don't fawn, I gush."

This gets a chuckle out of Oliver. "And the animal you'd want to own?" he asks.

"That would be a dog."

"A dog? That's fairly simple. Didn't you have one growing up?"

A bitter laugh escapes, surprising me. "My mother wasn't an animal person."

"Well, that's a right shame. Dogs are amazing. We had two growing up. Harold and Lady Sprinkles."

"Lady Sprinkles? Did someone eat a cookie right before naming her?"

"No, and she was actually a he. Sophie named him before knowing it was a boy, and she just really liked the name. She was three."

"That's adorable."

"Probably gave the poor bloke a complex."

I laugh loudly and receive several shushes. "One of the ladies in our building had a dog," I say. "She let me play with him and take him for walks. She knew how much I wanted a dog. His name was Caesar, and he was this white puffball of a dog. Some days he could have passed for a cotton ball."

"Now that would be something to see. A walking cotton ball."

"I have a picture." I pull out my phone and power it on. "She moved recently, so I haven't seen him in a while." I scroll through the photos, ignoring the near-constant buzz of notifications I knew would flood in. "Here it is." I hand the phone to him and lean over the table so I can see it, too. Our hands brush, and a fevered chill runs across my skin, goosebumps rising on my arms while my chest heats.

"Wow, you weren't kidding. He's so fluffy you can't even see his eyes."

"Let me see if I can find the one of him right after he decided a mud puddle was the best place for a nap." I pull the phone back towards me and start scrolling through the camera roll. A text vibrates in, the notification flashing across the top of my screen. I freeze when I see the message, my heart racing. "Shit."

"Remy? Everything alright? Did you delete all your photos?" he chuckles.

"I..." I stand quickly, nearly knocking over my chair. "I have to go."

"What? What's wrong?"

"I just have to go." I start backing away, shaking my head. I turn and bolt for the door, yanking it open and hurrying out into the heat.

Chapter Eight

Two Months Ago

"Him again?" Celia hands the vendor some money and I grab the tacos.

I nod and lead us to a seat at one of the tables next to the food truck. I'd shown up on Celia's doorstep the day after Gage and I had the huge blow-up, bag in hand and crying. I'd told her that we'd had a fight and that I needed a place to stay while we both cooled off. I hadn't wanted to go into much detail, and she didn't push me. She knows that it was more than just a typical fight, though. We had those all the time, and it didn't send me running to her place. Now, two days later, as we sit here eating our tacos, I brace myself for the questions I know she's about to ask.

"Are you ready to tell me what happened?" Celia asks, twisting the top off her soda.

I tear open a salsa pack with my teeth and squeeze it over my tacos. I take a bite and deliberately chew slowly, putting off answering.

Celia leans forward, waving a hand in front of my face. "Remy?"

I swallow my mouthful of taco and look at her. She's looking at me expectantly, not touching her food.

"When I came home the other night, he was passed out drunk," I say, taking a swig of my own soda.

"That's nothing new, though," Celia says, shrugging.

"He woke up and was a complete ass."

"Again, nothing new," Celia says. "What happened that was different?" I watch her eyes flash with anger. "Did he hit you?" Her eyes roam my body, searching for some bruise or wound she'd missed before.

"What? Celia, no."

"If he hit you, I'll—"

I hear the edge in her voice, the threat of what she'll do if Gage ever hit me.

"He didn't hit me, Celia." I say. "He was—he wanted me to have sex with him and I didn't want to. He got a little too pushy with it." I shrug. "I stopped him, and we said some things, and then I kicked him out." I take another drink. "I'm tired, Celia. I'm tired of coming home to find him drunk. I'm tired of him stumbling home drunk after a night out at his so-called business meetings."

Celia looks away, huffing in frustration.

"Look, I know what you're thinking," I say, trying to catch her eye. "You're trying to figure out why I'm still with him."

"Damn straight that's what I'm thinking. Remy, you're so un-happy, and he's such a fucking dick. I can't believe we're having this conversation...again."

I sigh, shaking my head. "Lately, he makes it hard to remember why I'm with him."

"Then leave!" Celia yells, attracting the looks of several surrounding people. "I have never understood why you've stayed with him. Just leave already."

I sigh, shaking my head. "You know it's not that easy."

"No, I don't know why it's not that easy," Celia says.

"It's just so complicated. But I'm not going to lie, I've been thinking about leaving."

Celia nods encouragingly, clearly liking the idea.

"It's just not that easy," I repeat.

Celia has always struggled to understand why I've stayed with Gage. When it was for college she was a little more understanding. However, this past year, since he proposed, she's become less understanding and more demanding of answers. Answers I can't give her.

"All you ever say is that it's complicated or not easy. You were all set to end things after graduation, and then the proposal happened. What aren't you telling me, Remy? Because I know there's something you're keeping from me."

I shake my head because I don't have an answer for her.

Celia sighs in frustration. "I just want you to be happy, Remy. Promise me that you won't go through with this wedding if you have even an ounce of doubt in you."

I can't promise her that. It's true that I've been thinking of leaving Gage, but I also know how much is at stake if I do. Celia grabs my hand on the table and squeezes it.

"Promise me, dammit." Celia stares at me, anxiously waiting for me to reply.

I look into her worry-filled eyes and nod.

❧ ···•··· ❧

The elevator doors slide open to reveal Gage sitting on the floor by Celia's apartment door. Her apartment is the only one on this floor, and it's keycard access only. His knees are drawn to his chest, and he's resting his head on his arms. Gage looks up as we step off the elevator.

"How the hell did you get up here?" Celia asks, taking a step forward and crossing her arms.

"The doorman let me up." Gage stands, shoving his hands into his pockets.

"I'll be sure to let him know the garbage goes to the basement, not my apartment."

"Retract the claws, Celia. I'm just here to talk to my fiancé."

"Did you ever stop to think that maybe she doesn't want to talk to you? Hence all of the unanswered calls and texts."

"Celia, it's ok." I step forward and put a hand on her shoulder. "I'll just be a minute."

Celia looks at me and then back at Gage. She shakes her head and steps around him to unlock the door before disappearing inside.

"She seems happy to see me," Gage says, rolling his eyes.

"What do you want, Gage?"

"That's all I get? No 'It's good to see you' or anything?"

I glare up at him, anger rising quickly. "What the hell do you want me to say, Gage? It's not good to see you. My patience for playing nice with you is running pretty low these days."

"Don't be dramatic."

My nostrils flare. "Ok, Sylvia." When Gage looks at me, confused, I continue. "You sound just like my mother."

"Do you think maybe she always told you that because you're always so dramatic?"

I throw my hands up. "I'm not doing this." I go to step around him, but he sidesteps, blocking the door.

"I'm sorry. Remy, I'm sorry. Please just hear me out."

"I'm getting real tired of your apologies, Gage."

"Please?" He reaches a hand out to touch my shoulder, and I take a step back.

"You were out of line the other night, Gage."

"Yeah, I was an ass. But I've been an ass before, and we've been just fine."

"I think that's the problem."

"What is?"

"You keep being an ass, I keep letting you be an ass, and then we just go on with our lives. Something needs to change. Gage, you..." I stop, not sure I can get the sentence out. "You realize what happened the other night, right? I need you to tell me what you think happened."

He sighs heavily, rolling his eyes as if this is all such a hassle for him. "I came home and passed out. Then I found you looking sexy in the closet. I thought I was going to get lucky with my fiancé. I said something stupid or dickish or both, and you kicked me out."

I stare at him, shaking my head in disbelief. "Wow." I turn and walk back towards the elevator. I don't know where I'm going, but I'm not sure I can stay here and have this conversation right now. I press the button and wait.

"What?" Gage asks. "Remy, where are you going? We're having a conversation."

I shake my head, glaring at the elevator doors, willing them to open.

"Remy, talk to me. I don't understand what the big deal is."

Anger explodes from me, and I whirl around. "You tried to force yourself on me, Gage!"

"Whoa, I wasn't forcing anything." He holds his hands up, shaking his head. "One whisper that I was trying to force myself on you, and our lives will be turned upside down."

"Ugh!" I run my hands through my hair. The elevator opens and I turn towards it.

"Remy, don't get on the elevator. Just stay and talk to me."

"You don't even remember what really happened, because you were so drunk," I say to the open elevator. The doors slide shut.

"I told you what happened."

I pull my shirt sleeve up and shove my arm in his face. "Do you see the bruises, Gage? That's where you kept yanking me towards you." I pull my shirt up in the back. "And that bruise is from where you pressed me into the doorframe when I tried to walk away." I put my shirt down and turn to face him. Gage stares at the bruises on my arm, a pained look in his eyes. "I wasn't into it, Gage. And, if you haven't noticed, our lives are already upside down."

Gage's head drops, and his shoulders sag. He slides down the wall and sits on the floor, burying his face in his hands. I watch as a slight tremble rolls through his shoulders.

"Gage?"

Another tremble. I sit on the floor in front of him, but he still doesn't look up. Silence surrounds us for a few minutes before, finally, he uncovers his face. His eyes are rimmed red, and there are tear streaks on his face. I stare at the tears continuing to roll down his cheeks, shocked. My trust in this man went out the window years ago, and I've come to question all of his motives. Is this real, or is it just another one of his games?

"I know it won't mean anything to you, but...I'm sorry." His voice sounds genuine, but he's such a good liar when he needs to be. "I know I've treated you like shit, and I'm horrible to you. I don't deserve you. My mom would be so disappointed in the man I've become."

I know how close Gage and his mom were before she died. After her death, he truly spiraled out of control and became this shell of a man. "If you're so worried about how disappointed your mom would be, maybe you should try changing."

Gage nods. "You're right. Dammit." Gage wipes at his face. "I want to be the man my mother wanted me to be. I don't know why you've stayed with me."

"You've not given me much of a choice, Gage."

He closes his eyes and pinches the bridge of his nose, nodding. "I know, I know. I don't want to lose you, Remy. I've put you through years of bullshit. I want to try. I want to try to be a better man. I don't want you to feel like you have to keep doing this, us. I want you to want to be in this relationship."

I stare at him, taking in his words, still unable to believe a single one of them. How can I? "How am I supposed to respond to that? Am I supposed to say that everything is ok, and we can live happily ever after?"

"No, of course not," he says, shaking his head. "Say...say you'll give me another chance."

"You've had chances, Gage, and you've taken them for granted."

Gage sighs, frustrated. "Can't you see that I'm trying here? That I'm putting forth an effort?"

"I see a guy who's done nothing but make one bullshit mistake after another, and now that he has to answer to it, he's scared. So, excuse me for not believing you, Gage. You've not given me a reason to buy into your bullshit for a while now."

Gage closes his eyes, and fresh tears stream down his face. He blows out a breath. "The fact that I forced you into that situation"—his voice is tight and he has to stop and swallow before continuing—"it's just unacceptable. The bruises, what I said to you…" he trails off, shaking his head. "I don't know who this person is. I feel like I've become some sort of monster, the villain of my own story. I don't want to be like that anymore."

"You remember what you said to me?"

Gage nods but doesn't speak or look at me.

"Do you know how much you're asking of me right now? You've done nothing but lie, cheat, and threaten me. You want to erase all of that now?"

Gage looks at me and shakes his head. "Not erase. I know it can never be wiped away, and it shouldn't. It needs to be there as a reminder of the person I am currently but no longer want to be. I want to move forward from this moment and try to be the man you deserve."

I stare at the wall behind him. I'm not sure what's happening right now. Maybe I fell asleep at the food truck or hit my head. Maybe I never woke up this morning, and this is all a dream—or would this be a nightmare? He talks as though I've had the choice to leave him all this time. Is he saying all this so I won't cause a scene with our parents? Or maybe he's worried it'll turn into a publicity nightmare if I'm not at the Johnson Foundation Cancer Benefit this weekend. Then again, he never really cared about the publicity. I don't know if I can believe that he really wants to change. After all, why would he need to change? He has all he could ever want.

An image tugs at my memory; a vulnerable young man spilling all his secrets to me as we hid away in his dad's study during his mom's funeral. With that image, a tiny sliver of doubt begins to creep in. Maybe there's still some part of that vulnerable boy inside the person in front of me. Maybe he is capable?

I take a deep breath. "This won't be easy," I say.

Gage looks at me, hope in his eyes.

I continue. "The drinking has to stop and so does the partying. The other girls—that's done too."

"I know," he nods, reaching over to take both of my hands in his—

But I pull away.

"We aren't there yet. I'm not there yet," I say.

"I understand. I'm sorry."

"I also want you to go to therapy."

"By myself? Or with you?"

I mull it over. "Both."

His eyebrows lift and he blows out a breath. "I don't know, Remy."

"It's not up for debate. If you want to make this work as badly as you say you do, you'll do it."

"I do want to make this work. Whatever you need, however you need me to be."

"Right now, I need you to go home, Gage. I'm staying the night with Celia. I'll be home tomorrow. Figure out how to have a normal, quiet night. Alone." I stand up and let myself into the apartment without another word.

Chapter Nine

"It's a bit early for the pier, Miss. Are you sure this is where you want to be dropped off?" The taxi driver turns around, a concerned fatherly look on his craggy face.

I'd called an Uber a few blocks from the coffee shop. The first place that came to mind when the app prompted a destination was Navy Pier. "Yeah, I'll be fine," I say, my hand on the door handle.

"The shops aren't even open yet."

"I'm fine, thanks."

The wind pushes me backward as the car pulls away, and I have to grab a post for balance. The ferris wheel is unmoving in the distance against the blue sky. As the driver has warned, most of the shops are either still closed or just showing signs of life inside. The water is choppy, crashing into the sides of the pier. Finally, I reach the end of the pier and look out over the fierce, churning waters of Lake Michigan. Despite it being early, people are already out on boats and jet skis, cutting through the angry waves. Birds swoop down on the water, rising again with their catch clasped tightly in their talons. The wind is stronger out here, whipping my ponytail around and pulling strands loose. It's cooler out here than on the city streets, and I welcome the sun as I tilt my face to it, letting the warmth soak into me. I take a deep breath and let it go.

"What are you doing, Remy?" I ask into the emptiness around me. But my question is swept away in the wind, unanswered.

As I stand here staring out at the cerulean water, my dress is hanging in the suite at the Plaza Hotel, the chairs are being placed neatly in rows, flowers are being delivered, and everything is getting set up for a wedding that is never going to happen. I should probably have knots in my stomach, a tightness in my chest, and maybe even a feeling of panic and guilt. However, for the first time, I feel a sense of peace. I feel like I finally made the right decision, for once.

Sure, I ran away from my life, from everything I've ever known, but I finally did something for myself. I know what Gage is going to do if he hasn't already and the repercussions that await me. I'm sure my mother is frantic by now. Her worry isn't for me, though. No, for me she'll just be angry. Her worry lies with herself and what to tell her friends and the guests of the wedding so that she doesn't look bad. I struggle to find the will to care about any of it.

Since the moment I turned it on, my phone has been buzzing. Every possible kind of notification I can get has been pouring into my inboxes. I pull it out of my pocket and look at them. There are countless numbers of voicemails from my mother, texts from Gage and Celia, and...I scroll down to see there are some from my Dad, too. The first voicemail is from last night, about half an hour after I left.

"Remy, Dear, it's your mother. Where have you gotten to? Everyone at the party is asking for you. You should be mingling with your guests. Call me back."

The next voicemail has fewer pleasantries, and her voice has more of an edge to it.

"Remy, it's your mother again. Your father said he saw you leave. Where are you? You're being rude and inconsiderate. Get back here, now!"

At least a dozen more through the night are in my inbox. The last message from her is from an hour ago, and she's in complete panic mode.

"Remy! This is, like, the millionth message I've left you. Where the hell are you? It's your wedding day. Your dress is here and ready, and you're not. People are asking for you. What am I supposed to tell them? Call me back immediately! You're embarrassing yourself and me."

I laugh at how predictably upset she is. There are a few texts from Celia as well.

Celia

> Did you ditch this party and not take me with you? What kind of friend does that? JK, text me back.

Celia

> Everyone is freaking out. Your dad said you left earlier and that you looked upset. Did it happen? Did the bird finally fly the nest?

Celia

> Girl, are you ok? Let me know you're ok. Luv you

I feel a little bad that I didn't let Celia know what was going on, but I know she'll forgive me. Gage's messages are next in line.

Gage

> Where'd you go, baby?

Gage

Everyone is worried about you…where are you?
Please answer me

Gage

It's our wedding day and you're not here…instead
you hopped a train to Chicago. That makes it a little
tricky for us to get married…guess I'll be seeing you
soon <3

The last message is the one that made my blood run cold at the coffee shop. How could he possibly know where I am? How long do I have before he shows up here? Should I just head for the train station or airport now? I see the voicemail from my dad and press play.

"Remy, my sweet girl, I don't know what's going on, or why you left here looking so upset, but I know that I love you and I just want to know you're ok. You know I support you no matter what. I love you, Remy. Please just let me know you're ok."

I swallow the lump in my throat. I wish I could save him from what is coming. I pull up Celia's number and FaceTime her. She answers on the second ring.

"You finally fucking did it." The smile on her face is huge, and her chocolate eyes are shining brightly. Her beautiful dark curls are pulled back into a bun, the stubborn ones curling tightly around her forehead. Whoever did her makeup chose a beautifully soft pink color to go with her dark skin.

I laugh because of course that's how she'd answer the phone. "I finally did it. Also, you look beautiful."

"I'm so proud of you, Babe. You finally got out. Where are you? It's loud. Also, thank you."

"I'm in Chicago, at Navy Pier by the water."

"Of all the places you could have picked in this world, you picked there?"

"I didn't pick here. Story for another time."

"No judgment. I'm just happy you're not in New York right now."

"Gage knows where I am." My stomach twists.

"How?"

"I don't know. He's Gage. He has his ways. But, Celia, he's coming here. He's coming after me. What should I do?"

"You owe him nothing, Remy. You're not his property. He's not your problem. So what if he shows up? Call the damn cops for harassment if you have to."

I think about what he's going to do and bite my lip because he's still a tiny bit my problem.

"There's still something you're not telling me." Celia stares at me through the phone, waiting.

"There is, but it's a lot."

"Give me the abbreviated version, then."

I sigh and look over the top of my phone at the water, trying to think of how I want to word this. "Look, I really can't get into details because it could take hours. So, please, just take what I'm about to say and leave it at that. Ok? No questions."

"No questions," Celia promises.

A deep breath, and I let the words spill out of me. "Gage is blackmailing me because he has dirt on my family."

Celia's face is frozen on the screen for so long that I start to wonder if the connection dropped. "Celia? You still there? You look frozen."

She blinks and shakes her head. "I don't think you understand how hard it is for me to refrain from asking you any questions right now. Just know that because you're my very best friend, I'm respecting your wishes. But damn! That's a bomb of information!"

I nod and blow out a breath. I can hear faint yelling in the background and Celia looks away. I think I recognize my mother's voice. "Where are you?" I ask.

"The hotel suite bathroom." Celia says. "Sylvia is running around like a tyrant yelling at the girls that they still need to be getting ready. She's in serious denial about there not being a wedding today. She still seems to think you're going to sashay through that door any second now."

"I have never in my life sashayed, and I don't intend to start now."

Celia laughs, but suddenly there's pounding at the door, and she falls silent. "Look," Celia whispers, "I have to go before she breaks the door down, and we both know she will. Be safe and keep me posted."

"I will. Can you..." I trail off.

"Can I what?" Celia asks, as more pounding sounds on her end.

"Can you let my...can you let Charles know I'm safe?"

Confusion crosses Celia's face. "Sure, I can do that. If you can do me a favor."

"What's that?" I ask.

"Take a risk. Live a little. Be happy." Celia blows me a kiss, and the call ends before I can respond.

I shove my phone back in my pocket and take one last long look at the water. I turn and retreat up the pier. I can't remember the last time I had nothing planned to do, nothing requiring my time and energy to be put into it. This level of freedom is exhilarating. I feel my phone go off again. I pull it out almost certain it's my mother, but am surprised to see I have a new message on my Instagram. I open the app and see that I also have a new follower, *Oliverse*. I click the profile and roll my eyes but find myself smiling too. Another buzz, another message. I open the messages.

Oliverse

Are you ok?

Oliverse

Did I do something to upset you?

I don't respond. I don't know how to put into words why I just ran out. I was genuinely having a good time with him.

An employee is unlocking the doors to the interior shops and eateries. I see a sign flashing 'open' at me in bright neon letters in the window of a candy store. I duck inside, and the cool air sends a flood of goosebumps down my arms. I make my way across the concourse and into the candy store. A small, older woman pulls a dolly of boxes through a door in the back. She startles at the sight of me.

"I'm sorry, I didn't hear the bell. What can I get ya, hun?" She brushes her hands against her apron and sidles over to the register.

I look around the shop, my eyes darting across the colorful wrappers and prettily packed chocolates. I pick up a small box containing just three dark chocolate and sea salt caramel truffles. My mouth waters just looking at the box. "I'll take a box of these and a bottle of water please."

"Those chocolates won't last long in that heat." The woman nods towards the pier.

"These chocolates won't last long in these hands."

The woman laughs a full belly laugh. "Good point, dear."

The bell chimes overhead signaling the door. The woman's eyes scan over the customer before returning to the register. I let my eyes roam around the shop looking at different displays when they land on the person who just came in.

Oliver is looking at a display of saltwater taffy. He looks up, and seems almost as surprised as I feel.

"This actually is starting to get creepy," I say. I wander over to him. "How the hell did you know I was here? Should I start calling you Joe Goldberg?"

Oliver's surprise changes to puzzlement. "Sorry, who's Joe?" he asks.

"Never mind. Seriously though, are you following me?"

"Absolutely not." He shakes his head.

"How do you explain this, then?" I wave my arms around to indicate the shop.

"Pure coincidence. I wanted to get taffy for my mum. She loves the stuff. I hear this is one of the best shops to get it."

"You heard correctly, young man."

We both turn to see the old woman nodding her head and smiling. I turn back to Oliver. "Wouldn't she be able to get it anytime?"

"How's that? I don't know what you mean," Oliver asks.

"Well, I would think, living in Chicago, she'd have pretty easy access to the stuff."

Oliver quirks an eyebrow. "I never said she lived in Chicago."

"But..." I pause, confused. "You said on the train that you were on your way to see your mom."

"Right you are. I, however, did not say that she lives in Chicago. This is just a stop along the way. Had to get the taffy." He rattles the box he's holding.

The woman clears her throat, sliding my water and chocolates over to me. "Here you are. Anything else I can get you?"

"No, I'm all set. Thank you."

"Yes, you are, dear." Her eyes roam over Oliver again and, clearing her throat, she asks, "Can I get you something, sir?"

Oliver steps up to the counter and places the taffy on it, paying and thanking the woman. We step back outside, and I work on tucking my water into the side of my bag.

"Why did you run?"

I stall, taking longer than necessary to get the bottle into the pocket. "I'm sorry," I finally say. "I shouldn't have run out on you like that. It was rude."

"Was it something I said?"

"No." I squint against the sun to see his face. "It wasn't anything to do with you."

Oliver eyes me like he's searching for something. "I guess it's really none of my business."

"Right. Thanks," I say, turning to continue up the pier towards the city skyline.

"Where are you headed?" Oliver catches up to me, stepping over a hose a custodian is using to clean the sidewalk.

I don't have a good answer for this because, I don't actually know. "Uh, a hotel I guess. You?"

"Might do some sightseeing but then head back to the hotel. I grabbed a room before coming here. I've got a ticket for first thing in the morning."

I stop walking and face him. "I guess this really is goodbye then." I put a hand out to shake his.

Oliver smirks, looking down at my hand. "Do you truly think this is goodbye, Remy?" He shakes my hand anyway, his hand strong in mine. "Maybe it is. But, listen, if you need anything before I leave tomorrow, you can shoot me a message on Instagram. Or if you're feeling really crazy and wanna tag along with me tomorrow, you're more than welcome to. Could be another good change of scenery for you." He winks.

"Thanks for the offer stalker, but I think I'm good. Good luck with the rest of your trip."

"You too, Remy. See you 'round." He smiles and heads in the direction I just came from, towards the gleaming water.

Chapter Ten

One Month Ago

I sit on a park bench watching the pigeons peck the ground. I laugh to myself remembering a book I read recently that had a billionaire who wanted to rescue all the pigeons. The park is crowded. It's the first truly nice spring day we've had so far this year. There's still a slight chill in the air, but it's not stopping anyone: bicycles roll by, people hurry past, and a man rollerblading trips over his own feet, rolling on to the soft grass next to him. I check my phone again.

He's twenty minutes late. My eyes scan the park in both directions but still no sign of him. He probably got held up in a meeting again.

I spot a hotdog cart and wander over.

"What can I get ya?" the vendor asks, his voice gruff as he spins the hotdog tongs in his hand.

I stare at the toppings menu, trying to decide. I can hear the vendor chomping on his gum.

"Are you ordering or not, lady? I ain't got all day."

I glance behind me and back at the vendor. "Yeah, because people are lined up down the street." I'm not usually so snarky, but I'm irritated today. "I'll take one please, with ketchup, mustard, and just a hint of relish."

The vendor grunts and starts to make my hotdog.

"I don't always like relish, but I'm kind of in the mood for it today." I have no idea why I just said this. It's not like the vendor cares about my day-to-day food preferences.

"Good for you. That'll be three dollars," he mumbles.

I hand him the money and return to the bench I'd been sitting on. I take a bite and am glad I went with the relish. Suddenly, a squirrel scrambles down the tree behind me and perches on the arm of the bench.

"Well, hello," I say to him. I assume it's a 'him'; it's not like I've brushed up on my squirrel-gender-identifying skills. He stands on his back legs, staring me down. I tear a piece of bread and toss it over to him. He hops down and onto the seat and grabs the bread, nibbling on it. "Must be nice, being a squirrel. Life is probably so easy for you. You can come down and look all cute, and people give you free food. No one has any expectations of you at all."

The squirrel just looks at me, and that's when I realize I'm talking to a squirrel. A woman hurries past, looking sideways at me, and I give her a smile. I try to ignore the furry creature next to me by smiling at everyone that goes by, but one peek out of the corner of my eye confirms he's still there.

"Oh fine." I take one final bite, leaving the end of the bun. I set it on the bench, and the squirrel snatches it up, climbing back up onto the arm of the bench to nibble on it.

"Remy!"

I look up and see him hurrying towards me, waving. I get up from the bench, toss my trash, and rush towards him, letting his arms wrap around me and pull me close. "You're late, Dad."

"I know, I'm sorry. The meeting ran late. Everyone is all 'Charles' this and 'Mr. Montgomery' that. Gage's father is quite the talker too. I hope you haven't been waiting too long."

"No, not long. I grabbed a hotdog and was swindled out of most of the bread by a squirrel."

Dad's eyebrows raise. "Is that so? Those Central Park squirrels can be quite cunning. Coffee?" He points in the direction of our favorite place.

"Absolutely," I say, looping my arm through his. This used to be a weekly thing for us, but as life has gotten busier and Dad's job has pulled his attention more these days, it's become more of a monthly thing.

We make our way towards the shop while he tells me about his day.

"How'd the trip to Sweden go?" I ask as Dad holds the door open for me. I duck inside and find our table by the window is empty. We sit and a waitress bustles over and takes our order. Once she's hurried off again, Dad finally answers.

"Uh, it was…" He trails off, and it seems like his face grows older, his eyes more tired. "I don't think it went well. We, well, we lost the account. I guess I should say, I lost the account."

"What happened?"

He just shakes his head. "Too many factors. I just dropped the ball on this one."

"Dad, I'm so sorry. I know that was an important trip for you."

He waves me off. "Enough about me. Business talk is annoying. I do it all day. How are you doing, sweetie? I feel like I never see you anymore. What's new?"

I take a deep breath. "Nothing, really. I've been doing a lot of work on the Johnson Foundation event...reading..." I trail off, shrugging.

"I have to admit, the last book you posted about was a good one. I totally agree with your assessment of the ending."

I stare at him, shocked.

"What?" he asks, chuckling.

"You watch my stuff?" I ask, astonished.

"Of course I do! I'm proud of you. I get some really interesting reading material from there. Stuff I would never have thought to read."

I smile. "That's pretty awesome, Dad." He and I have always been close. He's tried to spend as much time with me as possible. My mother hated this. She hated the attention my existence took away from her. Until now, it would seem. Now, she gets all the attention because I'm getting married.

Dad's phone beeps, and he looks down and rolls his eyes. "Your mother...again. Informing me that we have a fundraiser tomorrow evening." He sets his phone down again, rubbing his forehead in the exact same spot that I do. "Always something with her." He sighs.

I look at him, like really look at him. He's exhausted. Dark circles have taken up residence under his green eyes. His once copper hair has paled, dusted with a shower of grays. His mouth curves down into a frown.

"Dad, can I ask you a question?"

"I think you just did, kiddo." He winks. "What's up?"

I take a deep breath. How does someone ask their parent this kind of question?

"Remy?" Dad prompts.

"Would..." I stop. "Would you still be with Mom if she hadn't gotten pregnant with me?"

He splutters into his drink, looking at me in surprise. "Where on earth did that question come from?"

"You seem drained by her and by this world. I know that you guys had been dating, but I wonder if it would've worked out if I hadn't come along."

Dad sighs, smiling, but it doesn't reach his eyes. "That's a difficult question to answer, Remy. There is nothing in this world that I love and care about more than you. I care for your mother no matter how much of a chore she can be because she gave me you." He pauses, his expression shifting, like he's reaching back into some stored away memories. "I think you're old enough for the honest truth. Back then, your mother was a lot of fun to be with. I think I enjoyed her wildness—which contrasted so greatly with my reserved tendencies. Oh, the things she could convince me to do."

I hold up my hands, scrunching my nose. "I don't need the details, Dad."

He laughs. "Ok, ok." His face settles back into a thoughtful expression. "I do think that the lure of her wildness would have worn off, and I'd have been left to make a decision." He looks me in the eyes. "No, Remy, I don't think I would have stayed with her. I probably would have been the one to take over my family's business, like my dad had intended, instead of my sister."

My heart sinks. I'm the reason he's been so miserable this whole time. I'm responsible for his unhappiness. My thoughts and sadness show, because Dad scoots his chair closer to me and takes my hand.

"Don't you dare blame yourself, Remy. You are the only thing that has truly brought me happiness in life. If I didn't have you, I'd be lost. A raft floating in an endless sea. I chose to stay with her so that I could give you a whole family, not a broken one. I've never once regretted that decision." Dad swipes at a tear sliding down my cheek.

"I thought Grandpa forced you guys to marry?"

"When your mother told me she was pregnant with you, all I could think about was you and how excited and terrified I was that you were going to exist. At first, your mom didn't want to go through with having you. Grandma Montgomery wanted other options as well."

Dad winces and squeezes my hand. "I fought like hell against that. Your mom, well, she was hell-bent on not agreeing with anything her mom said. After Grandma Montgomery expressed her intentions on making other arrangements for the situation, your mom was determined to keep you. After that, your grandma suggested they raise you and leave me out of the picture. Again, your mom rebelled. So, we eloped, your grandfather offered me the job, and here we are."

Of course my mother had considered not going through with having me. I can't pretend I'm surprised by that. My entire life she's resented me for simply existing. Maybe, by trying to stick it to her own mom, she had realized what she'd done and it had been too late. Obviously she regretted going through with it.

Dad squeezes my hand again. "Remy, what's this really about?"

I shake my head and look out the window. My existence has caused so much trouble from the start with everyone in my life.

"Is this about your wedding? What are we, a month out?"

I wrinkle my nose and nod.

"What?" He looks at me knowingly. "I know that look."

"I dunno. The wedding. It's mostly Mother's thing. She's basically planned the whole thing."

"You know your mother, always the planner."

"Mmm," I reply, sipping my coffee.

"Does it bother you that she's done all the planning?"

"Ugh, no. Better her than me."

Dad looks at me, his eyes narrowing, and his brow furrowing. "Remy, are you happy?"

I don't answer the question. I think back over the last few months with Gage, over our last year. I think about the direction my life is taking. I can't remember the last time I was truly happy. Before I can answer, Dad chimes in.

"Should I ask you a different question? Do you really want to get married?"

I just stare at him, my throat tight, unable to form words. My brain unable to send the word 'no' that my brain is screaming to my mouth. He gives me a half smile, a sad smile, his eyes full of concern.

"I want—no, I need you to be happy," he says. "It's what I've worked so hard for your whole life. I wanted to ensure that you were happy and healthy. If you aren't happy, for whatever reason, I need you to change that. Ok? Life is too damn short to be anything but happy. I will love you and be so very proud of you, no matter what." He leans in and wraps me in a hug.

His phone rings, and he picks it up off the table. I see Mr. Donovan's face on the screen and I know he has to go. "It's ok, Dad."

"I'm so sorry, honey." He hugs me again. "I love you. Remember, find your happiness. No matter what." He kisses my forehead before hurrying from the café.

"I'm working on it," I say as the door swings shut behind him.

Chapter Eleven

Checking in at the hotel reminds me just how complicated Gage made everything. It always had to be this big ordeal with people rushing to greet us and taking our bags, and giving us all of the special treatment someone with a lot of money deserves. He always had to have the penthouse suite with all of the amenities and the best views. It's refreshing how simple it is for me. Today, I am just a normal person.

The room is simple with a king bed situated against one wall, a row of floor to ceiling windows to its left, and a desk and dresser across from the bed. The bathroom has a nice soaking tub perfect for the bubble bath I will more than likely take later. I look out at the city skyline and at the cars moving below through the streets like ants in sand. I flop backwards on the bed, sinking into the plush covers. A sigh of content escapes me as I lie staring at the sky through the window. With each ping of my phone, the thought of how close Gage might be to Chicago breaks into my mind. I wonder if the tabloids have picked up the story yet. I dig out my phone and type my name into the browser, and immediately there are a dozen headlines.

Anticipated Wedding of the Year Called Off!

Remy Montgomery on Self-Destructive Path with South American Kingpin!

Is Remy Montgomery Our Modern Day Runaway Bride?

Montgomery Family Shamed by Daughter's Disappearing Fiasco!

Gage Donovan: Picture of a Broken Man

Someone managed to capture a picture of Gage in his tux, a drink in hand, and him staring blankly across the room. The image tells the story of a broken-hearted man, but I know that's just what Gage looks like when he's plastered. I groan and throw my phone across the bed. I assumed the headlines would be bad, but these are just ridiculous. A South American Kingpin? Really? It occurs to me that the only thing in the headlines is the wedding, no other family drama. I don't know if that should worry me or not. Instead of letting myself lie here and wallow in all of the questions and what-ifs, I follow the sound of the bubble bath that's calling my name.

An hour and some pruney fingers later, I emerge from the steamy bathroom a little more relaxed. I kick back and start channel surfing when I hear my phone ring from the end of the bed. I lean forward to see Gage's name and picture flashing across the screen. My stomach drops, and I just stare at it until finally it falls quiet. I see half a dozen other missed calls and texts from my parents. The phone starts ringing again. Knowing I can't avoid it forever because he'll just keep calling, I answer it. Music blares through the speaker, and I yank the phone away from my ear.

"Hello?!" I yell into the phone.

"Hold on!"

I hear the music start to fade, and the line gets quiet.

"Remy, I'm glad you answered—finally. I've been worried about you." Gage's voice is sickly sweet, as though he hopes I'll get stuck to every word that comes out of his mouth.

"Yeah, it really sounds like you're worried. Drowning your sorrows in whiskey or tits? Wait, that's a silly question, both of course."

"Jealous are we?" Gage asks.

I make a retching sound. "Oh sorry, that was me throwing up in my mouth."

"Dammit, Remy, what's your problem? You've embarrassed our families, yourself, and me. You're being impossible. I'm coming to Chicago in the morning. This needs to end."

I cross to the window and stare out at the city. I can hear Gage muttering to someone.

"Remy? You there?"

"You know, Gage, you're right. This does need to end. I'm not going back with you. How do you even know where I am?"

"I have my ways of knowing, Remy. You should know that by now."

"Oh right, I must have forgotten you're the all powerful Oz. Shouldn't you be dick deep in some poor girl right now?" As if on cue, there's a burst of giggles and murmuring in the background. I hear a 'shh' before Gage starts talking again.

"You know what's going to happen if you don't come back with me."

I hear the hard edge in his voice, the threat. Dad's face floats into my mind and my heart squeezes. I know exactly what will happen if I don't go back. It's the same reason I agreed to marry him. Only, it's even more complicated than I thought. I can't keep myself trapped in that world anymore, though. I need to start living for myself. I turn away from the window and sit back down on the edge of the bed.

"Go to hell, Gage."

I'm sitting at the hotel bar, a rum and Coke in hand and an empty shot glass in front of me.

"Another?" the bartender points at the shot glass.

"Why not?" I throw my hands up. It'll be my third shot since sitting down an hour ago. I already devoured the BLT that I'd ordered the second it was placed in front of me.

He fills the shot glass with more Fireball, and I knock it back, chasing it down with my drink. After I'd hung up on Gage, I'd paced the room for a while, contemplating what to do. Then I'd lain down to think some more and must have fallen asleep. The next thing I knew it was almost dark outside my window. My stomach had been growling so fiercely I figured the best thing to do was grab some dinner.

I flip my phone over and over on the bar top. I've come to the conclusion that I have until at least noon tomorrow to get out of Chicago. Gage will be out all night partying, losing himself in some more than willing girl, and then sleeping it off late into the morning. I just have to figure out—between now and the time he rounds up his daddy's jet—where the hell I'm going, and how I'm getting there. I could take the train and head West, see where I end up. There's also the option of renting a car and going in any direction. An idea that I haven't even let myself consider—because it shouldn't be in my mind at all—jumps to the front: Oliver's words keeping coming back to me about joining him.

"You're being absurd, Remy. You don't even know the guy," I mutter to myself. The bartender shoots me a look but continues with what he's doing. I flip my phone a few more times before letting it rest screen up. I tap my fingers on the bar. "Just do it,

Remy." I glance at the bartender who, again, gives me a look like 'should I still be pouring you shots?'

I unlock my phone and open Instagram. I tap on my new follower, and it takes me to his profile. The most recent picture is from the train. The sun is backlighting the city skyline in the far distance. There's no caption with the picture, but I gather that he must have taken it right before I woke up. His other photos are a random mix of abstract photography, landscapes, and just a few of him with other people. I notice that none of his posts have captions and that he doesn't hashtag anything. I laugh as I see a picture of a giraffe staring the camera down, its tongue lolled out to the side, as though asking him for a treat. There's also a squirrel on a bench nibbling a snack, unaware its photo is even being taken.

I blow out a breath and open my messages. Oliver's messages of concern from earlier are at the top of my inbox. I lock my phone and put it back down on the counter and motion for the bartender to pour me another shot. I throw it back, chase it down, and stare at myself in the mirror. "Decision time, Remy." I narrow my eyes at my reflection. "You need to put your big girl panties on and decide what the hell you're doing."

The bartender has stopped and is just outright staring. He raises his eyebrows at me in question, and I just shrug, giving him a sheepish smile. I grab my phone and type a simple message—one that can't have any hidden meaning in it.

"Oh shit." I drop my phone on the counter and run my hands through my hair. "Oh shit, oh shit, oh shit. What did I just do?"

The bartender comes and stands in front of me, crossing his arms.

I point at him. "This is all your fault. You should really take phones away at a certain point. I mean, I could have just made a big mistake."

"Should I take your phone now?" He holds out his hand.

"A little late now, don't you think?"

He shrugs. "If I take it now, it could keep you from making any further potential mistakes."

I scowl at him. He turns and grabs the Fireball, holding it up to me, raising his eyebrows in question. I pause—but only for a moment—before waving him off. I open my phone and call the one person I know will calm me down. The phone barely rings before she answers.

"Remy, everything ok? Please tell me you're having fun." Celia's familiar voice comes through the phone.

"Define fun," I say, spinning my empty shot glass on the bar top. "I need advice."

"Lay it on me, girl. You know I've got your back."

"I'm not interrupting anything, am I?" The thought only just occurring to me that it's a Saturday night and she could be busy.

"If by 'anything' you mean my mud mask, glass of rosé and playing catch up on Bridgerton—then no, you're not interrupting. Ask away."

"I talked to Gage."

"That's not a question. But let's start there. When?"

"Earlier. He called me when I got to my hotel room. I tried ignoring it, but he wouldn't leave me alone so, I finally answered."

"What did he say?"

"That he was coming here tomorrow...to get me."

"Wow, no rush or anything," she deadpans. "Why, the delay?"

"He has to finish the party first."

"How dumb of me. I should have guessed that." Celia sighs. "So, what's this advice you're seeking?"

"Where do I go? I don't want to be in this city when he gets here."

"What are your options?"

I name off the ones I've come up with. "And..." I pause, not finishing the sentence.

"And what?"

I can practically hear Celia sitting up straighter, her eyes narrowing.

"What aren't you telling me?"

"I have another option."

"Annnnd?" she says. "Are you going to keep me in suspense, or are you going to tell me already? Wait, it's a guy isn't it? Oh my unicorns, it's a guy. Who is he? How? Tell me everything!" Her excitement bursts through my phone.

"First of all, you are way too excited. Or do you not remember that I was supposed to get married today?" This comment gains me another curious look from the bartender.

"Oh, whatever. You didn't love him. You're brain checked out of that relationship a long, long time ago. Details. Now."

"He was at the station in New York—"

"Go on."

I imagine Celia popping a piece of popcorn into her mouth and sipping her wine, eagerly waiting for more. "When I got to the train station I was—"

"Elated? Excited? Thrilled? Relieved?" Celia cuts me off.

"I was going to say 'overwhelmed'."

"Oh, well of course you were. Sorry, continue."

I smile and roll my eyes. "I was overwhelmed, and I had asked the lady at the ticket counter to print me a ticket to anywhere, I didn't care where. And she did."

"Ok? I'm not seeing a guy in this story yet," Celia prompts.

"I wasn't ready to look at my ticket and the destination yet. so I stood staring up at the departure boards trying to guess where I was going."

"Sounds like it would have been easier to just look at your ticket but, you do you."

"Anyways, this British guy pops up beside me, worried about having missed his train."

"Ooo British. Intrigued. Keep going."

"I pointed him in the right direction, but then I asked for his help keeping my trip a secret. So...he helped me to my train while I had my eyes closed and ear plugs in."

"Keeping that mystery alive...liking it. What happened next?"

"After the train got moving and I opened my eyes, he was there."

"Wait, on your train? Like he followed you? Ok, not liking this so much anymore. Or am I? I can't decide. I need more details."

"If you stop interrupting me, I can tell you the rest of the story." I laugh.

"Ok, lips are sealed, maybe."

"Anywho, he was on my train. Claims it was fate or, 'kismet' was the word he used. We didn't talk much on the ride. I fell asleep. He asked me to coffee when we first got to Chicago. I declined. But then, when I was having trouble getting a ride outside the station, he found me, offered to buy me coffee again—and I said yes."

"So, living life on the edge. About time. What happened next?"

"We went to coffee, played twenty questions. Gage texted me that he knew where I was. I freaked and bolted."

"That's it? How is this leading to another option for you?"

The bartender sidles over and waves a hand at my empty rum and Coke glass. I nod and push it towards him. "That's not it," I say into the phone. "After I bolted, I went to Navy Pier—as you know because I called you."

"Right, right."

"He was there."

"Gage?"

"No, not Gage. Oliver. The guy from the train."

"Even his name sounds British. Love it. Wait, don't you think it's sus that he was there, too?"

"I mean, a little weird." I shrug, even though she can't see me. "But he was getting taffy for his mom. Said it was the best shop in town to get it at."

"And did you two end up hooking up behind a shop or something?"

"What? Celia, no."

"You're losing me here, babe," Celia says, slurping her wine on the other end of the phone.

"He's leaving town on a bus tomorrow, on his way to see his mom. He invited me to go with him." For the first time during this conversation, there's silence on the other end. "Celia?"

"What kind of vibe do you get from him?"

"What kind of vibe?"

"Yeah, like, do you get serial-killer-stalker vibe? Or is it more of a this-is-my-epic-love-story-meetcute' vibe?"

"Ok—well, those are two extremes. I don't get either. I get more of a..." I pause, trying to find the words. "I dunno, a sweet, goofy, oddball?"

"Is he hot?" Celia asks. "'Cause that's a factor."

"He's definitely easy on the eyes," I say—those dimples and blue eyes flashing through my mind.

"Hmm. You know you could just jump on a plane and be in like Spain or something, right?"

"I know," I say, hesitating. "I'm just..." I don't know how to finish the thought.

"You like him," Celia says, a statement not a question.

"I'm intrigued by him," I respond, wiping at the sweat on my glass.

"Intrigued...wanting to screw his brains out. Is there really a difference?"

"Celia!" My face heats. I hear a ping in my ear and pull my phone away. It's a new message from Oliver. "He just messaged me," I blurt out.

"Not-bad-on-the-eyes-British-Oliver guy just messaged you?" Celia asks. "How?"

"Did I not mention that he started following me on Instagram?"

"You did not. Seriously, this guy is either really into you, or a serial killer. So hard to tell these days." She sighs. "Ok, all jokes aside, where is your head with this?"

It's my turn to sigh. "My head says I'm crazy, I don't know the guy, he could be a serial killer, and I should probably just go my own way."

"Mhmm. And what about your heart?"

My heart. I feel like I only recently started to really listen to my heart, and so far it has led me here. "My heart tells me to lean into the intrigue, to go with him, to take the leap, and go on the adventure." I hear Celia chuckle. "What?" I ask.

"I think you have your answer, Remy. Follow that heart—but use your head to make sure you're safe."

My stomach pinches— but whether with nerves or excitement I'm not sure. "But, isn't this crazy?" I ask, my inner monologue telling me over and over that it is.

"Maybe," Celia says. "But maybe crazy is what you need. To be a little reckless. Like I said earlier, live a little."

I blow out a breath and nod. "Thanks, Celia, for always being on the other end of the line."

"Always," Celia says. "But if you don't keep me updated, I'll be tracking you down myself."

"Ok, ok. I'll text you soon."

"Love you, girl."

"Love you too." I end the call. I pull the phone away from my ear and tap on the message waiting for me from Instagram.

Oliverse

How's the chocolate?

I laugh—because of all things he could have led with, he chose chocolates.

RemyisLIT…erary

Haven't tried them yet…I'm a dinner before dessert kind of girl.

Oliverse

That's a shame…taffy is delicious.

RemyisLIT…erary

You ate your mom's taffy?!

Oliverse

Just a piece! Had to make sure it wasn't poisoned.

RemyisLIT…erary

Riiiiight…well glad to know you weren't poisoned.

No new messages come in, and my screen goes black. Ten minutes pass. Then fifteen. I cash out and make my way to the elevator, my head buzzing from the alcohol. I stumble through the door of my room. Thick clouds pressing against the window obscure the skyline. I kick my shoes off, stumbling, and fall against the bed. My phone pings, and I struggle to pull it out of my pocket. I fumble with it, and it falls on the floor and under the bed.

"Shit," I groan, kneeling down to search for it. My fingers finally make contact, and I pull it out to see the message. It's from Oliver and I smile. "Stop smiling, Remy." I say to myself as I crawl onto the bed. "You shouldn't be smiling just because he sent you a message." I lie on my back, holding my phone above me.

Oliverse

Sooooo is everything alright?

I frown at his question, confused.

RemyisLIT...erary

What do you mean?

The little dots pop up, blinking on the screen, then disappear, then appear again. I wait for his reply.

Oliverse

I didn't expect to hear from you again.

RemyisLIT...erary

You mean to tell me after all that kismet bullshit you thought you'd never hear from the person you're fated to be with?

Oliverse

First off all, it's not bullshit. That stuff is real, so no mocking. Secondly, I figured we'd have some second chance meet-cute in the future. Just wasn't expecting it to be so soon.

RemyisLIT...erary

Sorry?

Oliverse

Don't be sorry for reaching out...ever. And you didn't answer my question, everything ok?

I set my phone down, unsure how I want to respond. Should I just come out and tell him what's going on? How would I even explain? Oh, hey, by the way, I'm trying to escape my ex fiancé who is coming tomorrow to try to drag me back to New York and force me to marry him. I laugh at the absurdity of it. It sounds like the plot of a bad romance novel. I decide to avoid his question and ask my own.

Hmm…Oliver, King of Curiosity.

I kinda like the sound of that.

Just so you know, I'm over here rolling my eyes lol

My grip slips on my phone, and before I know what's happening it smashes into my forehead. "Shit!" I clasp a hand to my forehead, massaging the spot where the phone hit. I pick my phone up, but this time roll onto my belly and prop myself up on my elbows.

Roll your eyes all you want but you know King Oliver sounds really good

Should I bow the next time I see you?

Also, just smashed my face with phone

I don't think bowing will be necessary

Ouch! you ok?

Might leave a mark.

How long before you get to see your mom?

Uh a bit. Long bus ride down.

Bus ride? Why the bus?

Oliverse

You know I don't do planes and the train wasn't going there.

RemyisLIT…erary

Rental car?

Oliverse

Nah, I'm ok with the bus.

you can meet some interesting people on public transportation. wink wink

RemyisLIT…erary

Point

We're both quiet, no little dots appear that he's typing. After a few minutes I think maybe he's gone to bed or something, but then a message alert lights up my screen.

Dots flash across my screen, disappear, and then are back again before Oliver's next message comes through.

I stare into the fog, letting my mind wrap around his question and trying to come up with an honest response. Just then a text from Gage flashes across the top of my screen. Hesitantly, I open it.

Shit. My timeline is off. My jaw sets, and I don't even think about what I'm doing—I just follow the feeling in my gut. I open my message thread with Oliver.

RemyisLIT…erary

Think there's an extra ticket for that bus?

Chapter Twelve

One Month Ago

It's been a month since Gage came to me, head in his hands and tears on his face, begging me for forgiveness. A month since he pleaded with me to give him another chance to stop being the inconsiderate selfish asshole he's always been and change. It's been a month since he almost got me to believe his bullshit.

That first week could have fooled anyone. Gage had been doting, loving, and caring. He made me breakfast in the mornings before work and spent the evenings curled up with me, watching movies on the couch. He took me to dinner and showed interest in my life for once. By week two though, I could see that his interest was fading and he was growing restless. He missed dinner for a meeting and skipped out on movie night to console a brokenhearted buddy. The only night he wasn't out late, he came home and got wasted in his office before passing out at his desk with his dick in his hand.

I can't let myself get sucked back into that life again—the vicious cycle of his bullshit and lies. The wedding is a month away, and if he's not going to change, then I need to change my future. I push my way through the revolving door at the bank. I'd made an appointment last week. My family is well known here—so someone is waiting, ready to assist me.

"Miss Montgomery, welcome! I'm John Fee, a senior banker here. Come on back to my office."

He leads me past the tellers and down a hall lined in gold carpeting and finally into an office. Mr. Fee motions for me to take a seat in one of the leather chairs as he positions himself behind the desk, his back to the giant window that looks out onto the busy street.

"How can we help you today, Miss Montgomery? We've heard from your mother that you'll be getting married soon. That's very exciting." He pushes his glasses up the bridge of his nose.

"Mmm, very. I'm here to open an account and move some money around."

His face scrunches in confusion. "But you already have an account. I don't understand. You've had it since you were born."

"I want to open a separate account. A private one."

"Alright, well, I'm sure I can help you with that. Any particular kind of account?"

"Just a private one." I've already put a lot of thought into this and the details. "I'd like you to transfer $15,000 from my savings account and deposit it into the new account."

Mr. Fee leans forward, folding his hands in front of himself on the desk. "Miss Montgomery, is everything ok?"

I level my gaze at him. "I'm perfectly fine, Mr. Fee. Just simply trying to open another account. If you're unable or unwilling to help me, I can take my business elsewhere."

He opens his mouth, closes it, and then opens it again, clearly stunned. Finally he composes himself. "Of course we want to help you. I didn't mean to offend you in any way. I just wanted to make sure everything was alright. I can get that account set up right away. Will there be anything else that I can help you with?"

"Yes. I would like the debit card printed right away, and I won't be needing checks."

Mr. Fee gets to work setting up the account. Half an hour later, he's shaking my hand and sending me on my way. I exit out onto the busy Manhattan street taking a deep breath of the early morning air, steeling myself for what comes next.

◆◆ ·· ·◆· ·◆◆

Gage is on the phone in the kitchen when I get back home. With as many numbers as he's throwing out, I'd say it's actually a work call. He looks up and sees me but doesn't acknowledge I'm there. I sit on one of the stools at the island, waiting for him to finish. The longer the call drags on, the antsier I grow. I go to the fridge and grab a bottle of water, leaning against the counter as I take a sip. Gage is pacing the length of the island, running his hand through his hair, his telltale sign of frustration. Finally, Gage hangs up but immediately begins looking at messages.

"Um, hello?" I push off the counter and circle around the other side of the island so I'm standing in front of him. "I'm literally standing right in front of you. Are you not going to acknowledge that I'm here?"

He rolls his eyes but looks up and says 'hi' before going back to his screen.

"I would say 'unbelievable'—but I know better than to expect anything else from you."

Gage continues to stand there, his face buried in his phone.

I push off the counter and walk away. "Fucking asshole," I mutter. And somehow, this gets his attention.

"What the fuck is wrong with you, Remy? Can't you see that I'm working?" Gage moves around the counter and picks up the jacket that's slung across the back of the couch. "Is it that time of the month or something? You always get a little bitchier around then."

I stare at him, unable to process the absurdity of that question. When I don't answer, Gage just shakes his head.

"Look, I've gotta run. I have meetings all day, and I'm already running late. I was going to try to take you to dinner tonight, but if you're going to be like this, maybe I'll just take a raincheck."

The front door closes, leaving me in the silence of the apartment. Not even the traffic outside floats in on the forty-eighth floor. I sit on the arm of the couch and look around me. The walls are stark white to contrast with the dark marble floors. The furniture, aside from the couch that I fought for, is all sharp angles and modern. The entire living area looks like it could be the lobby of a museum: cold and like there should be 'please do not touch' signs everywhere.

Gage bought the apartment as an investment property—not because he thought it would make a cozy home for the two of us. He brought in a designer, and this is what we ended up with. Gage got his office, and I fought for the measly bookshelves by the fireplace and a cozy couch. I've always felt confined by this place in more ways than one. I stand and walk over to the giant picture window that overlooks the city and Central Park. Even with a view like this, I still feel like I'm suffocating.

I pull my phone out of my pocket and call Celia, who answers immediately.

"I'll be with you in a moment Mrs. Grinsky," she calls out.

"Celia?" I say.

There's shuffling and I hear a door close and then silence. "Hello? Celia?" I say.

"Yeah, I'm here"—her voice is distant—"Hang on!"—more shuffling noises—"Ok, I'm here." Her voice is suddenly loud and I pull the phone away.

"Bad time?" I ask.

"No—I mean sort of—but, no. I'm at work, and I was on my way to the files dungeons with my arms full of shit when Mrs. Grinsky decided that it was the perfect time to try and call me into her office. Like, yes, let's totally ignore the two boxes of shit and stacks of papers that are literally falling from my arms."

"Bad day to work in a law firm."

"Every day is a bad day to work in a law firm." Celia chuckles. "So, what's up?"

I take a deep breath, trying to find the words. I already know Celia's reaction, and I know how it will go once I tell her. Getting the words out is the struggle. Up until this point, it's only been just a thought in my head playing on repeat, over and over, for the past couple of weeks.

"Remy? What's going on?"

I blow out a breath and blurt the words out. "I'm leaving." My heart is racing as I turn away from the window and begin to pace.

"Hooooly fuuuuck..." Celia drags the words out. "Oh my unicorns. Did you just say what I think you did?"

"Um, I guess that depends on what you think you hear." My voice is shaky. Where are these nerves coming from?

"You said you're leaving. Girl, are you finally leaving that asshole? Please tell me that you're finally leaving him."

"I'm finally leaving." The more I say it, the better I feel.

"When? How? Can I help? Do you need a place to stay?" Celia fires the questions at me at warp speed.

"I don't know."

"What do you mean you don't know? Remy, you're supposed to be getting married in a month."

"I'm aware how long it is until the wedding, Celia," I snap.

"What are you going to do, be a runaway bride? Leave him at the alter? Ooo...think of the scandal."

"Celia, this isn't helpful."

I hear her sigh on the other end, and her tone shifts immediately, becoming softer and quieter. "However you do it, whenever you do it, I'm here for you. Shit, even if you don't get out before the wedding, I'll be there to walk you through your first divorce."

I laugh, and the tension in my chest eases. I take another deep breath, and my next words come out quieter than I intend. "I just can't handle it anymore, Celia. I need more. I deserve more."

"Damn right. I've been waiting for you to figure that out for years. Can I do anything for you right now?"

"No, not right now. I just needed to tell someone and you're my someone. I know you need to get back to work."

"They can manage without me." As she says this, I hear a knock on her end. "Shit, I guess they can't. Text me if you need me. Love you."

"Love you."

"Remy?"

"Yeah?"

"I'm proud of you. So damn proud. And happy, too. You're making the right decision."

"Thanks, Celia."

I hang up and walk back over to the window, staring out at the big wide world and all of the possibilities it might hold.

Chapter Thirteen

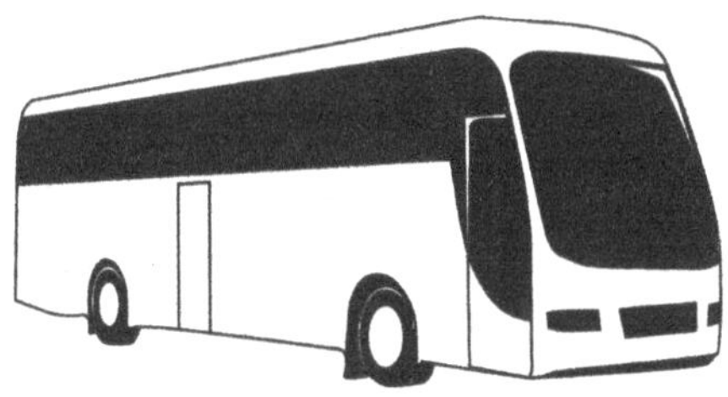

Headlights blind me as a car zips up the half-circle drive. It stops in front of me, its bold blue paint glinting in the lights from the hotel lobby. Oliver pops out from the backseat, a cheery smile on his face.

"Morning, sunshine! Ready for an adventure?" His enthusiasm this early in the morning is too much.

I groan in return, carrying my bags to the trunk.

"Not chipper and cheery this morning, are we?"

"Hotel is out of coffee. And this"—I wave my hand around his smiling face—"is too much for a non-caffeinated me."

He laughs. "Ah, well, lucky for you then that you're traveling with a thoughtful and chivalrous man."

I slide into the backseat to the smell of hot coffee and warm donuts. He really is starting the trip off right. I might even be able to get past his overenthusiastic morning attitude.

"Can you hand me those treats, mate?" Oliver asks the driver. "And could you kindly take us to the bus station, please?" The driver hands back a big pink box, followed by a drink carrier. Oliver lifts the lid on the box and gestures dramatically at the donuts inside. "Well? Huh? Impressive, right?" He smiles and wiggles his eyebrows. "I didn't know what you'd like, so I got one of everything."

"Ideally, there'd be one in there with cherry filling, but no one ever does cherry. They do strawberry, raspberry, blueberry and even lemon, but never cherry. It's a damn shame."

Oliver smiles slyly, biting his bottom lip. It's as though he has words that are ready to burst from him.

"What?" I ask.

"The lady said this one here, with the red and white icing, is cherry filled." Oliver's face is a look of triumph and pride.

"You're kidding!" I grab the donut and bite into it, the cherry flavor exploding in my mouth. A moan escapes my lips, and I sort of melt into the seat. "Oh. My. Unicorns. This is so good."

"Did you just say 'oh my unicorns'?"

"Yup." My lips smack on the 'p'. "It's a saying with a friend. And it kind of fits, seeing how this is the unicorn of donuts."

"Oh, it most definitely is. Why do you think you can never find them?"

I shrug in response, adjusting the lid on my coffee. "I forgive you." I say, taking a sip of the coffee, black, just the way I like it. He remembered.

"Did I need forgiving?"

"Your happy was too loud for me this morning. But you more than made up for it." I hold up the remains of my donut and my coffee cup.

Oliver beams and extends the box out to me. The rest of the Uber ride consists of us licking icing off our fingers and me going on about cherry donuts. When we arrive at the station, Oliver gifts the driver with the remaining donuts before we scoot out and gather our bags.

"Now I've spent my fair share of time on buses, and I know the proper place to sit." Oliver takes the lead, stepping onto the bus first. "You don't want to be all the way at the back, because it can be bumpy and there are quite a lot of chatty people back there. But you don't want to be at the front, because then you're subjected to a possible conversation with the driver—which can turn awkward. The middle is the sweet spot." When I don't respond, he looks over his shoulder. "What?" he asks, stopping midway down the bus and putting his bag in the overhead compartment.

"Nothing," I say, handing him my bag. "I just didn't realize there was a science to picking a seat on the bus."

"It's quite important, especially on longer trips. The wrong seat and you'll have a terrible trip."

"Right," I say, taking the seat by the window. "Oliver, no offense, but you're a little weird, and I'm currently questioning my decision to take this side adventure with you."

Oliver leans over to me, smiling. "We're all a little weird, Remy."

The cornfields of Indiana rush past in a blur as the bus cruises down the interstate. We're an hour into our bus ride, and I've spent the ride dozing in and out of sleep while Oliver reads on his phone. That is, until about fifteen minutes ago, when the kid behind me started kicking the back of my seat—ending all possibilities of more sleep.

"Well, that's heartbreaking."

"Hmm?" I pull my eyes away from my phone where I'm searching top cities to visit for relaxation.

"The ending to this book."

"What book?"

"It's called Gates of Smoke. It does not have a happily ever after." He shakes his head, brow furrowed. He slips his phone back into his pocket.

"Do you usually read books with happy endings?"

"Well, like I've said before, I'm a hopeless romantic. So, yes, I do love a book that has the big happily ever after. But I like historical fiction as well." He taps his pocket. "This was a historical fiction with some romance splattered in."

"I pegged you for more of a sci-fi reader," I say.

"I'm not opposed. Truly, I'm not a picky reader."

"Do you read a lot?" I ask, repositioning myself to face him a little better.

"When I can. Mostly on my phone."

I shake my head, giving him my best disappointed look.

"What?" he asks, raising an eyebrow.

"You're missing the best part about reading then."

"Isn't the best part of reading the story?"

"No—" I say, but before I can continue he cuts in.

"No? Somebody should really tell that to the writers then. They'll be relieved to not have to put so much into the story."

I roll my eyes. "Obviously the story is the best part of reading. But, as far as the act of reading goes, it's holding the book in your hands: the smell of ink on the pages, the feel of the paper between your fingers as you turn the pages…" I trail off. "I get that reading on your phone is more convenient, but nothing beats a physical book."

"I can't argue with you there." He holds up his hands in defeat.

"Do you remember your first book? The one that made you fall in love with reading and stories?" I watch as his face scrunches up in concentration.

"Peter Pan," he says, nodding. "I loved the magic that it brought to life. I could vividly picture everything happening in the story like I was there. I also remember the other kids around me loved the idea of living somewhere with no rules where you never had to grow up."

"I didn't really have a choice," I say, thinking back. "I was forced to grow up way too soon. I mean, my dad always tried to make sure I had a semi-normal childhood, but with the world we were in, it was hard." I shrug.

"A kid should always be allowed to be a kid. No matter the world they're brought up in. For me, it was different with that story. I remember thinking how sad I'd be if I didn't get back to my Mum eventually."

"Were you really close with your mom?"

"When I was younger." Oliver's jaw clenches, and it's clear he isn't going to elaborate. He looks over at my phone and nods. "What's that you're lookin' at?"

"Oh, um, it's a list of the top relaxing cities to visit. Trying to pick where I'm going to head off to once we get to New Orleans. I'm thinking somewhere with easy access to the ocean."

Surprise flashes across Oliver's face, but he quickly masks it. Oliver clears his throat and then asks, "You're taking off then? Right away?"

"Well...yeah...probably? I might explore a little. I'm not really sure. You'll have your mom to visit, and I don't know..." I just shrug, unable to give a good explanation. It would feel awkward sticking around as if I expect something from him in some way.

Oliver worries at his lower lip, his eyes trained on the land-scape outside. His eyes dart over to me and back to the window.

"What?" I ask, really unsure of where his thoughts could be.

"Nothing. I just, well, I just didn't expect you to leave so quickly. That's all."

I open my mouth to respond, but, as I do the, bus lurches and shudders. Several of the passengers around us scream out in shock. The kid behind me starts crying. Brown clouds of what I assume to be smoke billow around the sides of the bus from the rear. Slowly, the driver maneuvers the bus onto the shoulder of the road. The bus fills with the hum of chatter as the passengers begin speculating about what the issue is. We all watch as the driver exits the bus, walking to the rear. Minutes pass before he returns and gets on the loudspeaker.

"Ladies and gentlemen, it would appear that we are having some issues with the bus."

"I'd say that's blatantly obvious," Oliver whispers to me, and I shove his shoulder.

"I have radioed in, and there is another bus about twenty minutes away that has enough room to pick you all up and get you safely to the bus station in Indianapolis. Greyhound would like to apologize for any inconvenience this might cause to your travel plans. Just sit tight and we'll have you on your way soon."

Chapter Fourteen

"Folks, we're sorry to announce that your trip is being delayed by a few more hours."

A collective groan fills the bus. We spent an hour and a half waiting for the temporary bus to show, getting transitioned to it, and then finally arriving at the station. We were told to wait on the bus until we could be transferred to the next one for the second leg of our trip.

"It appears that the bus we were planning to transition you to is having some mechanical issues, and the next available bus won't be at the station for approximately four hours. There is a possibility that we will have you on a bus sooner, but there are no guarantees at this time. However, we invite you to go out and explore the great city of Indianapolis, Indiana. You can pick up some complimentary meal vouchers at our customer service counter. You will receive a thirty-minute warning notification before the bus leaves the station, allowing you time to return and load onto the bus. Again, we apologize for any inconvenience."

Oliver and I look at one another and shrug. After all, what else can we do? We gather our things and exit the bus into the balmy air. After grabbing the meal vouchers from inside and storing our bags in one of the lockers, we find ourselves out on a busy sidewalk.

"Right then, four hours to kill. That shouldn't be too difficult." Oliver glances over at me. "Any chance you know anything about this city?"

"Not a clue," I say, shaking my head and holding my hand up to shield my eyes from the sun.

"Hmm, ok." Oliver looks up and down the street. To our left is a dimly lit tunnel, and to our right is a whole lot of nothing. "Well, let's go that way. The crowd seems to be headed in that direction."

"Lead the way." I gesture for him to go first, not crazy about the idea of the tunnel. Once we're through the tunnel, Oliver turns around and faces me before starting to walk backward.

He starts pointing at different buildings. "And here we have a concrete building built at some point during the history of this city. And to your other side, you'll see a busy street that allows the cars to rush past us like they're being chased out of town by a zombie invasion."

I raise my hand in the air. "Tour guide Oliver, I have a question."

"Yes, lovely lady in the front." He points to me. "What is your question?"

The corners of my mouth curve into a small smile at his words. I settle my face into a curious expression, my eyebrows raised. "How do we know the cars are, in fact, not being chased by a zombie invasion?"

Oliver stops walking. "Good point." He begins beckoning at the crowd around us—waving, and prancing a bit. "Let's pick up the pace if we're going to finish this tour before possibly being eaten by zombies. Come along people, move your arses." The people around us cast confused looks our way, giving us a wide berth. Meanwhile, I'm half bent in hysterical laughter.

Oliver keeps up the tour guide charade all the way to a large intersection that has a glass atrium over the street. Across the road, I can see the entrance to a mall.

"And here we have," Oliver continues waving his arms above him, "a giant glass atrium arching out over yet another crowd-ed street."

A block past the mall the street turns to brick, and as we look down the street to our right, we see a monument set right smack dab in the center of a circle. The monument stands taller than the buildings surrounding it—wider at the base and narrowing as it reaches towards the sky.

"Now that looks interesting." I point towards it. "Let's go check that out."

"Right, this way you'll see—"

I cut him off. "Come on, you goof."

"Fired already. Shortest employment I've ever had." Oliver shakes his head, feigning disappointment.

As we approach the monument, an ice-blue fountain gushes water from one side and we can see people climbing stairs on either side of the monument. Carvings and statues, some soldiers, surround the base.

"Look, people are going inside. Reckon we have a look?" Oliver points to where a person is disappearing inside.

"Absolutely."

We cross the street and climb the steps. Craning my head back, the monument rises into the hazy blue sky. The cool air hits us as we step inside. It's dimly lit and small inside. An elevator is directly in front of us with a narrow staircase to its' side and a small counter is to our left.

"Hello, how can I help you today?" The lady behind the counter greets us with a smile.

"Oh, um, I don't know. We've never been here before," I say. "Where exactly are we?"

"Oh! Welcome, welcome. This is our Soldiers and Sailors Monument. It's Indiana's official monument to the Hoosiers who served in the Revolutionary War, the War of 1812, the Mexican War, the Civil War, the Frontier Wars, and the Spanish-American War." She pats the wall behind her. "The limestone used to build it is from an area about an hour south of here. The monument stands two hundred eighty-four feet and six inches high. That's only fifteen feet shorter than the Statue of Liberty." The woman nods enthusiastically. "You're currently standing in the gift shop and small museum. If you'd like to purchase tickets you can take the elevator to the observation deck. The steps are free, but I must warn you it's three hundred and thirty steps to the top. Only forty-nine if you take the elevator."

She finishes her speech and stands smiling at us, waiting for a decision. Oliver and I look at each other. I can say for certain that I am not into the idea of climbing three hundred and thirty stairs to the top.

Oliver can either read my mind or we're thinking the same thing because he steps forward. "Two for the elevator, please."

"Wonderful! You'll have 360-degree views of the city. It's truly quite a delight!" The woman doesn't stop smiling the entire time she prints the tickets and sends us on our way. Even as the elevator doors close, she has a smile on her face.

"Do you think she's required to smile that much, or is she genuinely that happy to work here?" Oliver asks.

"It's hard to say. But I know my face would be hurting after a full day of that."

The elevator chugs slowly upwards. Through the windows in the back of the elevator, we can see other visitors descending the stairs. Finally, we come to a stop and the doors open. We climb the narrow and final steps to the observatory, reaching the last landing and getting our first glimpse of the city sprawling out in all directions—a maze of streets and buildings through the windows. The observation deck is small. A narrow walkway leads all around the squared top, the cage of the staircase in middle.

"Now this is cool." Oliver walks around the empty observation deck. "I always enjoyed going to The View back home. It's at least double the height of this but I just love seeing a city from this vantage point. It really puts your world in perspective."

I start walking around the observation tower, staring out at it all. Oliver is on the opposite side doing the same. I lean forward and try to look straight down. I can see the cars circling the monument, racing off to their destinations, and the people hurrying up and down the sidewalks.

"Everyone always seems to be in a hurry," I say. "The world never seems to just pause for a moment and take a breath. We're always rushing, whether it be for a job or a date or just to get that cup of coffee. Sometimes it feels like I'm standing still and the entire world keeps moving forward."

"I don't think the world knows how to stand still." Oliver stops next to me, our shoulders just barely touching.

"Mmm, truth," I say, absentmindedly staring out the window. "Living in NYC, I can definitely attest to that."

"What was it like? Growing up there?" Oliver asks.

"Suffocating." The answer is out of my mouth before I even have a chance to think about it.

"How so?"

I take a deep breath, letting it out. "Just so many people. All the time. People on the sidewalks, in every building, in every nook and cranny of the city. You turn, and there's always another person practically in your face. And then there's my mother who's just there, always hovering, making sure I live the life she always wanted to have."

"Didn't she grow up in that world?"

"Oh no, she did," I say, laughing. "But I came along and messed up all of her plans."

Oliver doesn't say anything—but I feel him lean into my shoulder a little, and I feel his pinky brush against my hand on the railing. That tiny touch sends a shiver up my arm and down my back.

"What about you? What was it like growing up in London?"

"Um…" He pauses, thinking about it. "I mean, kind of the same, really. It's also a big city, people everywhere. You know how you said earlier you were forced to grow up too soon?"

I nod.

"It was kind of that way for me as well," he says, "With Sophie and—well, just everything."

Feet hammer against the metal stairs and yells from children below reach us on the deck. They get to the top and oooh and ahh over the sights of the city. The parents ascend and are discussing their day and plans for the afternoon.

"I just got an idea!" Oliver claps and rubs his hands together, a look of excitement on his face. "Come on, let's go."

"Go where?"

"You'll see."

We decide to take the 330 steps to the bottom and by the end my legs are a little shaky. When we step into the gift shop, it's more crowded than it had been when we came in.

"I'll meet you outside, just want to look at something right quick," Oliver waves me out the door, a giddy smile on his face.

I wait outside on the steps of the monument, watching the people run up and down them or sitting sprawled in the sun.

"Right then! We need a car. I'll call an Uber."

"What are you up to?" I narrow my eyes at him.

Oliver zips his lips and throws away an invisible key. Ten minutes later we're in the back of an Uber. Oliver asks the driver to take us to Row Your Mind. I have no idea what this place is or what he has in mind for us. The car dodges in and out of traffic, but before I know it we're pulling up to the curb outside of...

"A fire station?"

"Nope, it's behind it, love. At least that's what the lady said." We scramble out of the Uber and I follow Oliver around the side of the fire station to a set of stone stairs.

A shimmering canal with a gushing fountain waits at the bottom of the stairs. The canal winds between the city buildings, people strolling along the sidewalks on either side. "You're not deathly afraid of water or anything are you?" Oliver asks as we descend the steps. "Because I thought it could be fun to ride a paddle boat or kayak. I heard those people on the observation deck talking about it. I asked the lady at the ticket counter for directions."

I watch as people load onto the boats and kayaks, excited for their adventure down the canal. I've been kayaking a few times and loved it. Being on the water is such a freeing feeling when you feel trapped all of the time.

"Remy?" Oliver waves his hand in front of my face. "You ok? We don't have to do this, it was just an idea. I should have asked first, I'm sorry."

"No, no, I want to. It sounds really fun," I smile reassuringly at him.

Oliver beams and moves towards the ticket stand. "Two tickets for fun that will..." Oliver leans over and reads the logo, "row our minds, please." Oliver gives the guy in the booth an overexaggerated wink.

I cringe inwardly at the awful pun. The teenage boy in the booth just stares, unamused by Oliver. "Do you want a kayak or to ride a paddle boat?" his voice is monotone and he's clearly not in love with this job.

Oliver turns to me, raising his eyebrows.

"Um, kayak?" I say, only because I know what I'm doing with a kayak.

"Kayak it is, mate," Oliver says, turning back to the boy in the booth.

"Fantastic." The boy sounds like this is anything but fantastic. He pushes some buttons on the screen in front of him and two tickets pop out of the printer. "Make your way down to the canal and Hannah will help you get loaded into the kayaks. You're sure to have an adventure that will just row your mind."

A blonde girl about the same age as the boy in the booth stands at the edge of the canal near a pile of kayaks. She bounces on the balls of her feet, a grin stretched across her face. "Hey, you two! Welcome! Do we have kayaks or a paddle boat today?" Her enthusiasm is enough to compensate for the doom and gloom of the boy in the booth.

"Kayaks, please," Oliver responds.

The girls cheeks go pink as she looks Oliver over. She clears her throat. "Great! I'm going to go over some rules with you. Please be courteous to others on the canal. Swimming is prohibited. Once you're in the kayak we ask that you remain in it until you have returned here. Do not feed, hit, splash or interact with any wildlife. You may, however, take photographs. Your rental is by the hour, so when you finish, you will settle up your bill with Lucas in the ticket booth. Any questions?"

Oliver and I shake our heads and Hannah hurries around, getting the kayaks ready. We climb in and wait to be pushed off into the water.

"Alright, you two, go row your minds!" Hannah pushes us into the water and waves enthusiastically as we float away.

Chapter Fifteen

"Oh, bloody hell! What have I gotten myself into?" The look of panic on Oliver's face is priceless. His kayak rocks back and forth, threatening to dump him into the water as he tries to keep himself from tipping over. His muscles tense and release with each sway.

I laugh, shaking my head. "Have you never done this before?" I ask, shielding my eyes from the sun. "It was your idea."

"Uh, well, no. I thought it sounded fun, and I do love a good adventure." He scoots a little in his seat, and the kayak wobbles again. "Oh boy. Any tips?"

"Just relax. You really only need to use the upper portion of your body, so just keep your legs still."

Oliver blows out a breath, visibly trying to calm himself so he'll relax.

"There you go," I say encouragingly, and hold up my own double-sided paddle for a demonstration. "Now, you just dip the paddle in the water on the left side and drag it, and..."—I lower the paddle on the right side of the kayak—"then bring the other side down. And repeat."

Oliver works on paddling, and slowly he moves forward, his kayak staying steady with each stroke.

"Look at you go! Fast learner. Besides, if you tip over, we're in a canal—there's only so deep you can sink." I wink at him.

"How did you get so good at this?" Oliver asks, finally finding a rhythm with the paddle.

"My dad took me out a few times. When he actually had the time. Which was rare, since he worked so much."

"Workaholic type then?" Oliver asks, working to keep us side by side.

"Yeah, but not necessarily by choice."

Oliver looks like he wants to press me on that statement, but instead asks a different question. "You guys are close then?"

"Thick as thieves. Drives my mother nuts that we are so close."

"She doesn't like you being close to your dad? Seems odd."

"Anything that takes the focus off her is a bad thing. What about you?"

"Ah, now there's a complicated story." Oliver cringes a little.

"You don't have to talk about it."

"No, it's alright. Like I said before, when I was seven, my parents moved us to Liverpool. It was for my dad's job. He was a workaholic by choice. I really don't remember seeing much of him after the move. I was always angry with him for never being around. Eventually, my mum got tired of raising three kids alone." Oliver pauses, and we nod at some people paddling in the opposite direction.

"I imagine that couldn't have been easy for her."

"It wasn't." Oliver shakes his head. "When I was sixteen, she decided she wanted to leave him. My older brother, Jack, had already moved out, but me and my little sister, Sophie, were still at home. Mum moved us into a small flat in Westminster. My dad eventually stopped calling altogether. It was like her leaving had freed him up. He wasn't burdened by all of us anymore. Shortly before my eighteenth birthday, my mum took off to the States with some bloke she'd been seeing."

"What? That's crazy. What happened?"

"Well, Sophie was only fourteen at the time. The plan had been for her to live with Dad, but since he'd stopped coming 'round or calling that plan changed."

"Did she go with your mom?" I ask, bringing our kayaks to a halt under a bridge.

Oliver shakes his head. "I kept her with me and stuck around to finish raising her. Saw her off to college and everything."

I just stare at him, unable to form words. I can't imagine what he gave up to finish raising his sister. When I don't say anything, he looks over at me.

"What?" he asks, a blush creeping up his neck. "Why are you lookin' at me like that?"

"Oliver, you were only eighteen."

"So?" He doesn't say it rudely.

"So, not many people would do that."

"Do what?" he asks.

"Put their life on hold to raise their sibling."

He shrugs. "She's my sister." He says it so simply. "I couldn't just leave her to fend for herself. Our parents both had their heads too far up their own arseholes to give a shite—and I couldn't rely on Jack. Besides, I didn't completely put my life on hold. I did uni classes while she was in school."

A warm feeling spreads through my chest, and I feel a rush of emotions. My fondness for him deepens. I find myself reaching out, placing my hand atop his. "Oliver, know this..."—he stares down at where my hand touches his before bringing his eyes up to meet mine—"You are truly an incredible person. Your sister is lucky to have you as a brother."

He lifts one shoulder. "Eh, it was nothin'."

We paddle along the canal a little further, each in our own thoughts, before I ask, "So, what happened with your brother and your parents?"

"Jack is, and always has been, too busy for any of us. He met a girl while in school, and, last I heard, they were getting married. I still don't really talk to my dad. He sends a card at Christmas. For a very long time, I wouldn't speak to my mum either."

"But you're talking now? Since you're going to see her."

Oliver nods. "We never got quite as close as we used to be, but then again it is a little tricky to do when she lives across the world."

"Is that why you came to see her? To get close to her again?"

"Something like that." Oliver clenches his jaw and looks away from me. We paddle on in silence as the world floats by. "Remy, do you believe in second chances?" He glances sideways at me.

I think of all the second chances I gave to Gage—and how he threw them out the window. Clearly I believe in them enough to dish them out like free candy. "I do," I say. "But I think the person being given the second chance has to really want it."

Oliver nods. He maneuvers his kayak towards mine, the front ends bumping together. "Whoops," Oliver says, grabbing hold of my paddle.

"What are you doing?" I ask, laughing, trying to keep my kayak from rocking too much as he pulls us closer.

He sets his paddle down, his face growing serious. "Remy, there's something I want to tell you."

I study his face, confused by this sudden turn. "Um, ok?" I have no idea where this could be going.

He takes a deep breath. "I feel guilty about this. I—" Oliver is interrupted by his phone, and a second later mine starts chirping too. We both struggle to pull them out of our pockets, Oliver cursing his rocking kayak. "It's the bus," I say, slipping mine back into my pocket. "They're going to be ready soon."

"Right, I guess we should be getting back," Oliver says, picking up his paddle.

"What were you saying before the phones went off?" I ask, turning my kayak around while Oliver struggles with his.

"What?" he asks, distracted. "Oh, nothing. Not important right now." His brow furrows, and he bites his lip.

I can't tell if he's avoiding the topic or just concentrating really hard. I decide to let it drop. I'm sure if he wants to tell me, he'll bring it up again. We make it back, settle up our bill, and take a cab back to the bus station. Oliver is quiet the whole ride, staring out at the people on the sidewalks. We fight our way through the other passengers to the lockers and get our bags out.

The announcement comes over the intercom. "Now boarding for bus two-twenty: Indianapolis, Indiana to Nashville, Tennessee."

Finally, when we're standing in line to load onto the bus, Oliver speaks. "We forgot to use any of our meal vouchers." He throws his hands in the air. "If I complain on the bus that I'm hungry, I want you to smack me."

An unexpected relief washes over me at the comment. I hadn't realized how worried I was by his silence until then. Why had it bothered me, though? The question bounces around in my head until I hear my stomach growl. I look down at it. "I'm definitely not going to smack you, because I will, without a doubt, also be complaining of hunger."

"They better have a big, fat, juicy hamburger and chips waiting for me in Nashville," Oliver says, smacking his lips together.

"Or steak. Or shrimp. I could go for pizza. Or…" I trail off as another growl rumbles through my belly.

Oliver groans. "It's gonna be a long ride."

Chapter Sixteen

Oliver licks his lips. "Baked apple drizzled in caramel sauce."

"I think you have a bit of drool, just there." I point to his chin.

"No, no! Golden fried fish and crispy chips." He closes his eyes and inhales deeply as though he can smell it.

My stomach gives another rumble, and I groan. The driver said we were roughly fifteen minutes from our destination, but it feels like eternity with the hunger in my belly. Oliver and I have spent the entire ride talking about food and what sounds best to eat between our buses. "I've got one," I say, rubbing my hands together. "Root beer float, chili cheese dog, and fries."

"You know what I think?" Oliver asks. "I think we're both fans of torture, because that's exactly what we've done this entire ride." Oliver lays his head back on the seat. "Last one. My mum's shepherd's pie. Nobody makes it like her."

"Maybe she'll make you one when you get there," I say, nudging his shoulder.

Oliver lifts his head, and a brief half-smile flits across his face. "Yeah, maybe."

The bus exits the interstate and maneuvers through the streets of Nashville to the bus depot. Traffic is thick, and we manage to get stuck at what feels like every stoplight in town. As the bus turns into the station, Oliver lets out a whoop of excitement, which encourages other passengers to do the same. Before long the entire bus is cheering. The driver gives his final announcement, and we all exit the bus.

"Right, we've got 'bout an hour until the next bus. Let's go find some nosh," Oliver says.

⇒—·+·—⇐

"Can I get y'all anything else?" Our waitress stops by our table, motioning to our nearly empty glasses.

Oliver and I both nod, our mouths too full to speak. We chose a pizza place a few blocks away. Smelling the food cooking and waiting in a long line for a table was tough but worth it.

"This food is so good," I say, ripping off a piece of breadstick as though I'm a feral animal eating for the first time in days.

Oliver's mouth is too full to speak, but he nods his head eagerly. He chews quickly and swallows. "I can't tell if this is the best pizza ever or if I was really just that hungry," he says.

I laugh because I've had the same thought.

"What?" he asks, cocking his head to the side, giving me the impression of a puppy.

"Nothing, you're just kind of adorable," I say.

Oliver sets his fork down and leans back. "Oh, am I?"

I roll my eyes. "Don't make a big deal out of that statement," I say, and he grins.

"You think I'm adorable," he says.

I reach over and pluck a pepperoni off his slice of pizza and plop it into my mouth.

"Go ahead then," he says. "Have the whole piece if you want. See if I care. You think I'm adorable. Who needs pizza?"

"I take it back. I never should have said it," I say, laughing and shaking my head.

"Oh, but you did. It's out there. The universe knows." He whispers the last part, his eyes darting around.

Half a pizza and all of the breadsticks later, we're walking out of the restaurant full and content. Oliver pulls his phone out and suddenly stops walking.

"Damn!" he says.

"What?" I say.

"We weren't watching the time, Remy. We're going to miss the bus."

"Wait, what? We weren't in there that long." I pull his phone to me, and my eyes bulge. "We were in there that long?"

"Apparently," Oliver says. "We've got five minutes before the bus leaves."

"It's at least a ten-minute walk back," I say, worry starting to set in.

"I guess we ought to start runnin' then, yeah?"

We take off up the sidewalk, nearly sprinting. People jump out of our way as we bob and weave through them. Panting, we rush through the doors of the station and up to the nearest ticket agent.

"Bus...two-twenty-one...has it...left yet?" Oliver puffs out.

The man behind the counter looks up from his computer screen, eyeing us over his glasses. "I'm afraid to say you've missed it. It pulled out about a minute ago, young man."

I let my head drop and curse under my breath. "The one time public transportation actually leaves on time," I mutter.

Oliver turns to me with an unsaid apology in his eyes.

"Don't feel guilty, Oliver. It's not your fault. Since when does a bus leave on time anyways?"

Oliver doesn't argue but instead asks, "What should we do now?"

"The next bus for New Orleans doesn't leave until tomorrow evening," the man informs us. "Best if you two get a room for the night. Enjoy Music City a little." He gives a little shimmy in his seat.

⋙ ⋯•⋯ ⋘

The man at the bus station suggests a hotel right in the heart of the city. We cross through the city, following Oliver's GPS. The sidewalks are filled with people, even on a Sunday evening.

"Well, this is us," Oliver says, as we approach a multi-level building surrounded by hedges trimmed in shapes of guitars. We chuckle, and enter the lobby, looking for the reception area.

The woman at the counter greets us with a big smile.

"Welcome to Nashville!" Her voice has a definitive southern twang. "Are we checking in this evening?"

"Yes, we need two rooms, please," I say, digging my wallet out of my bag.

"And do we have a reservation?"

"Ummm, that would be a no," I say.

The woman clicks away at her computer and winces. "Whoops! I'm sorry, honey, but it looks like we are down to just our premium suite, which has a king bed and a pull out sofa."

"Oh, um, ok." My eyebrows shoot up, and I turn to Oliver, unsure what to do. "Should we just go to another hotel?" I whisper.

"Dunno," Oliver says, shrugging. "How do you feel about trekking around some more versus sharing a room for a night?"

I think about it. "Won't it be weird, though? Sharing a room?"

He shrugs. "I'm happy to take the pull out bed and I don't mind splitting the cost."

I chew my bottom lip, thinking it over. How awkward will it be to share a room with him? What's the likelihood of the next hotel also being close to capacity? At least with the suite we'll have a little more breathing room. I blow out a puff of air and turn back to the woman. "Ok, I guess we'll take the premium suite, please."

Chapter Seventeen

I stumble out of the bar laughing, a sheen of sweat covering my body. The crowd packed the bar wall to wall, making the room more of a sauna than a nightclub. I'm still laughing as Oliver shoots me an annoyed look, narrowing his eyes.

"Ok, ok," he says, putting his hands up in defense. "I picked the wrong pub."

"Are you sure you don't want to go back? It looked like the guys at the bar wanted to spend more time with you." I wiggle my eyebrows, and he rolls his eyes.

"Oh, ha ha," he deadpans.

I see that his cheeks are red with embarrassment, and I'm even more amused. He's downright cute when he's embarrassed.

"We didn't even have a drink," I say, adding a little whine to my voice.

"We took two shots," he corrects.

"Those were shots." I can still feel the alcohol from the back to back shots warming my body. "You promised me a drink, Oliver." I cross my arms and give him my best pouty stare.

His eyes travel down my face, first to my narrowed eyes, then to my scrunched up nose, and finally to my pouty lips. His gaze lingers on them, and I feel my own cheeks flood with heat as he licks his bottom lip. He looks away, glancing up and down the street. "Alright then, you think it's so bloody easy to find a good pub? You pick one." He holds his arms out, gesturing in both directions of Broadway Street.

I look around. There are people everywhere, the sidewalks all brimming with tourists looking for a good time. Neon signs flash at us, and music blares from the buildings around us, a different song playing through each open door and window. I pull my phone out to see what all is around us when Oliver snatches it from me.

"Nope," he says, holding my phone in the air. "Just pick one if it's so easy."

"Fine. Challenge accepted." I look around once more before walking in the opposite direction from where we'd started. I round a corner onto another street—one also teeming with people, though not quite as many as the main strip. "This one." I come to a stop in front of the least appealing building on the block. Nothing about it looks inviting, but the laughter and yells carrying out to the street from inside sound fun. The sign above the door reads 'Ten Gallon Saloon'.

"This one? Are you sure? Is it even a pub?" Oliver cranes his neck, eyes scanning the outside of the plain building. "You wouldn't rather go to that one?" He motions across the street to one with a big red sign outside and people spilling onto the sidewalk, smoking cigarettes and sipping drinks. "That one definitely looks less likely to be some sort of murder trap."

"You left it up to me—and I want this one." I pull open the door and the noise amplifies.

The inside is dim with the lights directed at the giant dance floor in the center of the room. A bluegrass band plays on the stage, while people line dance across the floor. A long bar stretches along the far wall, its stools topped with men and women tossing back shots. Oliver looks around the room, apprehensive. I chuckle and work my way around the edge of the dance floor. I feel Oliver put a hand on my shoulder, and despite the warm air, a chill runs through me. I approach the bar and squeeze between two bar stools. The couple to my left bump into me as their entanglement intensifies.

The bartender comes over and asks them to take it elsewhere before turning a cheery smile on me. "What can I get ya, honey?"

"Rum and Coke, please. And..."—I turn to Oliver—"What do you want? First round is on me."

"Gin and tonic."

I turn back to the bartender, but she's already busy making the drinks. I see a sign above the bar. *Ten Gallon Saloon Challenge: Finish Our Famous Cocktail from the Ten Gallon Hat in an Hour and Make it on the Wall of Our Most Wanted!* There are pictures of groups of people holding up the empty hat, cheering and smiling, proud of their accomplishment. The bartender hands over the drinks, and I pass her some cash.

Oliver takes a sip of his drink. "Wow! She knows how to make a drink."

I take a drink of my own and cough a little at the strength of it. We find a tall table near the back of the room and perch on stools. The dancers on the floor move perfectly in sync with each other. I've never attempted to line dance although I've never really had the opportunity to do so. I take a few more sips of my drink, still watching. Celia's voice floats into my head and I smile. I jump up, nearly spilling my drink.

"What are you doin'?" Oliver asks.

"Living a little," I say, smiling. "You coming?"

"What?"—realization dawns on him—"Oh no. Nope. Not gonna happen." He shakes his head. "I'll watch from right here. Guard the drinks and all."

"Suit yourself." I take another gulp of my drink, leaving a fingers worth.

I take a place at the back of the group of people on the floor and try to fall in step with the other dancers. As the feet in front of me move, I move my own, trying to keep pace with the person next to me. I toss my head back and laugh at just how bad I am. Oliver smiles at me from our corner, his phone pointing right at me, and I wave—which causes me to bump into the person next to me. I apologize, and refocus my attention on the dancing in front of me, finally picking up some of the steps. The song ends, and I fan my shirt trying to cool down. As the band gears up with another song, I fight my way back over to the table where I find a giant, red cowboy hat sitting in front of Oliver.

"Um, is that what I think it is?" I ask, circling the table. I can see a pitcher in the middle of the hat with two giant straws sticking out of it.

Just then, a bell rings throughout the bar and a voice comes through the speakers. "Attention, guys and gals! We have a couple brave enough to compete in our famous Ten Gallon Saloon challenge! If these two brave folks finish our special cocktail concoction in an hour or less, they'll get their photo on our wall of most wanted! Let's give these two a big yee-haw to wish them luck!"

A giant spotlight rotates and lands on our table, lighting us up. The entire bar yells a collective 'yee-haw' before the bartender comes back on the speaker. "Your time is here on the clock behind the bar. And it starts...now!" Red numbers start ticking down from one hour, and the bar erupts in cheers. The band starts up again, and the people start dancing again.

"What exactly is in this?" I ask, peering into the dark pitcher. I can't tell if the liquid inside is blue or black.

"Not quite sure," Oliver responds. "But since we're living a little"—he winks at me, pushing one of the straws towards me—"we best get moving. We've already lost two minutes."

I stare at the hat. The blue/black liquid stares back. Oliver wiggles the straw at me again. "What the hell," I say, taking the straw and sticking it between my teeth. I plant my hands on the table.

"Ready?" Oliver asks.

I shake my head but then nod my head, which makes him laugh.

"One, two, three. Go!" he says.

We both take a slurp from the pitcher—and cough. It's sickly sweet with a sour punch and burns my throat all the way down. I feel it settle in my belly, a warm pool of liquid. My eyes actually water from it, and when I look across at Oliver, I can see his eyes are a little watery, too.

"Well, that was terrible"—Oliver is shaking his head—"But bloody brilliant too. I never knew anything could be so bad—and yet so oddly good."

"You think this is good?" I say with raised eyebrows.

"Oddly. But also terrible."

"I'm questioning my judgment in you. So...what happens if we don't finish this?" I ask, raising my voice to be heard over the music.

"We go down in history as cowards—and we pay for the drink."

"I'm no coward, but I'm pretty sure we just ingested jet fuel."

"So you can feel it burning the lining of your stomach, too, yeah?" Oliver asks.

I nod. My head swims a little. The alcohol from tonight mixed with just one drink of this and I'm feeling it. Oliver takes another sip and winces, sticking his tongue out to reveal a dark stain.

This makes me laugh and the laughter doesn't stop. Giggles just continue to bubble up out of me.

"What's so funny?" Oliver asks.

"I...don't...know," I say through laughs, smacking my hand on the table. This makes Oliver start to laugh and before long we're both laughing so hard that tears are running down our faces. I look at the clock behind the bar. We've already wasted seventeen minutes. "I'm no coward," I say, wiping the tears from my face. "Let's do this."

Oliver nods, grabbing his straw and readying himself. "Right, let's go!"

We both start sipping on the drink, my eyes closing against the sourness. I get four giant slurps in before needing a break to breathe. "This isn't too awful, I s'pose," I say, my words slurring together. "Just gotta get usededid to it." I laugh. "Usededid. Usededid. Aw hell, you know what I mean."

Oliver stands straight, concentrating. "Used to it."

I slow clap. "Well, look at you talkin' all normal and stuff."

Oliver laughs. "I think I'm going to grab us water. We need some water." He points over his shoulder at the bar.

"But the time—"

He waves me off and heads to the bar. A moment later a guy in a cowboy hat leans across the table with what I'm sure he thinks is a seductive smile on his face.

"I saw you out there dancing. You looked real good."

I laugh. "Have you had your eyes checked? I looked anything but good."

"Wanna dance with me? I can teach you." He reaches across the table and places a hand on my arm.

Oliver reappears, waters in hand, and sets them on the table. "Sorry, mate, I think you've got the wrong table."

"You the boyfriend?" The guy looks at Oliver like he's trying to determine if he's a real threat.

Oliver's eyes slide over to me where I'm hiding a smile behind my hand. He looks back to the man before stepping closer to me, sliding an arm around my shoulders. "That's right—I'm the boyfriend."

My shoulders shake from the giggle I'm holding in, and my cheeks burn.

The guy looks between us, his eyes narrowing. "Boyfriend. Hmm." He scratches his beard. "Ya'll like pineapple?"

My eyes go wide. I can't believe he just asked that. "You can go now," I say. "Just go."

The man shakes his head and walks away. Oliver moves his arm from my shoulder and settles on the stool next to me. I take a deep drink of the water he has brought me.

"So, uh, why did he want to know our fruit preferences?" Oliver asks.

Water spews from my mouth and nose, and I cough.

"Is this a common thing for you? Choking on your drinks?" Oliver asks, handing me a napkin.

"Apparently only when you're around," I say, thumping at my chest a little, and wiping my face with the napkin."And do you really not know about pineapple? What rock have you been living under?"

"Um..." Oliver narrows his eyes. "Apparently a rather large boulder. Should I know what it means?"

"It's code for, for..."—my cheeks blaze red—"he wanted to know if we were into, um, swinging."

Oliver's face turns bright red, and his eyes go wide. "Bloody hell. I had no idea. I, I, I really thought he was just asking about fruit."

I giggle. "Yeah, no—that's not at all what he meant." I take a sip of water realizing just how badly I need it. "Thanks for the water...boyfriend."

This catches Oliver off guard, but he smiles. "No problem, sweetums." He says, and then cringes. "Terrible term of endearment."

"Agreed."

"What do you prefer?" he asks. "If I'm going to be your fake boyfriend, I need to know what to call you."

"Oh, um.." My voice gets quiet because—because*why*? Why am I suddenly feeling so vulnerable and shy? "I've never really thought about it, I guess. Never really had a reason to. My last relationship just used my name or nothing at all."

Oliver stares at me but then nods. "I guess we'll have to just try them out until we find one that fits. Is that ok with you, sugar?"

I scrunch my nose. "Not that one."

"Noted. See, we are making progress, cutie-pie."

"Nope."

"We'll get there," he says.

We sit sipping our water, and suddenly the bartender materializes beside us. She peers into the pitcher and shakes her head before bringing the microphone up to her mouth.

"And it looks like these two just couldn't get the job done! Better luck next time!" She lowers the microphone and talks to us. "Feel free to sip away on it. Honestly surprised you got as much down as you did. Just come collect your card from the bar at the end of the night." She says, directing this last line to Oliver, who nods.

"Well, I guess we failed," I say, my head still buzzing from the alcohol. "I'll split the cost with you."

Oliver waves me off. "No worries—was a fun experience."

The band announces they're taking a little break but that they'll be back in a bit. A slow song comes through the speakers, and people pair off—swaying to the music, holding each other close.

Oliver clears his throat, leaning close, his breath tickling my ear. "Will you dance with me, honey?"

"Um..." I look at the couples embracing each other. "First of all, also a bad name and second of all, I thought you didn't want to dance."

"Slow I can do. I'm throwing in a 'please'." He winks at me. "What's the worst that can happen?"

I smile at his choice of words. "Ok, but only because you said 'please'."

Oliver stands, grinning, his eyes bright with happiness. He holds a hand out to me, and I take it, letting him lead me to the dance floor. Just the touch of his hand sends a shiver through me that races up my arm, across my chest, and down my spine. Oliver slips between couples, guiding us to the middle of the dance floor. He turns to face me, smiling down at me as he gently pulls me close to him. He wraps an arm around my lower back while his other holds my free hand. I feel a slight tremor in his hand. Is he nervous? I wrap my other hand around the back of his neck, and he pulls me closer to his chest. My body seems to mold perfectly to his, and I lay my head on his chest. I can hear his heart beating just as quickly as mine. I take in his scent of cedarwood and lavender with each breath I take.

I lift my head and look into his face. His eyes are soft and gentle as he stares back down at me. His lips pull into a crooked smile, and I smile back before laying my head against his chest again. I feel his head rest atop mine, and we sway to the music, lost in our own world, just the two of us.

At least two songs pass, but we don't stop, even when the rhythm is slightly faster. I feel completely at ease in his arms despite my racing heart. Being here, like this, I feel safe. He lifts his head, and I look up at him. Oliver is looking down at me, his eyes intense, filled with want. I swallow hard, my heart beating faster—if that's even possible. He rests my hand against his chest before letting go and trailing his hand up my arm and to my face, caressing my cheek and brushing a thumb along my bottom lip. His fingers leave a trail of fire behind on my skin. I feel like a mixture of fire and ice are racing through my veins, settling low in my belly. Oliver moves his hand to the back of my neck, his fingers entwining with my hair. Somewhere in the back of my mind I'm aware that we've stopped moving. His eyes search mine, darting down to my mouth. I can feel my breathing speed up at the same time that I feel myself lifting onto my toes, moving closer to his mouth.

"Yeeeehaaaa!"

We both jump and spring apart, looking around for the source of the yell. A woman with big hair and cowgirl boots stands on the stage. "Are we ready to kick this party up a notch?"

The crowd noise swells in agreement and people move in to form lines. Oliver grabs my hand, and we push against the bodies back to our table.

"I think I wanna step outside for some fresh air." I fan my face. "I'm really warm."

Oliver nods, following my lead as we make our way outside.

Chapter Eighteen

ool night air fills my lungs and helps to clear my head as I take a deep breath in. My body is still buzzing with the electricity that seemed to flow from Oliver's body to mine on the dance floor. We walk up the street away from the hoards of people and loud music. To our left is a ramp that says it leads to a pedestrian bridge, so we wander up and are greeted by an arching bridge twinkling against the night sky. Oliver keeps pace beside me as we walk in silence listening to the sounds of the music fading behind us. We pass others who are walking up and down the bridge, taking in the city lights dancing on the dark water below us. I spot a bench and take a seat facing the skyline.

Oliver is the one to break the silence. "So, that was..." he trails off.

I look over at him and watch as he stares out at the hidden waters below, his face pulled into confused concentration.

"I enjoyed dancing with you," I offer, pulling his attention away from the water.

"Yeah?" he asks, genuinely curious. He comes and sits down on the bench beside me.

"I haven't felt that calm and happy in a really long time." I shiver as a cool breeze blows past us. It tousles Oliver's hair, leaving it disheveled, and I laugh.

"What?" he asks, as I continue to stare up at his mussed up hair. "Are you laughing at me?"

"No—" I reach up tentatively. "The wind made a mess of your hair. Can I?" My hand hovers in midair.

"Oh…right, sure."

I reach up and gently comb my fingers through his hair. It's soft and silky against my fingers. It finally decides to behave and lay mostly right. I slowly bring my hand down, and our eyes lock—the same electricity sparking to life again inside of me.

"Better?" he asks, his voice low.

I clear my throat. "Yep." Another breeze comes off the water, and I shiver again.

"Chilly? Wanna head back to the hotel?" Oliver moves to stand up, but I grab his arm to stop him.

"Not yet. I like being near the water. It's soothing. I can't quite describe how it makes me feel other than at peace. If there's water, you can bet on finding me there." Another shiver runs through me.

Oliver scoots closer and starts to put his arm around me. "Oh, um, is this ok?"

I smile at his hesitation and nod, huddling closer to him. His hand moves up and down my shoulder, trying to keep me warm. He leans his head on top of mine, and I hear him sigh. I pull back to see a big goofy grin on his face. Just seeing those dimples warms me inside, and I'm smiling back at him. There's just something about his smile—about him really—that fills me with happiness.

Oliver's smile fades a little, the same desire from the dance floor back in his eyes. He slowly brings a hand to my chin, tilting my face up towards his. His thumb brushes my bottom lip again—and just like on the dance floor—my skin ignites from the touch.

Oliver leans his forehead against mine and closes his eyes. My heart hammers in my chest, my breaths uneven. I don't know what's going through his mind, but I know what's inside of mine. I want him to lean forward, to bring his mouth to mine. At the same time I feel foolish for wanting that, for wanting him. I close my eyes, trying to separate my thoughts, when I feel him take my face in his hands.

My eyes flutter open in surprise and meet his deep blue eyes. Our noses are close enough that they just barely brush against each other.

"Remy..."—his whisper falls against my lips—"Is this ok?"

I answer by pressing my lips against his. Heat spreads through every part of my body, and I forget about the chill I'd felt just moments before. My head swims as his lips move against mine, soft and gentle. His tongue slowly brushes against my lower lip, coaxing my mouth open and deepening the kiss. I tangle my fingers in his hair, pulling him closer to me, letting myself become completely lost in the kiss.

Oliver pulls back, planting small kisses on my lips, cheeks, and nose before resting his forehead against mine. My head swims, the kiss leaving me a little woozy.

"I've been thinking 'bout that kiss since the moment I first laid eyes on you," he whispers. "It's everything I thought it would be and more." He kisses the tip of my nose, pulling back and searching my face. "You ok?"

I nod my head. "I don't really have words." A giggle comes out, surprising me. "Oh, wow. I don't know what that was. I don't giggle. I am definitely not the giggling type."

Oliver leans in, kissing me softly on the lips. "I reckon I've left your brain all muddled then, yeah? Good to know my kisses have that effect."

I grin at him, shaking my head and rolling my eyes. "Don't get too big an ego now." I kiss him again, and another chill runs through me, this time from the heavy breeze.

"Should we nip back to the hotel then?"

I nod. "Yeah, let's head back."

The hotel lobby is quiet, but a gentle hum of voices floats out from the café area. We take a spot at the back of the elevator as others follow us on.

"What floor?" the man at the front asks.

"Top floor, please, mate."

The man looks between us and then turns with a smirk to hit the button. The elevator stops a couple of times for people to get off. At the last stop before ours, the man turns, a smirk still on his face, and winks.

"Have fun, you two," he says, before exiting.

Oliver and I exchange awkward glances and wait patiently for the elevator to reach our floor. As we enter our room, I'm still caught off guard by its spaciousness. Here I had been expecting just a simple room but instead we're in one twice the size of a normal hotel room. A frosted glass partition blocks off the bed while a sectional couch sits facing a flat screen on the wall. A small kitchenette area is tucked into the corner near the window with a dining table set for four.

"Right then, whatcha wanna do?" Oliver asks.

"I think I'm going to change and maybe grab some hot chocolate from the café," I say.

Oliver nods but doesn't answer. His hands are shoved into his pockets, and he bounces a little on the balls of his feet. I round the glass partition and start grabbing clothes from my suitcase to change into. I slip into a pair of cotton shorts and a too big sweatshirt. When I step back around the partition, Oliver hasn't moved, his face a look of deep concentration.

"Everything ok?" I ask, tugging at the neck of my sweatshirt to keep it from feeling like it's choking me.

"Everything's brilliant," Oliver responds. His eyes travel down my body, taking me in and sweeping back up, everywhere they linger catching fire. His shoulders drop, and he shakes his head. "Fuck it." Oliver crosses the room in a few quick strides and wraps his hands in my hair, pulling me to him.

This kiss is different from the one on the bench. His lips are fervent, the kiss deeper, filled with a longing, a need to be closer to me. He walks me backward, pressing my back into the partition. My hands slide up his back, clenching his shirt. His mouth wanders hungrily across my jaw and down my neck. He nips at my neck, and I grip his shirt, tugging up in an attempt to remove it.

Oliver steps back and yanks his shirt over his head, tossing it to the floor. My eyes slide over his lean torso, and I run my fingers across his chest. I shift sideways and start walking backward, pulling Oliver along with my kiss. The back of my knees hit the edge of the bed, and we stumble backward. We laugh, and Oliver looks down at me, his eyes warm. He trails kisses up my neck, and I leave a trail of my own across his chest.

Oliver's hand glides up my bare leg, his eyes following its progress—over my hip, up my side, and finally coming to rest on my jaw. "You are so beautiful."

I feel myself blush, but I reach up and pull his lips back to mine in answer. Our kiss deepens again, becoming more hectic. I can feel Oliver against me, and my insides clench. I wrap a leg around his waist and pull him closer to me, raising my hips to meet his. Suddenly, I feel his body tense and he stops kissing me.

His head drops onto my shoulder, and he shakes it. "Remy, I can't..."

He pauses, and before he can continue, I begin to pull myself out from under him. "Oh, um, it's fine. This was stupid." I scoot across the bed and wrap my arms around my knees.

Oliver's expression is pained, realizing what he's done. He scoots closer to me. "No, Remy. Blimey, it's not you."

I scoff. "I get it. Look, Oliver it's fine." I feel shame and embarrassment and just want to curl into a ball and forget any of this happened.

"Dammit," Oliver says, more to himself. "I'm mucking this all up. Remy, there's something I need to tell you. I don't want...I can't...I just need to tell you something."

My stomach clenches, full of nerves. Oliver moves to sit in front of me, but at the same moment my phone rings. Oliver curses under his breath and I wave it off.

"Ignore it," I say. "Tell me."

The phone keeps ringing. When the call ends, it starts to ring again.

"You keep your ringer on?" Oliver teases. "Answer it. I'm not going anywhere." Oliver brushes a piece of hair back from my face.

I find my bag and pull my phone out. Ice fills my veins as I see the image on the screen. The call ends but immediately starts to ring again.

I answer. "Gage?"

"About time you answered." Gage's voice is low. "I was beginning to think you were avoiding me. You're not in Chicago, Remy."

"What an astute observation. Figure that one out all on your own?"

"Feisty."

"What do you want?" I ask.

"You, Remy. I want you. I thought I made that clear already."

"Oh, you made it abundantly clear while you were fucking some girl at our rehearsal dinner!" I hiss into the phone. "I thought I made it clear that I don't want you or that life by not showing up to the wedding."

"Dammit, Remy. Why do you have to make everything so complicated. We were almost at the finish line. What changed?"

"Everything changed, Gage. You were just too drunk to notice."

I hear him huff in frustration. "You know what's at stake. Are you really willing to take that risk?"

"Honestly, Gage, I'm surprised you haven't done it already. I told you, I'm out. Done. I want nothing to do with you, my mother, or anything else in your fucked up plans for me. Do whatever the hell you want, Gage. You usually do. We're done."

Before I get the chance to hang up on him, Gage responds. "You want some honesty, Remy?"

I snort. "You've never bothered being honest before, why start now?" I hang up and throw my phone on the couch. I sit on the arm and drop my head into my hands, which are shaking from the anger coursing through me.

"Sorry, I wasn't trying to eavesdrop."

I look up to find Oliver peaking his head around the partition.

"You sounded so upset," he says, coming a little closer.

"Uh, yeah. A little." I give a half-hearted laugh. "It's hard to not get upset when talking to him."

"Him?"

I shake my head. "Not important."

Oliver stands in front of me and tilts my head up to meet his eyes. "It sounded important. Did you split?"

"Trust me, it was over years ago." I pause. "Actually, it never really existed, not for me anyways." I sigh, rubbing the spot between my brows. "It's hard to explain."

"It's really none of my business, and I won't pry. But, just so you know, I'm here to listen if you need. I've got spectacular listening skills."

I've never talked about the real relationship, the whole truth of it, with anyone. I've always kept it to myself, bottled up, weathering the storm alone, worried about the repercussions if the truth got out. Not even Celia knows the truth, which has caused so many rifts between the two of us over the years. I'm tired of it having control of my life and of having it woven into every inch of my being. Maybe if I just talk about it—let it all out—I can finally let it go and put it all behind me.

Chapter Nineteen

Oliver and I sit in the hotel lounge in a corner as far removed from everyone as possible. A pot of tea and two steaming mugs sit in front of us. We sit in silence, sipping our drinks, Oliver patiently waiting for me to be ready to talk. I watch the people around us. Couples clearly on their first date sit huddled together, whispers passing between them, men in suits with their ties loosened and an amber drink in hand, unwinding after a long day of business, and the random family laughing loudly as they play a board game. I think back and can't bring to mind a single time that Gage and I ever sat down to play a game.

"Gage and I never played board games," I say, still staring at the family, as if that's the reason my whole life went up in flames.

Oliver glances over his shoulder and watches them too.

"That's his name. Gage." I laugh. "Gage Elliot Donovan. Everything about him is pretentious, from his expensive suits right down to his name."

"Sounds like the name for a real wanker," Oliver lifts his cup to me.

I snort into my tea. "You're not wrong there. He's probably the biggest one of them all."

"So, how did you meet him?" Oliver rests his chin on his hand, watching me intently.

"Our parents were friends. Well, friends is a generous term. They ran in the same social circle. You see, the world I'm from, it's all about who you are and who you know." I roll my eyes. "It's cutthroat, even from a young age. I can remember how mean the girls were—trying to make sure they were the most popular because of who their parents were."

"I know you said your life is nothing like Gossip Girl, but you're not helping the case." Oliver winks, and I stick my tongue out at him.

"We were forced together, Gage and I, growing up. We'd been sent to the same private school, and then, of course, we were made to keep each other company with the other kids at our parents' parties. I couldn't stand him. He always acted every bit the privileged asshole his father was raising him to be. His mom tried so hard to discourage that side of him as much as possible." I pause, sipping my tea.

"When his mom passed away, his dad brought him back from boarding school and he seemed like he'd changed somehow. Like maybe his mom dying had been some eye-opening life-changing experience for him. A reality check, maybe? He'd always been closer to her than his dad, despite taking after his dad. We started dating shortly after that, and it was pretty great at first."

I think back to all the stolen moments hidden away at parties and events. It had been so thrilling and exciting.

"What changed?" Oliver asks.

"So many things, really. But the main thing was that I found out he'd been sleeping around the entire two years of our relationship."

"Called the wanker part, then." Oliver slaps the tabletop, turning a couple of heads our way.

I nod. "I must have been pretty naïve or stupid not to see it."

"Or, and this is just a theory, he was just that big of a prick."

"I tried to end it, when I found out. Because what sane person would want to stay in a relationship like that? My mother wouldn't stand for it. She thought it would look bad for the family and hurt the company."

"Wait, she wouldn't let you break up with the bloke?"

"Nope." I shake my head, laughing bitterly.

"How is that even possible? How does one force a person to stay in a relationship like that?"

"If anyone is capable, it would be Sylvia Montgomery." I roll my eyes. "But I had one card to play in that game. My mother wanted me to go straight into the life of being an Upper East side wife."

"What does that even mean?" Oliver asks, scratching his head.

"Parties, events, charities, looking pretty, being arm candy for you husband, doing good for the world with our money—but not too much good because then we won't have money. Do just enough to make us look like saints."

"That's just..." Oliver shakes his head, pinching the bridge of his nose. "I don't even have words."

"I wanted to go to college. Follow my love of books and literature, and she knew that. She used it to bargain with. She offered me something I couldn't pass up. So I made a deal with her. If she paid for me to go through college, I would stay with Gage."

Oliver's face scrunches. "Couldn't you have gone without her help? There's financial help out there, yeah?"

"There is." I trace a scratch on the table, feeling his gaze on me.

Oliver reaches a hand across the table and gently covers mine. I still don't look at him. "What aren't you saying?" he asks, squeezing my hand.

I sigh, pulling my hand away, and bury my face in my hands, rubbing at my eyes. "Just, just don't judge me, ok?" I finally look at him and am surprised to see hurt in his eyes.

"Why would I ever judge you?"

"I don't know." I drop my hands to the table. "As much as I loathed Gage, I think I loathed that world more. I wanted to be free of it completely. So I figured what was a few more years? I knew there was a trust fund waiting for me, but I didn't want it. I wanted to be able to walk away free once those four years were up. I didn't want a mountain of debt, so I figured why not let her pay for my college after the way she'd treated me all those years." I cringe. "Ugh, that makes me sound so bad, doesn't it?"

"No, not at all. First of all, you shouldn't have had to bargain with your mum to go to uni. Secondly, she shouldn't have used college as a way to make you stay with some bloke who was clearly a bad guy just so you didn't make the family look bad. And lastly, from the sounds of it, paying for your college was the least she could do for you. Where was your dad in all of this?"

My face softens, but my throat tightens thinking about him. "He was there." I nod. "He only wanted me to be happy. It's all he's ever wanted for me. He tried to speak up, tried to tell my mother that they could just pay for my college and leave my love life alone. He really didn't think it would make a huge deal with the merger in the long wrong. After all, why should the outcome of two companies be determined by the love lives of teens?"

"That's great that he had your back."

I smile. "He always does."

"I'm taking it your mum didn't listen to him?"

"Nope. She pointed out that it was her family's money and company and my poor dad was shamed into silence by that. He's put his whole self into that company, but she's never let him forget that it's her family's money."

Oliver shakes his head, looking around the lounge. "So, you got to go to uni but had to still be with the stupid prat. Stupid question, I'm sure, but did he get better in college?"

I laugh, shaking my head. "If anything, he got worse. Openly cheated on me, not even bothering to hide it. The good news with that, though, is it meant I didn't have to deal with him too often. He was too busy partying and sleeping around. I only came into the picture for public outings."

Oliver rolls his eyes, clearly irritated by all of it. "You got yourself through uni, yeah?"

"I did." I grin. "Majored in English Lit and minored in business."

"So, you dropped him after that, yeah?" Oliver asks.

I wince. "I just wanted to get through college, get the degree, and then I knew I'd be free. Just four years and I'd be free. But then graduation came and went and..." I trail off.

"And what?"

"He proposed."

Oliver's eyes nearly pop out of his head. He just blinks at me. "You're joking!" he says, astonished.

All I can do is shrug, unsure of how else to respond.

"Why the hell would he propose? I mean, clearly he didn't respect you, right? He obviously wasn't invested in the relationship." Oliver shifts around, agitated. He takes a deep breath, calming himself. "What did you say?"

It's my turn to take a deep breath. "Well, seeing how yesterday was supposed to be my wedding day, what do you think?"

He squeezes the bridge of his nose and mutters something to himself, too low for me to hear. "You really did say 'yes' to him? After all the shit he put you through?"

"Wow, what happened to not judging me?" I ask, bitterly.

Oliver closes his eyes and shakes his head. "I'm so sorry. I'm not judging you. I just, I don't understand."

"It's complicated." The words are harsh and I feel my shoulders sag as soon as they leave my mouth. I feel the exhaustion from that overused excuse filling my entire body. "I'm so tired of saying that," I whisper. Oliver leans forward to hear me better. "Telling people it's complicated."

"You don't have to use that excuse with me," Oliver says.

"Well," I say. "It boils down to him being the same person he's always been—and my world being as fucked up as it's always been." I chuckle half-heartedly. "Ok, yeah, it's complicated for sure." I rest my forehead on the palm of my hand.

Oliver once again squeezes my hand, giving me a reassuring smile. "I'm sure I can keep up."

Chapter Twenty

One Year Ago

"Babe, we should go celebrate." Gage's voice drifts from the bathroom and reaches me on the bed.

"Why?" I curl into myself, pulling the sheet tight around my naked body, and stare out of the window at the sky, tinted yellow from the city lights.

"We just graduated college. It's kind of a big deal. Everyone celebrates, why wouldn't we?"

"I dunno. I don't feel like it." I think about my already packed suitcase hidden in the spare bedroom closet.

Gage emerges from the bathroom, a towel wrapped around his waist. Water drips from the tips of his hair onto his shoulders before rolling down his hard abs. There's no questioning why the girls all throw themselves at him.

"I didn't mean tonight. I meant like next week or something."

"And I meant I didn't really feel like going and celebrating with everyone. You go celebrate. I'm sure the D Squad would love to have another reason to party. I would just bring them down."

"No." Gage shakes his head, coming to sit on the edge of the bed. "I don't want to celebrate with them. I want it to be just us." He reaches down, brushing the hair out of my face, gently caressing my cheek.

I raise an eyebrow at him, pulling back slightly and sitting up a little. This isn't Gage. He isn't affectionate like this with me unless he wants to sleep with me—and he already got that. I cringe inwardly, already regretting having given in to my own sexual needs and sleeping with him. It's been three days since graduation. I should have taken my packed bag and gotten the hell out of here. Why was I sticking around?

"What's that look for?" he asks, pulling his hand away. "Can't a guy want to spend an evening with his girl?"

I stare at him, suspicion growing with every passing second. What is he up to? I sit up fully, holding on to the sheet. "What's going on, Gage? Are you up to something?"

His brow furrows. "What do you mean?"

"No offense, but this isn't you. The sweet, affectionate guy who wants to spend some solo time with his girl when it isn't just for sex."

"Offense taken." Gage stands up. "Damn, Remy. I just want to take you to celebrate. You've worked really hard, and you deserve this. But if it's such a big fucking deal, then never mind." Gage stalks back to the bathroom, muttering.

I roll my eyes at his outburst and crawl out of bed, wrapping myself up in the sheet and crossing the plush carpet to the bathroom. Gage is standing at the mirror, razor in hand. His eyes meet mine in the mirror before he returns to the task at hand.

"I'm sorry," I say, leaning against the door frame. I don't know why I'm apologizing. It's not like I said anything other than the truth—and he knows it.

"Just forget it," he says.

"You have to admit though, this is out of character for you. You always want to go out with the guys. I can literally count on one hand the number of times you willingly wanted to take me out to dinner."

"Fuck, I get it, alright? I'm not perfect—we both know that. I was just trying to do something nice. Dinner, that's all. But forget it."

I study him in the mirror as he carefully moves the razor up his neck, rinses, and repeats. His eyes shift to me a couple of times, but he says nothing. "Just dinner?" I ask. "This won't end with us at some random club and the guys there and I'm forgotten in some corner?"

He rolls his eyes but nods, turning towards me. "Just dinner." He puts the razor down and steps closer to me. "No guys, no clubs. Just us." He runs a hand down my shoulder and back up to my cheek. "You deserve this, Remy."

I look into his eyes, soft and sweet. Why can't he be this man all of the time? My mind drifts back to the closet with my suitcase. I should just grab it and go. But I don't. "Ok, dinner." I watch as his lips curl into a smile, and he dips his head to kiss me, getting shaving cream on my chin.

"Great! Friday night. I'll plan everything. Don't worry about a single thing." He kisses me again and turns back to finish shaving, still smiling.

⋙ ⋯•⋯ ⋘

Friday arrives and, as promised, Gage has taken care of everything. A new dress, shoes, and jewelry sit wrapped in a beautiful box on the bed when I return from the spa day he sent me to. I get ready, taking my time. One last look in the mirror...and I smile, knowing I look good. At 8:30 I get a call that my ride is waiting downstairs. I emerge onto the sidewalk to find a limo waiting with Gage smiling from the backseat. He has rose petals scattered around the back of the limo and a chilled bottle of champagne waiting.

"Gage, what is all of this?"

"A celebration." He hands me a glass and holds up his own to toast me. "To us—you mainly—for making it through these last four years like a champ."

I sip the liquid, the bubbles tickling my nose and throat.

"You look stunning tonight, Remy." Gage runs his hand along my thigh and back down to my knee, leaving it to rest there.

"Thank you. You did a good job picking out the dress."

Gage smiles, proud of himself. "I know my girl well."

The statement doesn't land well with me, but I let it go. The limo moves through Friday-night traffic, horns blaring, and the lights of the city are just starting to glimmer in the twilight. We finally arrive at our destination and clamber out of the limo. Gage hurries me inside the building and onto the waiting elevator. He bounces on the balls of his feet, excitement bubbling out of him. The elevator springs upwards, rising higher and higher. The bell dings and the doors open, revealing a set of double doors standing wide open to the rooftop. The purple sky from the setting sun is visible beyond the ledge.

"Gage, is this for real? This is for us?" A table with candles and more roses is set in the middle of the rooftop. "I thought you said just dinner."

"It is just dinner. I just added a little ambiance to it."

I move to the ledge and stare out at the city, the buildings cast in purple hues. I can see the Hudson River shimmering in the distance. A prickling sensation to walk away runs through me, but before I can dissect the feeling, Gage is at my side handing me a glass of wine.

"This all seems a bit much just to celebrate graduation, Gage."

"I wanted to do something special for you," he says. "I know"—he pauses, grabbing my hand—"Well, I know that I'm a dick and hard to love. This is me trying. You deserve tonight."

He guides me back to the table, pulling out my chair, and I sit. In the far corner of the rooftop a small string quartet plays a gentle melody that drifts over to us on the evening breeze. Tea light candles are scattered across the rooftop. When the waiter appears to take our order, Gage waves him off, telling him to bring us the chef's special.

I stare at him, marveling at the man before me and at all that he has done. This isn't the real Gage—the one who comes home drunk, smelling of other women. This is the man I thought he always could have been. Again, I feel that tug, that prickling to get up and walk away—but I push it aside for now.

Our dinner arrives and we eat while easy conversation flows between us about what's going on in our lives. He tells me what's been happening at work, and since Gage is usually so absent from my life, there is a lot that I'm able to fill him in on.

"Wait, so you're telling me"—he pauses, laughing—"that your teacher's assistant was caught with the librarian?"

"Apparently." I shrug, laughing with him.

"Wait, you don't mean..."

"Yup, that one."

Gage nearly spits his wine out. "Stop, just stop. I can't. She's, like, eighty—right?" He's laughing so hard that tears well in his eyes.

I try to remember the last time he was this carefree, this engrossed in what I have to say. It must have been shortly after his mom passed away, way back when we first started talking.

Dinner winds down, and I notice that Gage is growing paler by the second. He takes a sip of wine and then wipes his hands on his pants. His eyes dart around, landing on anything but me.

"Are you ok? Did dinner not sit right?" I ask, leaning forward and placing a gentle hand on his arm.

His gaze finally lands on me, and he smiles. He takes a deep breath but stops, the words not coming out. He tries again. "Remy, we've known each other for years. We had the hottest whirlwind of a romance when we first met."

I laugh, rolling my eyes. "Uh, yeah, I guess." I sip my wine.

The waiter comes out with our dessert and hurries away when Gage throws him an annoyed look. Gage takes another deep breath and starts again. "I know things haven't always been perfect between us."

I raise an eyebrow, but I don't say anything.

"I'm not there for you like I should be—and I'm always such an ass."

"You could say that." I think back to just last week when he came home with lipstick smeared on his neck. I shift in my seat as that prickling picks up again. I suddenly feel flushed, like the night air suddenly turned sticky.

Gage swallows, looking away before scooting his chair closer. He grabs my hand, and finally it all makes sense. Oh shit. Oh shit, oh shit, oh shit. My stomach drops and my chest tightens.

"Remy, I want to spend the rest of our lives trying to be a better man for you."

"Gage..." My voice is raspy, my throat having gone dry. Panic flutters in my chest.

"Hold on Remy, just hear me out. I want to be there for you, support you, love you. I want to be the man that you have always thought I could be." Gage slips down onto one knee, and I think I might faint from shock.

What the actual fuck? This can't be happening.

"Remy Montgomery, will you marry me?"

All I can do is stare at him. The music in the background floats around us, and the stars are twinkling somewhere above the city lights—but all I can do is stare. My mouth moves soundlessly, my heart hammering in my chest. Is this really happening? This isn't how this is supposed to go. Actually, this isn't supposed to be happening at all. I've graduated. I'm supposed to be free. Free from my mother, from Gage, from this life. I suffered the last four years of him. I'm not supposed to be in this situation right now. How could I be so stupid? Why did I let myself get to this point? The bag was packed, why didn't I just leave? Questions swirl in my head—an endless cycle of torture.

"Remy?" Gage squeezes my hand, trying to get me to focus on him.

I wonder if I look like a trapped animal—my eyes wide with fear, darting around trying to find a way to escape from here.

"Remy, did you hear me?"

"Gage, I..." My eyes finally find their way to him. "Why?"

"What?" His brow knits. "Did you just ask me why? Remy, I don't think you heard me. I asked you to marry me."

"I heard what you asked me." I try to shift in my seat, but I'm trapped between the table and Gage. "But why? Why are you asking me to marry you?"

Gage drops his head, shaking it before rising and sitting in his chair. Shock and anger flash in his eyes as he motions for the waiter, who hurries up at once, looking awkward. "Can you clear the rooftop please? We need a moment."

"Right away, sir."

The waiter rushes away, ushering the musicians away. Once they're all gone, Gage runs a hand down his face, frustration building.

"Remy, I asked you to marry me. I want to take care of you, and I want you to be my wife."

I don't reply. I sit there, my leg bouncing, chewing on the inside of my lip. Gage slams his hand on the table, and I jump.

"Say something, Remy! Usually, when someone is proposed to there are tears or joy, maybe some squeals and words. What's the problem? Better offer?"

Anger flares in me. "Maybe." How dare he get shitty with me after just springing this on me. "Maybe I have a kind, honest, faithful man waiting to whisk me away." I shove away from the table and walk towards the ledge.

"Oh give me a fucking break, Remy. You don't have anyone else."

I cross my arms against my chest and stare out at the city.

"Just say you'll marry me," he demands.

I let a moment pass by before slowly turning to face him, setting my jaw. "No."

"Excuse me?"

"I know you don't often hear the word, Gage—but no. I will not marry you."

Gage jumps up from his seat, knocking it over, and grabs the wine bottle, pressing it to his lips. *Glug, glug, glug.* I watch as the contents vanish. He wipes his mouth and sets the bottle back down. "I'm going to ask you one more time, Remy."

I shake my head and grab my purse, shoving past him—but he grabs my arm and turns me to face him.

"Will you marry me? Please, be my forever girl,"—his tone softens, but his eyes are still full of anger and frustration—"Please, be my forever girl."

I start laughing and push him away. "This is so fucking unbelievable that it's believable enough. I should have walked away from all of this a long time ago. I should have told my mother to go to hell and loaded myself down with student debt. I regret ever agreeing to be a part of this life a second longer than I had to. So no, Gage, I won't marry you."

"Alright, fine." He throws his hands in the air. "I didn't want it to have to come to this, but you're going to marry me after what I'm about to tell you."

I scoff and roll my eyes. I grab the wine glass off the table and take a swig. "There isn't a damn thing you can say that will make me want to marry you. Not today or any day. You don't scare me, Gage. Thanks for"—I wave the wine glass around—"all of this." I finish the contents of the glass and start to leave again. I'm about to step through the doors when he speaks again.

"Your mother is a whore." His words reverberate around the roof.

Slowly, I turn towards him. "What did you just say?"

"Your mother is a filthy, lying, cheating whore." His eyes glint menacingly.

I'm not my mother's biggest fan. In fact, there have been many times in my life where I've wished she weren't my mother at all—but who is he to talk about her like that? "Who the hell do you think you are? What gives you the right to talk about her that way?"

"I only speak the truth." He grins, wickedly, as though he's already won. "Besides, when have you ever defended your mother?"

I walk back towards him, stopping just short of his smug face. "My mother might be a lot of things, but she's not a whore. You're pathetic, Gage, for stooping that low. And why do you think telling me my mother is a whore would get me to marry you?"

He chuckles, scratching his chin. "Oh, I didn't think that part was going to get you to marry me." He shakes a finger at me. "No, that was just to get your attention. You see, right now your mother is probably fucking my dear old dad."

The absurdity of that statement makes me burst out laughing. "Right, and you aren't screwing any other girls."

"You think I'm lying?"

"You are lying. You're always lying, Gage."

"Am I lying this time, though? Because the long forgotten hidden nanny cam would beg to differ. I caught them. A month ago."

I cross my arms, anger coursing through my veins. "Fine, I'll play. Say you are telling the truth. How would that force me into marrying you? It's their business."

He smiles, opening the other bottle of wine at the table, and pours himself a glass. "Funny you should use that word"—he takes a drink—"Business." Gage takes another sip, turning and walking to the edge of the roof, peering out at the city. "Our fathers are in business together, are they not?"

My mind jumps into action trying to decipher where he might be going with this, but between the wine and my anger, I can't put two and two together. What kind of twisted plan has he concocted in his sick mind?

"Thank you, Captain Obvious. Stop playing games already, Gage. What the hell are you getting at?"

"The company is fragile right now. I think we can thank your father for that one. That deal in Sweden should have been a piece of cake, and yet"—Gage turns, shrugging—"he managed to fuck it all up. And now, because my dad decided it was a smart investment to merge with your family's company, his company is hurting."

"So?" I spit, my whole body buzzing with frustration and anger.

"So, do you know how devastating it would be if word were to get out that he was having an affair your mother—with his partner's wife? Imagine how that would make him look as a person. People might not trust him anymore, and he probably would lose a bunch of clients. Hell, I'd bet stocks would plunge, and the company would be truly hurting."

"Yeah, I imagine that would be very bad for business," I say dryly, narrowing my eyes at him, still not sure where this is going.

"I know I don't want that information coming out." Gage pulls a small blue box from his pocket and turns it over in his hands. "I know my father, and I know he wouldn't want his reputation ruined if this footage got leaked."

"Gage, you'd be the person leaking it," I say, exasperated.

"Indeed, I would. Which is why I'd advise my father that instead of taking such a great risk to just pull out of the company, he should take all of the money he used to save your family's pathetic company and take the clients with him as well."

"You wouldn't do that," I say through clenched teeth.

"Oh, but I would."

I clench my fists at my side and take a deep breath. "Why the hell would your father allow himself to be blackmailed by his asshole son?"

"Because I'm guessing he really doesn't want that video to be released. There's more on it than what I've told you so far."

"Where does that leave you, Gage? If your father refuses to listen to you, and you release the video, and it ends badly for the company—the one you're supposed to take over—where does that leave you? Where will all your fun money come from?"

"I have my trust fund to hold me over. I already have possible job offers lined up. I never wanted to take over the family business. Not my style. I'll be fine. You see, I want you to marry me—"

"Why?" I yell, cutting him off. "What the fuck does my marrying you have anything to do with you blackmailing your dad?"

"Details." Gage waves me off. "As much as my dad and I butt heads, I don't want to see him humiliated. I'm sure you'd like to save your father—whom you adore so dearly—not only the humiliation of finding out that his wife is cheating on him with his business partner, but also the shame of losing the company." He chuckles as though he's being so clever. "Imagine him losing a company that wasn't even his to begin with—and how it'd look—him, just a kept man who can't even hold onto his wife's family's money." No matter how it plays out, your father loses—and so do you."

"But if you release the footage, everyone loses. You, your father, my parents, and me. You don't get your trust fund until you're twenty-five."

Gage mulls this over, tilting his head back and forth. "You make a good point. In order for me to win, I can't leak the footage." He pauses again, thinking. "How about this, if you don't marry me, I'll still leak the information to the press that your mother is a cheating lying whore. Maybe I'll even doctor the video to disguise my father so I don't have to expose who she's with. This, of course will ruin your parents' sham of a marriage. My father won't want to be associated with such a bad reputation, and I'll suggest he buy out your family's side of the company and oust your dad—cutting ties with you altogether."

I shriek and throw my wine glass at him, but it misses and shatters against the stone wall behind him. I grind my teeth, glaring at him. Did I suddenly end up in the middle of some plot line of a book? "You're a real asshole, Gage."

"Yeah, you covered that. Will you just agree to marry me already?"

I rub my forehead and huff out in frustration. "I still don't understand why you're trying so damn hard to get me to marry you. It's not like you love me. I'm just some arm candy that looks good at events and that holds a good family name. You and I both know you don't need me for anything. You sleep around and do as you please. Imagine how much easier life would be without me dragging you down? Why marry me, Gage? Can you just answer that?"

Gage clutches his heart. "I'm truly hurt. Don't love you? I care deeply for you, Remy."

"On what planet?" I scoff.

His nostrils flare, and he rolls his neck, annoyed. "I'm done explaining this to you. I want to marry you. I want to be a better man for you—"

"Great start." I laugh. "Blackmailing me into marrying you."

"Fine." Gage walks up to me. "You forget how well I know the relationship you have with your dad." He pulls out his phone and swipes through the screens before looking up at me. He opens the blue box in his hand to reveal the biggest, tackiest diamond I've ever seen. In his other hand he turns the phone to show me a video starting to play. Even at the low quality, it's clear what it is, who it is.

I turn my head, resisting the urge to heave. "Turn it off." The image of our parents will be forever burned into my brain. The video continues to play, and I cover my ears trying to block out the sound.

Gage speaks loudly so I can hear him over the video. "I don't want to blackmail you into marrying me. I want you to want to marry me. I need time to prove to you that I want to be a better man. If this is what it takes—then so be it. These are your options, Remy. Marry me—or I use what I've learned from this to ruin your precious father's life. It's that simple."

The video keeps playing, and the sound makes my ears feel like they're going to bleed. The world blurs around me, and I sway a little on the spot. How did I end up here? How is this real life? How could my mother put us in this kind of situation? This is anything but simple. My father's sweet smile and kind eyes float into my mind. He's bent over backwards for us. Dad has always done everything he can to love me, make me happy, and protect me.

Gage shakes both objects in front of my face. "What's it going to be?"

It's my turn to protect Dad. At least until I can figure out a way to put an end to this once and for all. I clench my jaw and turn my cold, hard gaze on Gage. "Fine."

Gage stops the video and puts his phone away. He holds the ring box out to me. "Fine what?"

I take a deep breath and look out at the city shrouded in darkness—the buildings' lights creating a cheap imitation of the stars we can't see. This prison that has held me captive here for so long doesn't seem ready to let me go just yet.

I close my eyes, and a tear slides down my cheek—but I swipe it away quickly.

"Fine, I'll marry you."

Chapter Twenty-One

My eyes are heavy from lack of sleep. Oliver and I stayed in the lobby past midnight talking. He'd listened patiently to my story about how I'd gotten engaged—and let me rant a while about it all. Our conversation eventually segued into favorite music, past relationships, and even a lively debate on which is better, coffee or tea.

I can say with certainty that it was one of the easiest conversations I've had in a long time—the words flowing easily between us. It was also the most I've smiled in a long time. By the time we'd dragged ourselves upstairs, my body felt lighter—like all of the tension I'd been carrying had melted away. I fell asleep listening to the sound of Oliver's steady breathing as he drifted off, a smile still on my face thinking about our evening.

"Are you hungry?"

Oliver's voice pulls me out of my trance. I drag my eyes away from the rain-streaked car window to look at the clock. We've been on the road for a few hours now. Not wanting to wait for the bus, we decided to rent a car instead. The GPS shows us somewhere in the middle of Alabama.

"Remy?" Oliver reaches over, squeezing my hand. "How's your head?"

I woke up with a headache from hell this morning—no doubt the direct result of too much alcohol and not enough water. "Still sucks. Food could be good though."

"Right. On it." Oliver takes the next exit and pulls into a truck stop. "Want me to go get you something?"

"You don't have to do that. I can go in with you."

Oliver shakes his head. "Honestly, I don't mind. What would you like?"

"Um...a Snickers bar, a bag of Cool Ranch Doritos, and a bottle of water."

"That's not food, that's snacks."

"That is my-head-hurts-and-I-just-want-junk-food food."

"Right then." Oliver smiles, shaking his head. He gives my hand one more squeeze before going inside.

Just as he disappears through the doors, my phone starts to ring. I close my eyes and groan. I swear if the caller ID shows Gage's stupid face I'm marching over to that trash can and dumping this phone. I dig around in my purse until I finally find it on the bottom and pull it out. Celia's goofy picture fills my screen, and I sigh in relief.

"Hello?" I answer.

"Girl, are you sitting down?"

"Since I'm in a vehicle, standing would be a bit awkward. Why?"

"Have you been on social media at all? Watched the news? Talked to your family? Anything?"

"Um, no? I've been trying to lay low. Be away from it all. Seriously, what's going on?"

"It's been all over that your mom is having an affair with some mystery man and that she filed for divorce. The Woolington's Fashions stocks are plunging—but Mr. Donovan swooped in and bought out your family's side. But he had your dad ousted. Said it was because of some sour deal in Sweden."

I close my eyes, the anguish over all that my dad is going through right now filling me from head to toe.

"And..." Celia starts, but falls silent.

"And what, Celia?" I don't usually have to drag information from her like this.

"Shit, I don't know if I can be the one to tell you this, Remy. They're saying..." She stops again. "They're saying that your dad—"

"Stop!" I snap, the word loud and harsh. I don't need to hear the end of that sentence.

"You already know, don't you?" Celia asks, her voice soft.

I watch through the window of the truck stop. Oliver seems to be debating over snacks.

"Remy?"

"Yeah, I'm here."

"You knew about all of it, didn't you?" Celia is calm and gentle, like someone speaking to a scared animal.

"Yeah, kinda." I sigh, frustrated. "Look, I swear I'm going to tell you everything—because now I can—but right now it's the last thing I want to talk or think about. Tell me something happy."

Celia hesitates. I can picture her now, chewing on her thumbnail, debating on whether to drop the subject or not. I know she's dying to ask more questions, but, thankfully, she knows me well enough to leave it alone. "Something happy? Oh! You know that girl from my gym that I've been crushing on for weeks?"

"You mean the one you've been stalking?"

"I'm not stalking her! But yes, her."

"Did you she finally discover you've been stalking her and take out a restraining order?"

"Now, how would that be happy news? No!—well, sort of?"

"You sort of have a restraining order? How does that work?"

"No, no restraining order." She huffs, and I laugh. "We left the gym at the same time and ended up at the same coffee shop again."

"The same coffee shop that is in the opposite direction of where you live? So, you ended up there at the same time by accident?"

"Maybe, maybe not. It could have been by coincidence that the coffee shop is so close to the gym. Regardless, she asked me out! We have a date for this weekend."

"Celia, that's great! So, she doesn't mind dating a stalker?"

"I'm not a stalker." Celia laughs on her end. "Where are you anyways? See, I'd know the answer to that if I were a real stalker."

"Somewhere in Alabama."

"Alabama? What the hell is in Alabama?"

"Nothing is in Alabama. Just passing through."

"To?"

"New Orleans."

"Birthplace of Jazz. Alone?" Celia has her sleuthing voice on.

"What? Sorry, the rain is loud," I say, trying to avoid the question.

"Are you on this trip to New Orleans alone? Because last I knew you were trying to decide if you wanted to hop on a bus with that Oliver guy."

"I'm not alone."

"Is it the Oliver guy or have you been kidnapped? If you need help say 'pickle'—and I'll send a rescue team."

"I've not been kidnapped. I can assure you, I'm perfectly safe and healthy."

"Details, please. You've failed to update me thus far, and I'm disappointed."

I crane my neck to try and see where Oliver is, and I can see him on the far side of the truck stop in conversation with an employee. "Well, we took a bus to—well, it was supposed to be to Nashville, but we got stopped in Indianapolis because our bus broke down."

"Don't really know anything about the place," Celia says. "Go on."

"We went kayaking on the canal. He nearly tipped over. Several times. It was pretty amusing. And we went line dancing in Nashville."

"You better have video. If not, then the disappointment is growing. You better have some really juicy details that you're holding back."

"Well…" I say, trying to keep an eye on Oliver in the store.

"I knew it! Spill!"

"We kissed. Ok—we more than kissed. We full-on made out last night. Like my legs wrapped around his waist pulling him against me."

"Shut up! No—don't shut up. Way to bury the lead! How was it?"

"Confusing."

"Um, what? Why?"

"Celia, two days ago I was supposed to be getting married—and last night I was making out with some guy I just met. Doesn't that seem a little wrong?"

"Girl, you listen to me and you listen to me good. You've been with that ass of a guy since high school. You've not had the opportunity to date anyone else. You weren't in love with him, and you didn't want to be with him. Marrying him definitely wasn't on your wish list. Think of it this way, ok—you were just released from a very long, very bad prison sentence, and you finally get to start living your life. This is a good thing. I don't think it's too fast. It sounds fun and flirty and sexy."

I watch as Oliver steps into line to finally pay for the basketful of stuff he's gathered. There are a few people ahead of him. "Celia, he's—I haven't smiled this much in so long. The tension just goes away. It's easy with Oliver."

"Ooo girl! See, this is exactly what you need. Is he a good kisser?"

"Oh very. But…" I trail off thinking back to last night.

"But what?" she asks.

"He stopped the kiss."

"Wait, what? What do you mean he stopped the kiss?"

"Just as I wrapped my legs around him he froze and pulled away. He said he needed to tell me something."

"What? What did he need to tell you?"

"I have no idea."

"Maybe he was trying to warn you about the giant cocklesaurus rex inside his pants."

"Celia! Can you not right now," I say, but laugh at her absurdity. "I doubt that's what he was trying to tell me. He was trying to tell me while we were kayaking, too. But we keep getting interrupted."

"Maybe it's his strong feelings for you?"

"Maybe?" Oliver is pushing open the truck stop door, bags in both hands. "Look, he's coming back to the car. I should probably hop off of here."

Oliver opens the car door and gets in, setting the bags on his lap.

"Ok, ok. You go and enjoy your adventure. If anyone deserves this, it's you. Sorry about the shit with your family."

"It's ok. Thanks for calling. I miss you already."

"I miss you too. I'll call you this weekend to fill you in on all the details of the date. And I'm sure you'll have an update for me." I can hear the smirk in her voice.

"Love you," I say into the phone.

"Love you too, girl."

The line goes dead, and I set the phone in my lap. I look over at Oliver who's going through the bags. "Did you buy the entire store?"

"Not quite. I got some friendly advice on what helps with headaches and fatigue. I got a little bit of everything." He hands me a bottle of water. "Everything alright there?" He nods at my phone.

"Oh, yeah. That was Celia, my best friend. She was calling to see if I'd seen the news."

"What news?"

I've pulled up the news app, and there it is, right at the top.

Woolington's Fashions Closing Shops after a Century of Business.

The next one reads...

Sylvia Montgomery Files for Divorce Amid Affair Scandal.

I read the next one...

Donovan Enterprises Buys Out Woolington's Fashions and Fires Co-CEO Charles Montgomery.

I catch a glimpse at the next headline, but lock my phone, unable to bring myself to read the whole thing. I close my eyes against the anger-fueled tears pricking at the corners of my eyelids.

"Is everything alright? What news?" Oliver asks again.

"My family—they're in the headlines. Again. First it was me with the wedding and then me not showing up for the wedding and now this. I had the power to keep it all from happening. It's my fault." I pick at the edge of my phone case. A surge of anger courses through me, and I hurl my phone against the floor of the car. I can feel my throat tightening, the ball of tears threatening to spill out.

Oliver starts the car and moves to the side of the building, out of view of everyone coming and going from the truck stop.

He turns to face me, taking one of my hands in his. "I don't understand. You're going to have to give me a little more. What is your fault?"

"No, you wouldn't understand, Oliver," I snap. "My life is a fucking mangled ugly mess."

Oliver looks at me, pain and concern etched all over his face.

I blow out a big breath. "I'm sorry, you didn't deserve that. You're not the one I should be snapping at."

"Snap at me all you need, love." He brushes a lone tear away with his thumb.

I take a deep breath. "I told you how Gage got me to agree to marry him. He had all the pieces to bring my whole family down. Well, he finally did it. He pulled the trigger."

Oliver shakes his head. "I still don't get why he was so hell-bent on getting you to marry him. Not that I don't think you're fit for marrying. You're very fit for marrying. Not that I'm saying..." Oliver trails off.

I look up to see that his face is red and he's chewing his bottom lip. I laugh, but my heart isn't in it. "I know," I say quietly.

"What?"

"I know why Gage wanted to marry me so badly." I don't look at Oliver, unable to meet his eyes.

"You know why the bastard wanted to marry you? Why?" He shakes his head. "I'm still confused how any of this is your fault."

"I didn't marry him. I left. He made good on his threat. My family's company is done. My mom left my dad who was already publicly humiliated from the company debacle and the affair scandal." I rub my forehead. "That's not even the worst of it."

"How is that not the worst of it? What else could there be?"

I don't reply as I watch a semi driver attempt to back into a spot too narrow for his truck, an overwhelming feeling of grief washing over me.

"Remy?" Oliver's voice is soft as he lifts my chin, bringing my eyes level with his soft gaze—willing me to talk to him. "Why did you run?"

Chapter Twenty-Two

The room is stuffy, much like the people that fill it. My dress is digging in on one side, making every movement just a little more uncomfortable. The rehearsal dinner started three hours ago and is somehow still going strong. My feet hurt, and I could really use a break from all of these people. I edge around the outside of the room towards the exit, trying to go undetected, when a hand lands on my shoulder.

"Remy, my dear! Congratulations! Really couldn't be happier for you." The purple face of my great Uncle Theo presses too close to mine, the smell of too much alcohol drifting up my nose.

Usually the only time I'm forced to be in his company is during the holidays—thank God—because I've learned he loves to drink and can get handsy. "Thank you, Uncle Theo." I work to pull my shoulder out from under his grasp, but he's not letting go.

"That young man of yours seems like a fine gentleman. Reminds me a little of me at his age. Just the type to treat you respectably, the way you deserve." Theo's hand slides down my arm, and he tries to grab onto my hip.

I sidestep, managing to avoid his roaming fingers. "He's something alright." I scan the room, noting Gage is still nowhere to be seen.

A glass tinkles somewhere in the room as a spoon is tapped on its edge. The room grows quiet, and I see my dad standing on the stage near the front. I use this distraction as an excuse to escape Theo and move further along the outside of the room. I pause next to the exit, watching my dad.

"I want to thank all of you for being here this evening to celebrate my sweet little girl's big day tomorrow. I know some of you won't be able to make it to the actual wedding and reception tomorrow, but we're glad to see you here at the rehearsal." He pauses. "I can't believe my little Remy is all grown up and getting married. It seems like just yesterday she was running through the house, butt naked, screaming about not wanting a bath."

My cheeks flush red and my eyes widen as laughter rolls through the onlookers. Dad's eyes sweep the room, finding me, and he grins and winks.

"Remy, you know it's my job to embarrass you. All I've ever wanted is for you to be happy." He swallows, his expression turning serious as his eyes stay focused on me. "Your happiness means more to me than anything else in this world." Tears well in his eyes as he pauses again. A sad kind of smile spreads across his face as he clears his throat. "I won't bore you all tonight with a long speech. That's what tomorrow is for." A few guests chuckle. "I just wanted to thank you for being here, and I hope you enjoy the rest of the evening."

The guests begin to applaud, and I use this as my opportunity to escape the hotel ballroom for a breather. I hurry out and make my way to the bank of elevators. The lobby is quiet and the air cooler. The doors open and I step on, letting it carry me to the penthouse suite. I slip my shoes off, my feet nearly groaning in relief. The doors slide open to reveal a short, dimly lit hallway with plush carpet separating the elevator from the door to the room. As I approach, I notice the door to the suite is ajar and heated voices carry out into the hall. I move a little closer, recognizing the voices at once. Through the crack, I spot Gage, shirt unbuttoned and hanging open, his hair a disheveled mess. My mother steps into view, and I back into the corner, listening.

"Gage, what the hell is the matter with you?"

"From what all the therapists say, a lot." I can hear the humor in his voice at what he thinks is a clever comeback.

"Oh grow up. It's not time to be a sarcastic asshole. It's the night before your wedding. You're at your rehearsal dinner for fuck's sake. Have you no decency?"

"I just stepped away for some air, Sylvia. Haven't you ever needed to step away?" He puts emphasis on the last two words.

"Right, stepped away. And did you just happen to bump into that girl while stepping away?"

"Oh, I bumped into her more than once."

My eyes close, and I hang my head, anger and humiliation coursing through me.

"Ugh," Sylvia scoffs. "You're an absolute pig. Would you talk to your mother like that?"

"Well, she's dead, so I guess we'll never find out." I see him tug on the back of his neck. "Come on, Sylvia. Don't be a prude. I was just blowing off a little pre-wedding jitters. And she was blowing"—he pauses—"well, me." Gage laughs. "Remy won't mind because she'll never even know."

"I'm fairly certain Remy would mind."

I roll my eyes at the thought of my mother thinking she knows me at all—despite her being right in this moment.

"You're obviously too busy being a selfish bitch and fucking my dad to know your daughter very well. Or anything about our life for that matter."

Gage has one thing right, she doesn't know me or our life.

"What's that supposed to mean?" Sylvia asks.

"Nothing. What did you come up here for anyways? My dad isn't here."

I cringe at the thought of my mother and Mr. Donovan. Almost a year later and the thought still makes my stomach heave. I hear the unmistakable sound of ice clinking into a glass. I lean forward to see Gage pouring an amber liquid into the crystal glass.

"I wasn't looking for your father, I—"

"Oh, that's right," Gage interrupts, "you already got what you needed from him earlier. Drink?"

My mother clears her throat. "I came to find the groom actually." She brushes off his question. "The room full of people downstairs has been asking for you. Only, I find you with some girl bent over the sofa. I have to say, though, it was awfully considerate of you to offer her your shower." Sylvia's voice drips with sarcasm.

"Well, I'm nothing if not a gentleman."

I grind my teeth. Even with Gage's extracurricular activities, he's never been so bold as to bring them home. I guess, to his credit, this isn't home.

"You're marrying my daughter tomorrow, and while she and I haven't always gotten along, I do expect you to respect her enough to not fuck someone else on the wedding night."

Gage laughs a deep, long laugh. "You're one to talk, Sylvia. I wouldn't even be in this situation if it weren't for you."

My brow furrows in confusion. Inching closer, I listen harder to what they're saying, trying to watch them through the sliver of an opening in the door.

"If I hadn't discovered the little secret between you and my father, I wouldn't be here tonight."

"Don't be dramatic, Gage."

I know that tone. It's her 'I don't have time for your crap' tone. I get it all too often. But I still smile, hearing her tell someone else to not be dramatic for once.

"I'm not being dramatic, Sylvia. Just honest."

"You weren't leaving her, and you know it. She's everything you need in our circle."

Gage nods. "I'll give you that one. She fits the part so well. But it was Remy who was on the way out the door."

"Seems you managed to do something right to convince her to marry you."

"Well, you and my father made me an offer I couldn't pass up. That kind of money made marrying her worth it."

"Oh please, Gage. You make it sounds like she's some kind of hired whore. You've never been worried about the money. Sure, the money is great—but admit it, you weren't leaving her. You need her. It's not like you can walk around with an actual whore on your arm."

Gage walks in a slow circle around my mother. "I wonder if Charles realizes what kind of whore he has on his arm."

I work to steady my breathing as the anger and shock bubbles inside of me. It takes every ounce of control I have to not go bursting into that room.

"Watch yourself, Gage." Sylvia's voice is low, measured.

"No, Sylvia, you watch yourself. Because if your other dirty little secret gets out, you're whole world is finished. We both know what secret you're really paying to protect."

"Remy would never forgive you."

"Forgive me? I'm not concerned with her forgiving me. If this secret gets out, I won't be the one who needs to be looking for forgiveness. You're the one who's been lying to her for twenty-two years."

"I haven't been lying to her," Sylvia retorts, but I can actually hear a tremor in her voice. Is she scared?

"Stretching the truth? White lies? Whatever bullshit you want to wrap up and tie with a pretty bow so you can sleep at night. You've been lying to her about who her father really is for her entire life—and it's you she'll never forgive."

The air leaves my lungs in a whoosh as though I've been punched in the chest. I lean against the wall for support, closing my eyes, trying to steady myself. My ears are buzzing, and my heart feels as though it's going to pound right out of my chest.

"I never lied about it, Gage. I just didn't tell her." Sylvia's words are muddled as I try to get my heart and breathing to slow down.

"Same damn thing!" Gage bellows. "And for the cherry on top, your own husband doesn't even know he's not the father. Your whoring around got you into trouble twenty-two years ago—and it's gotten you into trouble now. It seems you can't learn from your mistakes. I wouldn't be walking down that aisle tomorrow if you and my father hadn't offered me a deal I couldn't refuse."

"And if you remember right, that deal includes you keeping your mouth shut about the affair and her father."

"A little late for the first one."

Sylvia throws her hands up. "What the fuck, Gage?"

"How the hell do you think I got her to agree to marry me?"

Sylvia scoffs. "Nice, Gage. Real classy. Blackmail?"

"Must run in the family." He shrugs.

"Fine, Gage. But if you want her trust fund in your bank account, plus the $10,000 a month for life, you'll not say a damn word about her father. Otherwise, you're out on your ass, broke, and cut off," Sylvia hisses.

"Let's not forget me filling the second CEO position. Charles has been making a few too many mistakes of late."

I inch away from the door, unable to hear anymore. I shake my head as if I can clear away everything they just said, like an Etch-a-Sketch. I trail my hand along the wall for support. My mind and body are numb and whirring all at the same time. I retreat into the elevator, a swirl of emotions warring inside of me. Everything they just said begins to hammer into my brain over and over. My blood pulses, and I clench my fists as the fury begins to course through me. Angry tears spring to my eyes and spill down my cheeks. As the doors open, I can hear the distant sounds of the party. I step into the lobby, tears dripping off my chin and onto my dress. A voice calls to me from the direction of the ballroom.

"Remy?"

I turn to see my father—or the man who I've always thought to be my father—walking towards me, worry etched on his face. "Is everything ok?"

Panic and sadness take hold of me, squeezing until there's hardly any air left. I can't be here. I can't do this. "I'm so sorry," I say to him while shaking my head, the words barely audible as I back away. I watch as his face turns to confusion. I shake my head again. "I can't. I'm sorry." I turn and hurry out of the hotel, not stopping for anything.

Chapter Twenty-Three

I am full on ugly crying. If someone were to look up the definition of ugly crying, it would say 'see Remy Montgomery'. Tears spill from my eyes and speckle the front of my shirt. Oliver clumsily climbs into the back seat, his long legs getting stuck on the console. He reaches forward, taking my hand and gently tugging, a silent gesture for me to join him. I unbuckle my seatbelt and clamber into the back, landing harder on the seat than I'd intended. Oliver scoots closer to me, wrapping both arms around me in a tight hug, pulling me to his chest. Giant sobs claw their way out of my throat as every emotion I've trapped inside of me fights to break free. I can feel Oliver's head resting against the top of mine, his steady breathing against my side as he just lets me cry.

"My whole life," I sob. "My whole life has been a lie." I hiccup. "And something to manipulate into what my mother wanted."

Oliver smooths my hair, still not saying anything.

"How could she do this to me?" Hiccup. "She lied to me about who my father is, and she blackmailed her own daughter into marrying a guy she knew I didn't want to be with." More hard sobs burst free as I clench Oliver's shirt in my fists. "I was never enough for her. Never. She never wanted me, but she figured..." I choke a little and cough. Oliver pats my back. "She figured if she had to have me, she'd make sure I lived the life she'd wanted. The one I'd stolen from her—that Dad..." Another hiccup. "The one Charles had stolen from her."

"What life had she wanted?" Oliver asks quietly.

I don't answer right away, thinking about the question. My mother had always found a way to point out all of the things she didn't get when she'd gone through with having me. She didn't get the man she'd always dreamed of having or the villa in Italy or to get away from her own parents. That was the biggest hypocrisy of it all. "She's such a fucking hypocrite."

"How so?"

"She hated her family. Loved their money but hated them. She wanted to be free of them. She'd planned to marry a man with enough money to take her away from them." I sniffle as another hiccup escapes. "She wanted to live in a villa in Italy and be drunk on the world's finest wines. With her family's connections, she really didn't think it would be all that hard to track down such a man. Although, I feel like anyone with that kind of money is going to pull you into a world just like that no matter where in the world you are." I try to lean back, but Oliver holds me to his chest, so I sink further into him.

"Why did she marry Charles?"

"Because she was pregnant with me, of course. Her mother wanted me taken care of, but any chance of Grandma having control over her life, my mother rebelled. So, they eloped. Grandpa said he would give Dad—Charles—a job, and that they'd all be taken care of."

"So, she got the money she'd wanted but was trapped." It wasn't a question. "Why would she try to do the same to you? Why would she trap you in the world she hated so much?"

The tears have slowed some, and I take a deep breath. "I don't think she hated that world. Just her family. I mean, my grandma wasn't a walk in the park, that's for sure. But, like I said, she loved the money and with the money comes that world." I stare at the back of the passenger seat, my vision blurred with fresh tears spilling over and down my cheeks. "He didn't deserve this." I shake my head, another sob escaping me. "He didn't deserve this, dammit!" I yell. I feel Oliver tighten his arms around me, and for a moment we just sit there, the rain beating down on the car, muffling the sounds of my anguish. "It's my fault that he's living through hell right now. If I'd just..." I trail off, not able to finish the thought.

Oliver pulls back for the first time and looks me in the eyes. "If you'd what? Married a bloke you didn't love? Married someone who you couldn't stand? Married someone who mistreated you every single day? If you'd agreed to live a life you never wanted? Remy, you have to believe me when I say this one thing—none of this is your fault. The fault lies solely on your mum." Oliver looks at me, searching my face for a sign of doubt. "Your mum should never have lied to you in the first place. She's been lying to a lot of people for a long time, it seems."

"But, I could have kept my dad—I mean..." I exhale in frustration. "I could have kept him from all of this hurt."

"How? Remy, I need you to explain to me how you could have prevented any of this from happening that didn't end with you trapped."

I look away from him, searching for the answer in the rain-drenched windshield. Beads of raindrops splash against the glass, bouncing off and sliding down to get caught in the wiper blades.

"Let's run through scenarios, Love. Let's play what if. Ok? Ready?" Oliver asks.

I nod my head.

"Right, here we go. What if you'd told your dad about the affair when you'd found out? What do you reckon would have happened?"

I think back to when Gage proposed. His dad had been wanting to acquire another company that was based in Sweden. He'd sent Charles to close the deal, and it had gone poorly. "I don't think it would've gone very well. Charles had a really bad business deal and lost a major account. He was beating himself up for weeks. He was in such a dark place, drinking more than usual. I think if I'd told him about the affair—well, I don't know what he would have done. It would've devastated him."

"Right, so if you'd told him about the affair, it would have been bad."

"But at least he would have been hearing it from me, someone he loves and knows cares about him, instead of the damn media mongrels and gossip pages."

"True, but he still would have been hurt and crushed. May have even taken it out on you unintentionally. Bearer of bad news and all. Do you see what I'm trying to say here? Remy, it doesn't matter if you'd told your dad a year ago or let it come out the way it did—either way he was going to get hurt. It wasn't your responsibility to clean up your mum's mess—and he knows that."

I know deep down that he's right, but it still doesn't completely banish the doubt and guilt I feel for the hurt I know he must be going through right now. I know I've only added to that hurt by disappearing on him.

"When my mum and dad were going through their divorce"—Oliver shifts a little so he can look at me from a normal angle, still keeping an arm around me—"it wasn't a good divorce. Divorces never really are, but my parents were both pretty selfish."

"How so?" I wipe my face off, last night's makeup smearing my fingertips.

"At first, my mum went on about how the divorce was because of the amount of time my dad spent working instead of with his family. She wasn't wrong about that, but then she started blaming us kids."

"What? Why?" I ask, lacing my fingers through his.

He shrugs. "She blamed us for never getting to spend time with him. If we weren't around, she'd have been able to go to more work events, or they would have been able to go on more holidays."

"But she could have gotten a sitter or done a family trip."

"I know." He nods. "When my brother told me he knew my dad was cheating on Mum, I was shocked. I wanted to tell her, to protect her, but my brother made me swear to not get in the middle of it. Later, Mum found out. She started blaming us more. It's part of what started the wedge between us. My little sister actually believed the words coming from her mouth. Sophie truly thought the divorce was our fault."

"That's just awful."

"I know now that Mum blamed us because she was hurting. It was the easiest way for her to deal with the pain."

"But—"

Oliver holds up a finger, cutting me off.

"My point is, my mum was hurting from the divorce. I could have told her about the cheating sooner, but she would have been hurt just as much either way. It wouldn't have mattered. She would have just been hurtin' more a little sooner. It doesn't matter if your dad had known sooner or not. He still would be hurting all the same. There is nothing you could have done to save him from this hurt. Eventually, it would have come out."

There's no denying the words coming out of his mouth. He's right. It doesn't matter when the truth came out, or how—the truth was always going to be there. But, there is still something there, tugging at my brain. "If I'd told him about the affair when I'd found out, I could have finally been free. There wouldn't have been anything Gage could have held over my head."

"He knew the truth about your dad, though. The bastard would have found a way to use that against you in the end, because he knows how much you care for your father. You would have wanted to protect him."

"Point," I say, knowing Oliver is right again. Again, the sound of the rain fills the silence around us. I stare at our tangled fingers, marveling at how I ended up here.

"If you want to put a positive spin on all of this heartache and hurt, look where it's led you. In some backward strange turn of events, it brought us together."

I look at him and the half-crooked smile on his face. His eyes are warm and gentle. I glance down to see the giant spot of tears and snot on his shirt. "I snotted up your shirt." The words are quiet.

"I don't care." He, too, is almost whispering. "Muck up my shirt as much as you need, Love."

My eyes find him again, and he's still looking at me—but this time his gaze is on my lips. He reaches up and brushes my hair back, wrapping his arm a little tighter around me. He slides his hand into my hair, and I press my cheek into his palm, feeling the warmth of it against my skin. Oliver leans down and gently kisses me. It's slow, deliberate, and filled with words and meaning that he's never said, but that I can feel, in this one kiss, are true. Oliver pulls back enough to look me in the eyes. His kiss leaves me feeling adored—a feeling I've never felt before. He leaves a delicate kiss on the tip of my nose before pulling me to him again, wrapping me in both of his arms and holding me tight.

Chapter Twenty-Four

Rain beats against the windshield, the wipers furiously working to make the road in front of us visible. Oliver had held me in the backseat for what felt like hours as we let the sound of the rain wash away the pain and the world around us. I felt safe and secure wrapped in his arms, and now, in spite of the blinding rain, I feel a sense of peace.

"Do you see the exit? I can't see a bloody thing in this rain. I'm from London. It rains a lot there you know, so you'd think this would be a piece of cake." Oliver leans over the steering wheel, squinting through the windshield.

I lean forward, eyes straining to read the signs on the side of the road. We're nearly passing it when I spot it. "There!" I jab a finger to the right of us.

Oliver maneuvers the car onto the exit ramp, and the GPS guides us through the narrow streets of the soggy French Quarter. At last, Oliver is able to put the car in park in the driveway of our AirBnB. I watch him let out a sigh of relief, but can't actually hear it because of the deafening rain pounding on the roof of the car.

"Right, then!" Oliver shouts to be heard over the rain. "Our flat is on the second floor!" He points towards the house, and we both lean forward to peer at it. The door seems impossibly far.

"Should we save the bags for later?" I yell back.

Oliver shakes his head. "We might want to change once we're inside and out of this deluge."

I nod. "On the count of three then?" I look at Oliver who nods back.

"One!" He holds up a finger, turns off the car, and pushes the button to open the trunk.

"Two!" I yell, as we unbuckle our seatbelts.

"Three!" We both shout it at the same time as we swing our car doors open.

I jump out and run around to the already open trunk and start grabbing bags. Oliver grabs most of them and makes for the stairs as I pick up the remaining ones and slam the trunk shut. I slip and slide on the wet wood as I run up the stairs. Oliver is attempting to enter the entry code to the door, but is met with a red error light. He tries again, but gets the same error message.

"What's the code?" I yell.

"Zero-two-two-zero. I must be doing something wrong."

"Did you hit the unlock button after you put the code in?" I brush my drenched hair out of my face.

Water drips into Oliver's eyes and down his face as he bites his lower lip and winces. He turns back to the lock again, finally gets the green light, and pushes the door open. We stand just inside, water dripping off both us and our bags.

"Is the air set to arctic in here?" I shiver as goosebumps spread over my skin.

"Towels. We need towels. Here, give me those bags, and I'll set them in the bath so they don't get water all over the floor." Oliver takes all of the bags and hurries away to find the bathroom. He comes back through the trail of water he left behind, his t-shirt sticking to his skin in all the right places. He hands me a towel and steps back, stripping his shirt off. My eyes linger on his body, taking him in. A faint outline of abs covers his torso, and when he turns around I see the muscles in his shoulders roll with every movement. I realize I've been staring and look away, hurrying to try and dry myself off, but I'm shivering too much. My teeth are chattering.

"You'd probably have an easier time getting dry if you took off the wet clothes," Oliver says, tousling his hair with the towel. "Maybe a warm shower might help?"

I try to nod, but the shivering has taken control of all of my muscles.

"There's a second bath, in the main bedroom. Come on then, and take a warm shower." Oliver takes my hand and leads me down a short hallway, into the main bedroom, and through to a bathroom. A giant glass shower sits in one corner and a clawfoot tub in another. "I'll be out here if you need me."

I raise an eyebrow at him and attempt to smirk. His cheeks flush.

"Right—not that you'll need me in the bath." He clears his throat. "Right then, I'll just be, um, enjoy." Oliver backs out of the room and closes the door.

I turn on the hot water and let the steam fill the bathroom as I peel the wet clothes off and toss them in the sink. When the water hits my cold skin, I nearly gasp at how wonderful it feels—like being wrapped in a warm blanket. I stand under the hot stream, letting it chase away the cold. Soon, my teeth stop chattering and my muscles relax. When the water begins to cool, I turn it off and slip out, wrapping in a big fluffy towel. It's then that I realize that I have no clothes to change into.

I crack the door open and peer around the room. "Oliver?" It takes a second, but he comes into the bedroom. "Um, I don't have any clothes to change into. Can you get my bag?"

"Sure thing." He leaves and comes back with my bag, which is completely soaked still. "I'm not sure if you're going to find anything dry in here."

"How are your clothes dry?" I ask, taking in the appearance of his shorts and t-shirt.

"I had a trash bag in there for dirty clothes. I think it helped protect some of them." He grimaces. "Want me to see if there's something in there you can wear?"

"Uh...yeah, that's probably best. But, um, can I still have my bag?"

He cocks his head.

"Under clothes," I say, opening the door a little more and holding out my hand. He hands me the bag and retreats from the room. I unzip it and take stock of what survived the rain. Pretty much everything on top is completely soaked through. I dig to the bottom and find panties I can wear—but no usable clothes or bra.

Oliver knocks gently on the door. "I have a t-shirt. It's quite large. Might be more like a dressing gown on you."

I open the door enough to take the shirt. "Thanks. Just give me a minute." I get dressed, and the shirt is really big, coming almost to my knees. I swing the door open and step out, the steam rolling out behind me. "Why do you have such a big shirt?" I notice Oliver staring at my legs. "Oliver?"

He tears his eyes away from my legs. "Oh, um, dunno. For backup, I guess. I started a fire in the living room, if you're still chilly."

"That sounds perfect," I say as a clap of thunder sounds overhead.

Oliver leads me into the living room, and I see the fireplace, flames dancing inside. I pull a blanket off the couch and sit on the rug in front of it, closing my eyes and letting the heat wrap around me. Oliver pushes the couch closer so I can lean against it, before sitting beside me, his knee resting against mine. I can see the rain still falling outside the window and listen to the slow roll of thunder filling the silence. I stretch my legs out, leaning against the couch.

Oliver pulls me against him. "Is this ok?" he asks, uncertain.

I nod and rest my head against his chest, staring into the fire. *This, I think to myself, this is my happy place. Not our location, or the weather, but this...with Oliver, feeling his heartbeat and his arms around me. This makes me happy.* Oliver's thumb brushes back and forth against my thigh where the shirt has ridden up, and chills run through me.

"I'm happy," I whisper against his chest.

"Yeah?" he asks, his voice a whisper, too—as though both of us are scared to break this peaceful bubble around us.

I nod before shifting so I can look up at him. "You make me happy."

I watch as the briefest moment of pain flashes through his eyes before they soften, and he brings a hand up to my chin. "You make me happy too, Remy." He runs his thumb along my lower lip before sliding his hand into my hair. He dips his head and lightly brushes his lips against mine. He pulls back and whispers, "The happiest." He kisses me again, running his tongue along my bottom lip.

Heat spreads through my body, pooling in my stomach. I bring my hand up to his cheek, feeling the stubble beneath my fingers. I trace a finger down his nose, over his top lip, and along his bottom lip. I take his chin and pull him towards me, pressing my lips to his, sliding my fingers into his still damp hair.

Oliver deepens the kiss, gently parting my lips. His fingers tighten in my hair, pulling me closer to him. I use my other hand to push myself up and slide my leg across his lap, straddling him.

He breaks the kiss, cradling my face in both of his hands. He rests his forehead against mine.

"Remy, I..." he whispers, his eyes pressing closed.

I shake my head and tug at the hem of his shirt until it's up and over his head and toss it on the couch. "Just kiss me," I whisper into his neck as I run my tongue along his ear.

I feel the muscles in his chest tighten under my touch, and his heart races beneath my fingers. I trail soft kisses across his chest from one side to the other. Oliver runs his hands up my thighs, pushing the shirt up and leaving trails of fire in their wake. Pulling back, I look into his eyes—and they're burning with desire. It's the kind that makes your stomach drop and your heart skip. The kind that leaves you without any doubts, questions, or fears.

Oliver leans forward, pulling me towards him and crushing his lips to mine, tangling his fingers in my hair, frantic, like this might all disappear if he doesn't kiss me. His tongue flicks across my lips like a flame, parting them and slipping inside. I feel him tug at my shirt, and we part only long enough for him to pull it over my head and toss it aside before we're pulled back together like magnets.

A groan slips past his lips as my bare breasts press against his bare chest. He leans back, and I watch as his eyes drag down my mostly naked body, coming back up to land on my chest. He takes my nipple into his mouth and sucks. My eyes roll closed, my breath hitching. He does the same to the other side and then leans back, brushing his thumb back and forth against the sensitive skin. I can't stop the moan that falls from my mouth.

Oliver's mouth is against mine again, hungry and needy. I pull at his hair, trying to bring him closer, and his mouth falls to my neck, biting and kissing across it.

He shifts, his arms bracing me as he tries to gently lay me back on the carpet—but we lose our balance and topple over, Oliver landing on top of me. We're both laughing, and I reach up to press kisses against his cheeks, nose, and lips. Oliver pushes up, a smile still on his face, and kneels over me, his eyes roaming down my body and back up to meet my eyes. He stares at me with a look that I've only ever seen in the movies, only ever read about in books. It's a look of pure adoration and desire.

"Remy, you're so gorgeous." Oliver's voice is hoarse.

A lump forms in my throat, but I swallow it down as I reach a hand up to the back of his neck, pulling him towards me, bringing our lips together. Our mouths are eager, and our hands move hungrily, exploring each other's bodies. I tug him closer, wrapping my legs around him, and a little moan escapes him. I push back slightly, needing a breath of air, and his lips find my neck, moving down to my breasts. He flicks his tongue across my nipple, and I moan. Taking it in his mouth he sucks and teases as I squirm beneath him.

"Oliver," I breathe out.

Another moan. "I love the sound of my name in your mouth." He shifts off me and drags his hand down my body, feather-light. He stops at the top of my panties, running his finger back and forth, teasing, before sliding it under the fabric. His fingers brush over my slit before he spreads me and glides a finger over my clit.

My back arches, and I gasp, unable to find words.

Oliver lowers his head to my ear. "You're so wet," he whispers. "I love knowing I do that to you." He keeps running his finger over that sensitive bundle of nerves until I'm panting. He pulls his hand out and grabs my hand. "This is what you do to me, love."

Oh. My. God. He's rock hard, and I can feel the girth of him through his shorts. He really does have a giant trouser titan going on in there. I swallow hard. "Wow," I breathe.

He chuckles. "That's all? Just wow?"

"Brain....not braining," I say, shaking my head.

He chuckles again as he stands, sliding out of his shorts, and I get a full view of him. And *damn!* he's sexy as hell.

"Panties," he says, pointing to me. "They need to bugger off."

I shimmy out of them and toss them aside. Oliver kneels over me once more, and I yank him towards me, greedily taking his mouth with mine, wrapping my legs around him, pulling him closer.

"Protection?" he whispers.

"Birth control," I say between kissing him. I wrap my legs around him again and pull him closer. I feel his cock slide against me, and it drives me crazy. "I want you. Inside of me."

"Demanding, are we?" he asks, licking my nipple, gently biting it, sending pleasure through my whole body in ripples. "You didn't ask nicely." He thrusts himself against me. I feel him rub against my clit, and I moan. "Only good girls get what they want." He bites at my ear. "Say it nicely." His breath on my ear sends shivers across my skin.

"Oliver, I..." He rubs against me again, making it almost impossible to think.

"Yes?" he says, smiling, knowing damn well what he's doing.

"I need you," I say, breathless.

"What's the magic word, love?"

"Fuck me, please!" I yell out in frustration.

I feel him push into me, and I gasp not expecting it, my eyes rolling closed as I dig my nails into his back.

"Good girl," he growls in my ear.

His rhythm is slow at first as he watches me, brushing kisses against my lips as I sigh into his. Every nerve in my body is on fire, setting everywhere he touches ablaze. Once again he brushes a thumb across my nipple, and my back arches off the floor as I whimper, an ache pulsing through me. Oliver slides a hand down my side and between my legs; his fingers circle around and around, each stroke of my clit a torturous ecstasy.

"Yes," I moan out, bringing my hips up to meet his touch.

He brings his hand back up to my breast, his pace picking up. Each thrust becoming harder and faster, grinding into me. It's as though there is no him or me—our bodies are just one, moving together. He moans as he kisses me, the vibration traveling all the way through my body. I wrap my legs tighter around him, pulling him as close as I can, meeting each thrust with a grind of my hips. The heat deep inside of me builds until it feels like I might explode. Oliver must sense that I'm right there, on the verge of shattering. He kisses his way up my neck, his moans resonating into me.

"Remy," he moans into my ear. "Touch yourself."

I don't think, I just do. Following his commands like they are the law. Using my fingers, I circle my clit as he continues to thrust into me. "Oh, god, Oliver..." I start to fall apart, and I wrap myself tighter around him as my body gives into him, coming unraveled.

He buries his face in my hair, and I feel his body shudder as he calls out my name again. His movements slow and then stop, but our breathing continues fast and hard, a sheen of sweat covering our skin. Oliver lies next to me, pulling me to his chest, and wraps his arms around me. I lay my head on him and feel his racing heart and the rise and fall of his chest as he works to get his breathing to a normal pace. We lie in silence, words escaping us both.

Finally, he lifts my chin so he can see my face. "I've never felt anything like that before. I've"—he pauses, searching for the right words—"I've never felt so close, so connected to a person."

All I can do is nod as I trace circles on his chest with my finger. "I've never had someone make me feel so"—I pause and swallow the lump in my throat—"wanted before." I look up at him.

His brow furrows, and he dips his head, placing a gentle kiss on my lips before pressing his lips to my forehead, pulling me tighter to him. "Stay." Oliver's voice is barely a whisper.

It's such a simple word. One syllable. Four letters. Yet it holds so much meaning. I pull back and look into his piercing blue eyes, glowing in the light of the fire.

"Stay," he says again. Don't leave tomorrow morning. Wait for me. I'll go with you—wherever you want to go, I'll go. When we're together, everything makes sense to me."

I lay my head against his chest again, breathing in his scent. Our hearts beat to the same rhythm. I could say no, and continue alone on this journey that I set out to take on my own. I could find a place that my heart loves and build a life for myself there. I could make new friends, get a job, have a life that is just for me. Or...

I think about what it might be like to say yes. To have Oliver come with me and see where we end up. To get to feel his arms around me every day. Maybe we can find a place that our hearts love and build a life there. Make new friends together. Continue on this crazy adventure fate seems to be sending us on.

Fate...

The girl who doesn't believe in fate, realizing that fate might really be what brought us together.

I feel Oliver take a deep breath beneath me, and I know what my answer is.

"Ok," I whisper, nuzzling in and letting my eyes fall closed.

Chapter Twenty-Five

I wake up confused. The floor next to me is empty and sun pours in through the rain dappled window, basking the living room in the warm glow of the afternoon sun. I sit up and wrap myself in the blanket and look around. I can hear Oliver's muffled voice coming from the bedroom. I stand, stretching, and go to find him. The door of the bedroom is ajar, and as I get closer, Oliver's voice gets clearer.

"I told you before that I couldn't do it anymore." His voice has an edge to it.

Silence follows, and I peer through the crack in the door to see him pacing back and forth across the room, wearing nothing but shorts. My heart races a little, and my stomach tightens, flashes of the rehearsal dinner going through my head.

"Look, you're just going to have to find another way. I tried telling you this days ago." He pauses. "You think I don't know what that means?" Another pause. "Right then, if you can't leave it be, then piss off and leave me the hell out of it," he spits out, ending the call and continuing to pace back and forth, his fists clenched. "Fuck." It comes out through clenched teeth, and he runs his fingers through his hair a few times before dialing another number.

I push the door open, stepping into the room, and lean against the wall.

"Hey, Henry, is Mum around?" Oliver turns and sees me, a brief smile flits across his face before he turns to pace the other direction. "'Ello, Mum, how are you?" He pauses, listening to her reply. "Well, aren't you the card shark? Listen, I wanted to let you know I'm planning to come 'round for dinner, yeah? If that's alright?" His eyes find mine again, and this time he gives me a warmer smile. "Yeah, in a couple hours...brilliant. Um, listen, is it ok if I bring someone along?" Oliver pauses, a hint of a smile on his lips before he rolls his eyes. "Yes, Mum, a girl." Another pause. "Right, see you soon. Miss you too, Mum."

He ends the call and turns his attention to me, planting a gentle kiss on my forehead before stepping back to look at me. "How'd you sleep?" he asks, rubbing my arms.

"A little stiff from the floor, but I'm fine." I shrug, taking a step closer to him. "You ok?" I put a hand on his chest, feeling his steady heartbeat.

"I'm ok," he replies, brushing a thumb across my bottom lip.

"Your phone call, though..." I trail off, trying to find the right words.

"That was just my mum and Henry."

"No, the other phone call."

Oliver shifts, looking away. "It was nothing."

"You seemed upset." I search his face, concerned by the sudden change in his expression.

"It was no one that matters." He meets my gaze with a hardened expression.

It's my turn to look away, and I hear him blow out a heavy breath. Out of the corner of my eye I watch him run his hands through his hair and down his face.

"It was just—"

I shake my head and hold up a hand to cut him off. "It's none of my business. I shouldn't have asked. I'm sorry." I turn to go back into the living room, searching for my clothes. I can sense Oliver behind me, but I continue to hunt for my bra, before I remember I wasn't wearing one. I turn to find Oliver watching me.

"I'm sorry, Remy. I didn't mean to be short with you. I just..." he trails off and shakes his head. "It was just something I thought I'd already dealt with. Work-ish stuff."

I sigh, but I'm not sure if I'm relieved or frustrated by his answer. "You do remember me telling you about all of the shit I've been through, right? Everything that's made it so incredibly hard for me to trust people?"

Oliver steps closer to me. "I do, love. I'm sorry. Look, I can spell it all out for you right now if you'd like."

I don't know what I want. Do I want to hear what he has to say? Is this what he's been trying to tell me this whole trip? I don't want to ruin the good the last couple of days has brought us, so I just let the subject drop, shaking my head to clear it away. "Let's just drop it. I shouldn't have pried," I say, waving it off. "So, you're going to have dinner with your mom?"

He nods, still looking unsure at just dropping the subject. "And I'd like you to come with me. If you want."

"Meeting a parent already? You move fast, Oliver Adley."

"You don't have to come along," he says, a hint of worry in his voice. "I don't want you to feel pressured to go."

An involuntary smile crosses my face. "You're adorable, you know that?"

"What? Why?"

"You just are. I'm fine with going."

"You sure? Because you really don't have to."

"Positive." I lift up on my toes and plant a kiss on his lips, which makes him smile. "Besides, you already told her you were bringing someone."

"Right then, I should probably grab a shower."

"You know," I say, stepping backwards, "I could really use another shower too." I drop the blanket from around me, my clothes falling to the floor with it. "Whoopsie."

It takes Oliver a second to tear his eyes away from my naked body and up to my eyes. "That will never get old. Well, we should get you in there, then." He swoops down and scoops me up and over his shoulder, pulling a little scream from me. Oliver laughs, swatting me on the ass as he hauls me off to the bathroom.

⸎ — ◆ — ⸎

Oliver drives us across Lake Pontchartrain, one hand on the steering wheel, the other on my leg. I watch the waves churn and crash as the waters try to calm themselves after the storm. We drive across the bridge for what feels like hours before finally exiting and heading down a side street. Oliver follows the GPS and winds through a neighborhood not far from the lake. We pull up outside of a cute, sunny-yellow bungalow on stilts. Under the house, on the concrete patio, a grill billows smoke into the face of the man standing over it. He coughs, waving away the smoke, and takes a step back into cleaner air space. Oliver and I get out, and as I close my door, the man turns at the sound, his face lighting up.

"Oliver!" he says with a strong southern twang as he walks forward, arms spread wide, welcoming Oliver with a hug.

I watch this exchange and see the stiffness in Oliver's shoulders, the tightness in his muscles as Henry wraps him in a hug. The man pats Oliver on the back a couple of times before pulling back and holding him at arm's length, smiling—his white teeth a stark contrast against his suntanned skin. His soft brown hair is thinning at the front, but he definitely keeps himself in shape—judging by the fit of his shirt across his broad chest and shoulders.

"How are you?" he asks Oliver, finally stepping back.

"I'm alright. How're you, Henry?"

"Can't complain." Henry beams. His smiles is contagious, and I find myself smiling too.

"And, um, how's Mum?" Oliver asks.

Henry's warm brown eyes slide past Oliver—his smile never wavering—to me and back to Oliver, who gives a minute shake of his head. Henry clears his throat. "She's good! Upstairs prepping the rest of dinner. Says steak isn't enough for a meal." He glances between us. "Hope you all like steak."

We both nod.

"And this is the girl we've been hearing so much about?" Henry steps around Oliver to shake my hand.

I try to keep myself from smiling as Oliver shakes his head, clearly embarrassed.

"I mentioned her once," Oliver says.

"Twice, thrice, four or more." A faded British accented voice floats down from the top of the stairs, and I watch as a set of sandaled feet descend down. She's carrying a tray ladened down with bowls.

Oliver jumps forward, reaching for the tray. "Let me get that, Mum." He takes the tray from her, setting it on the table, and turns back, wrapping her in a giant hug. He holds her there a moment before she starts fussing at him to let her go. Oliver turns to me. "Remy, this is my mum, Eliza. Mum, this is Remy—the girl I've mentioned maybe once or twice."

Eliza gathers me into her arms, giving me a tight hug. She's thin and boney, but her hug is full of warmth and love. She pulls back and takes my face in her hands, smiling at me, her blue eyes the same striking blue as Oliver's, shining bright with happiness.

Her blonde hair, streaked with gray, is pulled back into a loose ponytail at the nape of her neck. "I'm so pleased to meet you, Remy. From what Oliver has told us, you sound exactly like the kind of girl he needs in his life. "

"Mum, stop." Oliver's cheeks are rosy red, and it makes me laugh.

"What?" Eliza puts her hands up in defense. "Only speaking the truth." She looks at Oliver, who's still pink. "Alright, fine. I'm done. Henry? Where are the steaks?"

"Nearly done, dear."

"Lovely," Eliza says, busying herself with setting the table.

I notice her hands shaking as she sets the bowls of food in the middle of the table.

"Can I help?" I ask, stepping up to the table.

"Aren't you sweet?" Eliza hands me some plates, and I start placing them around the table. Oliver and Henry begin pulling the steaks off the grill and add them to the mix of food on the table.

"Bottomless pit reporting for duty," Oliver says, rubbing his belly.

We all laugh, taking our seats.

"You always were my biggest eater. No idea where you put it all, but you were always hungry. 'Mummy, can I have a snack? Mummy, I'm hungry.' Didn't matter if we'd just eaten, you'd always want more."

"I was a growing boy," Oliver says with a shrug, spearing a steak with his fork and slapping it on his plate. "Which one do you want, love?" he asks, pointing at the plate. I point to one, and he spears it and drops it on my plate.

"So, Remy, we hear you're on an adventure across the states," Henry says, slicing into his steak.

I glance at Oliver, unsure of how much he's told them. "Um, yeah, something like that." I rub the spot between my eyebrows. "Just kinda looking for a fresh start, I guess."

"Sounds exciting," Eliza says, leaning in close. "Any idea where you're headed next?"

"I've got a couple of ideas in mind, but nothing concrete."

"Do share!" Eliza exclaims, excitement gleaming in her eyes.

"Oh, um..." I look around the table. "I looked at the Pacific Northwest. The Oregon coastline looks beautiful, and I love the idea of the rain. I also like the look of Savannah."

"That's two different sides of the country. Two extremes. How will you choose?" Eliza asks.

I glance at Oliver and smile. "Maybe I'll let fate decide."

"Oliver, do you plan to chase after her?" Henry asks.

Oliver clears his throat and shifts in his seat. "I wouldn't call it chasing. But, if she'll have me, yeah, I'd like to tag along." He winks at me, and I feel myself blush.

Eliza and Henry share a smile with each other before Eliza steers the conversation in another direction. "I talked to your sister," Eliza throws in. "She seems to be doing really well. The guy she's with—it seems serious."

"Yeah, he's a nice bloke. They've come 'round for dinner a few times."

Eliza purses her lips, looking torn. "Is she happy?" she asks. Worry lines crease her forehead, but her face smooths as quickly as they'd appeared.

"She's very happy, Mum." Oliver's voice is tight with an emotion I can't quite pinpoint.

"And your brother seems to be doing well, too. I haven't been able to get him on the phone, but I saw his post about he and Julia purchasing a home in the country."

Oliver sighs. "Mum, you know they'd have come 'round if they could. They just have a lot going on right now."

Eliza's smile is rueful and a little sad as she nods. "Of course," she says, waving Oliver off. "I know that." She clears her throat and takes a sip of her wine, making a quick swipe under her eye.

"How's your steak, Remy?" Henry reaches across the table pointing to my steak with his knife that could cut the tension in the air. "I got them at the farmer's market this morning."

Oliver and Eliza keep their eyes on their plates. I wonder how long it's been since Eliza has seen all of her kids in person. It seems to truly pain her that they're not here with Oliver. Are they really busy, or did they never fully forgive her behavior from all those years ago?

"Remy? Is everything alright?" Henry waves a hand in front of my face.

I blink and bring the world back into focus. "Yeah, sorry. Spaced out for a second. The steak is amazing. It's seasoned and cooked to perfection."

"Henry likes to call himself the Grill Master," Eliza chimes in.

We all chuckle and dinner continues with more chewing than talking. After we finish, I help Eliza clear the table, carrying the bowls and plates up to the kitchen. As I'm setting the last of the dishes into the dishwasher, Eliza pauses, leaning against the sink, both hands gripping it, her knuckles white.

"Are you ok?" I ask, placing a hand on her shoulder.

She breathes through her nose, eyes shut tight. "Dinner must not be agreeing with me. Give me a moment."

I watch as Eliza disappears into the bedroom and closes the bathroom door. Faint retching noises reach me in the kitchen, so I move through the bedroom and knock gently on the door. "Eliza? Are you sure you're ok? Should I get Henry?" I hear the sink running and the sound of gargling.

The door opens and Eliza's pale face appears. She's smiling, but it's weak and strained, not reaching her eyes. "I'm fine. Not to worry." She pats my cheek and then leads me out of the bedroom and back downstairs. Eliza is slower on the steps than earlier, holding onto the railing.

As we reach the bottom I see Henry stretched in the hammock and Oliver sitting in the chair next to him. When Henry sees Eliza's pale face he hurries to stand.

"Honey, are you alright?"

"I'm fine, just fine." Eliza waves him off. "Don't think dinner agreed with me. Made me a little woozy."

Oliver stands. "Are you sure—"

"Remy, dear," Eliza cuts in, "would you mind terribly if I steal Oliver away for a bit? I want to walk him down and show him the docks."

"Are you sure you're up for a walk, Mum?"

Eliza takes Oliver's hand, patting it. "Of course I am, now hush." She turns back to me, waiting for an answer.

"I don't mind at all. Please, take your time."

Eliza loops her arm through Oliver's. "We'll be back. Henry, don't bore the poor girl." She winks at me.

Oliver gives me a small kiss on the cheek before linking his arm with Eliza's, strolling towards the street, and disappearing around the corner. I feel Henry touch my shoulder and I realize I've been staring at an empty sunset-filled street for too long.

"Drink?" Henry holds up an empty wine glass.

"Sure?" I take the glass and sit on one of the lounge chairs while Henry trots upstairs and brings back three bottles of wine. I laugh. "I thought you said a drink. Emphasis on the 'a'."

"I didn't know if you were a red or a white. So I brought one of each—and a rosé for the middle option." He shrugs. "Preference?"

"Rosé actually sounds great, thanks." I hold my glass out as Henry pours the blush-colored wine.

He sits the bottle down and takes a seat across from me, groaning as he sits. I look back down the street in the direction that Oliver and Eliza vanished.

"It's been hard on Eliza."

I look over to Henry, and he sees the question on my face, so he continues.

"Being away from the kids, it's been hard on her."

"Has she gone back to see them?"

"We went over about five years ago, when Sophie was graduating high school. Eliza knew it wouldn't be easy, but she didn't imagine it to be as hard as it was." Henry sips his wine. "I don't know how much Oliver has told you, but Eliza was less than kind to the kids after the divorce."

"Oliver mentioned how she blamed them for it."

Henry nods. "She regrets that every single day of her life. She was hurting so much after the divorce, and pain can make you react in strange ways."

"But she left them. How could she just walk away from her children?" I can't mask the judgment in my voice.

Henry sighs and rubs the back of his neck. "I'm not going to defend what she did. In fact, back then I tried to convince her to act differently—but she was so full of anger and hurt that she was blinded to what she was doing." He takes a sip of his drink. "I tried to stay in contact with Oliver. He fought me on it, of course. Blamed me for his mom leaving. I sent him checks, from his mom, to help care for Sophie."

"That was awfully kind of you. You didn't really know the kids all that well, did you?"

"No, not really. But it wasn't from a lack of want on my end. Eliza had introduced me to them, and I'd seen them a few times—but she tried to keep it all separated."

"Oliver seems to have warmed up to you." I place my glass on the little table next to me, curling my legs under me. The twinkling lights strung above our heads kick on in the dimming evening light.

"Some," Henry responds. "I'm sure you can still see some of his leftover reservations for me, the tension he had when I hugged him. And I don't blame him for that. But I think he's come to realize I'm not the enemy. Sophie"—he grimaces—"she was the most hurt in the whole situation. Eliza acting the way she did before leaving...and her father not stepping in—it really took a toll on her. She still holds a bit of a grudge. And their brother, Jack, was already out of the house when Eliza left—but from what I could tell, he'd been trying to distance himself from the family for quite some time."

"And Oliver? I'm assuming by the fact that I'm sitting here that he must have forgiven her at some point."

Henry nods. "It was about a year and half after we'd made the trip over for the graduation. I'd been sending the checks, and Oliver had at least stopped blaming me by that point. I kept dropping into our conversations, as brief as they were, how much Eliza missed him, and how he should try to put the past behind him and..." Henry pauses, his eyes thoughtful. "I told him that he needed to try to put the past behind him and create a future he could look back on and be proud of—not one that he would regret."

I stare at Henry, feeling a strange sense of gratitude towards this man I've only just met. "You must really care about them."

"Eliza is my world, my everything. I knew the moment I saw her that my life would never be the same and that I didn't want to go a second longer not knowing her. I would do absolutely any-thing for her. And once I met her kids"—he chuckles—"despite their loathing for me, I fell in love with them as if they were my own."

"You must be rubbing off on Oliver."

"Why do you say that?" Henry looks curiously at me, his brow furrowed.

"He talks a lot like you do about love. Believes in fate and destiny."

"You're not a believer?"

I shrug. "I didn't used to be. But Oliver can be pretty con-vincing." An unexpected smile spreads across my face. "For someone to go through what he did, to see love unravel the way it did with his parents and still have the belief in fate and destiny—it's catching."

Before Henry can respond, we hear laughter from the street. Oliver and Eliza are rounding the corner, strolling into the driveway, and coming to a stop on the patio. Immediately, I notice their red-rimmed eyes despite the smiles on their faces.

"I hope Henry didn't bore you too much," Eliza says, going to stand behind him and wrapping her arms around his shoulders.

"Not at all. Any situation where there's good wine can never be boring." I smile at Henry, and he winks at me.

"Anyone up for dessert and maybe a board game?" Eliza asks. "I made my famous blueberry crumble."

The corners of Oliver's mouth twitch as he tries hard not to smile. He looks down at me as I give him puppy dog eyes, and he laughs.

"I don't know about you," I say, standing up, "but I would love some blueberry crumble."

"That's the spirit!" Eliza says, eyes shining bright.

"Can I help with anything?" I offer.

"Absolutely not. Henry, dear, come upstairs and help me get the stuff. You two make yourselves comfortable at the table."

Eliza and Henry disappear upstairs, and Oliver steps closer to me, wrapping his arms around my waist and pulling me close. His eyes still have a hint of red to them.

"You ok?" I ask, raising my hand to gently stroke my thumb beneath his eye.

Oliver just nods, his eyes never leaving mine. He dips his head and gently presses his lips to mine. One hand tightens on my back, pulling me closer to him, while the other tangles in my hair as he deepens the kiss. He walks me backward and lifts me so I'm sitting on the table, still kissing me. A shiver runs down my body, and Oliver pulls back, staring intently into my eyes.

"I don't think this is what your mom meant when she said to make ourselves comfortable at the table." I smirk.

He smiles, but takes my face in his hands. "You are an incredible woman, Remy Montgomery—and don't you forget it."

I pull back. "What brought that on?"

Oliver shakes his head. "I just needed you to know. Speaking of you knowing things, there's something I've been trying to tell you. I don't want to wait any longer to tell you. I—" Oliver is cut off as Eliza and Henry's feet appear at the top of the stairs.

"Tell me later?" I ask, planting a soft kiss on his cheek.

He's unable to hide the disappointment on his face as he nods, turning to find a seat at the table. Henry sets the game up as Eliza serves up dessert. I look around the table at the smiles and laughs being shared and happiness fills me. Oliver and I may come from two screwed-up, broken lives, but here we are—and I can't remember ever feeling more whole.

Chapter Twenty-Six

Standing at the sink in the bathroom, I hear someone knocking at the front door and arch an eyebrow in confusion. Who could be here? Oliver's mom and Henry? I can't imagine it would be them. We were there fairly late last night playing board games until I could barely keep my eyes open. Oliver had gotten us back to the apartment and tucked me in. He'd gotten up earlier this morning, letting me sleep late and freshen up with a shower before we ventured out to explore the city a little.

"Hey Oliver, can you get that?" I call out, returning to adding the finishing touches on my makeup. The knock comes again. "Oliver?"

When he doesn't answer, I step out of the bathroom into an empty bedroom. I go out to the living room and find the entire apartment empty. Another knock. I peer through the peephole in the door and am both confused and amused when I see who's on the other side. Laughing, I open the door, and there stands Oliver, a bouquet of sunflowers in his hand and a devastatingly handsome grin on his face.

"Whoa." A blush creeps across Oliver's face as he takes me in, his eyes roaming over every inch of my body. "You look"—Oliver clears his throat—"Wow…absolutely stunning."

It's my turn to blush. "Thank you." I open the door a little wider, and Oliver steps inside. "But how did you—? When did you—?" I point at the door, then to him, and then back at the door again. "I'm so confused."

Oliver laughs, holding the flowers out to me. "While you were in the shower, I snuck off to grab these. Wouldn't be a proper date without them."

I take them and turn to close the door. I hear an intake of breath behind me and smile knowing he's just seen the keyhole opening in the back of my dress. It goes from my shoulders to my low back. I face him and take in his attire. He's dressed in a deep blue suit with a dark red tie pulling it all together. He can truly pull a suit off spectacularly, looking so damn sexy in it. I can't stop myself from letting my eyes roam over him, remembering the feel of his body against mine.

"You're staring," Oliver says, a small smirk on his face.

I shake my head and bring my eyes up to his and find myself blushing again. I turn away from him and go to the kitchen, taking a cup from one of the cabinets to put the flowers in. I need to give my hands something to do other than ripping his suit off.

"So, I made reservations at Muriel's in Jackson Square. It's supposed to be amazing," he says.

"I've read about that place in travel blogs. It's on my list of places to try," he says.

"I'm ready when you are." Oliver holds a hand out to me.

"Ready." I smile and take his hand, letting him lead me from the apartment.

We're sitting on the balcony overlooking Jackson Square, and the view is gorgeous. We've gotten to watch the sun set and the lights of the city come on as we've enjoyed our dinner.

"I can't eat another bite." I say, groaning, my dress tighter than when we'd sat down. "How can you keep eating?"

"Bottomless pit." Oliver pats his stomach. "Sure you don't want anymore?"

I shake my head, groaning again. He proceeds to finish the dessert down to the very last crumb. After a three course meal and dessert, I feel like I could fall asleep right where I'm at. My eyelids are heavy, and I feel completely relaxed.

"I was thinking we could walk down to the river, see the cathedral from that platform over there." Oliver points to a spot in the distance.

"You might have to carry me," I say, my eyelids drooping closed. "All of that food, and I'm ready for sleep."

"I'd carry you if you asked me to," Oliver says.

I stretch and shake my head. "I think walking will do me good. Dinner was delicious, thank you again."

"My pleasure," Oliver says, taking my hand and kissing it.

We exit onto the crowded sidewalk. Tourists bustle around taking pictures of the famous landmarks, while artists sell their wares and musicians play to those walking by. Oliver wraps an arm around me, pulling me close. As we approach the busy intersection, the smell of the delicious café au lait and beignets fill our noses, wafting from Café Du Monde. The line stretches down the sidewalk as people wait for one of the many packed tables to open up. We reach Artillery Park Plaza, and Oliver drops his arm from my waist, taking my hand in his. We climb to the top and turn to see the beauty that is the cathedral, a bright spot in the dark night sky.

"It's so beautiful," I say, unable to pull my eyes away from it.

"Yes, very beautiful."

I turn to find Oliver isn't looking at the cathedral at all, but at me. He kisses me, cupping my face in his hand. He pulls back just enough to look into my eyes. "Incredibly sexy even." He smiles and kisses me again.

"Finding architecture sexy? Maybe you picked the wrong profession."

Oliver rolls his eyes, shaking his head. I feel his hand run up my back, his fingers brushing against the exposed skin. I shiver and lean up to press a kiss to the side of his neck, and I hear him sigh. The putt-putt of an engine behind us pulls our attention to the water, and we walk across the plaza and down the steps towards the river. The lights of a boat move along the water as it chugs slowly past us. We sit as close to the water as we can without actually having our feet in it. There are only two other couples spread out along the steps in the dimly lit darkness. We sit quietly huddled together listening to the water lap against the steps. Oliver laughs, and I look questioningly at him, which only makes him laugh more.

"What's so funny?"

"This. All of this. I never in a million dreams would have imagined this trip turning out like this. You truly are a work of fate."

"There you go with that fate business." I hold up a hand as Oliver tries to defend it. "You might just be making a believer out of me, though." I smile and lean in, softly kissing him before nuzzling my head into his neck.

"That's something I never thought I'd hear leave your lips."

"What can I say? You can be very convincing." I pull back and look at him. The same look that had crossed Oliver's face on the canal, in the hotel room, and standing outside Eliza and Henry's house, shadows his face now. "What? That look has been a ghost in your eyes since Indiana. What's going on?"

"Remy, there's something I need to tell you. I've been trying to find a way to tell you the whole time. It's never the right time, or something keeps getting in the way..." He pauses, looking out at the water.

"Well, there's nothing in our way here."

He shakes his head. "Let's go back to the flat."

"Can't you tell me here? Before something else gets in the way?"

He presses his eyes closed. "Please, let's go back to the flat. It will be better there."

I stare at him a second longer before replying. "Ok," I say, and before I can even stand up, Oliver is already hovering above me, pulling me to my feet.

We head back up the stairs, and I try to catch his eye—but he's not paying attention, lost in whatever it is he needs to tell me. I squeeze his hand to let him know I'm here, and he glances at me, giving me a half-smile and pulling me to his side. Oliver wraps his arm around me, and I feel him press a kiss into the top of my head. Halfway across the plaza, a voice calls out—

"Well, isn't that just an adorable sight?"

A doctor would probably pronounce me dead, because my heart stops at the sound of his voice. I spin around as Gage pushes off the statue he's leaning against and casually walks towards us.

Chapter Twenty-Seven

"Gage? How are you—? Why are you—?" I can't seem to form a full thought, and my heart is pounding hard in my chest.

"I never thought I'd see the day that you couldn't put together a sentence, Remy. It's amusing to watch you stutter with shock." He smirks, looking cockier than ever.

"What are you doing here, Gage?" I manage to get out at last.

His eyes slide over to Oliver and back to me. "So, not happy to see me then?" Gage pouts mockingly. "Pity. Not exactly the warm and fuzzy greeting I would have expected from the woman I was supposed to marry."

"What greeting did you expect, Gage? For me to leap into your arms and ask you to whisk me away back to that world? Why are you here?"

Gage pretends to mull it over. "No, not exactly. But a warmer greeting than this one. I just wanted to clear the air, clarify a few things. Call it a truce, if you want."

I narrow my eyes at him, knowing full well he's up to something. "What's left to clarify? I left, Gage." I say this loud and slow, so that maybe it'll get through to him. "Can't you just let me go? Leave me alone and let me live my life."

Gage looks at Oliver again before speaking. "Looks like you're living your life, alright. Just days ago you were supposed to be marrying me—and here you've already moved on with someone else. You're more like your mother than you think," he says with a sneer.

I feel Oliver shift behind me, and I reach back to grab his hand.

Gage's eyes don't miss a thing, and he smirks. "Look, just let me say my peace, and I'll leave." He holds his hands up.

"Forget it, Gage. I heard all I'll ever need to hear in the hotel suite at the rehearsal dinner. I'm done—and I'm tired of telling you just how done with you I am. I don't want anything to do with you. Do I need to spell it out with alcohol bottles? How about naked girls holding signs?" I turn to Oliver. "Come on, Oliver, let's go. I'm not wasting another second on this asshole."

Gage moves to block our path. "Oliver? Oliver Adley?" Gage puts a hand out to him. "It's so good to finally put a face to the name."

Confusion roots me in place as a sense of unease rolls through my body. I look back and forth between the two of them as my stomach squeezes with nerves.

"You're taller than I thought you'd be," Gage says, chuckling to himself.

"How do you know his name?" I'm still looking between the two of them as though I'm watching a tennis match. Oliver still hasn't moved as he continues to stare at Gage, jaw tense.

"You should know by now, Remy, I have my ways," Gage says.

A thought occurs to me. "Of course," I say, shaking my head. "You hired some PI to follow me around, didn't you? That's how you knew where I was and how you know who Oliver is. Unbelievable." I throw my hands into the air. "Actually, no, it's not. It's just believable enough with you. Did you use that sleazy old man your dad usually uses?"

Oliver finally moves, stepping in front of me, blocking Gage from view and lifting my chin to meet his gaze. "We need to go...now. I really need to talk to you." Oliver's eyes are pleading, but I pull away and step around him.

I look at Gage, who is smirking. "What, Gage? Just what?" I look back at Oliver, whose whole body is tense, worry shadowing his face.

"I told you, Remy, I just wanted to clear some things up. But, you know, having Oliver here will be a big help. He can help me with some of the story." Gage looks Oliver up and down appraisingly. "Doesn't look like a sleazy old guy to me," he says, and shrugs.

My stomach tightens and rolls and I step back as Gage's words play through my head. I look at Oliver, but his eyes aren't on me. He's staring at the ground, shaking his head.

"You hit the nail on the head," Gage says. "I did have you followed. Did you think I wouldn't find out about the secret bank account? Where did the money come from anyways?"

I swipe a traitor tear as it rolls down my cheek. "I have my ways," I respond, throwing his own words back at him.

Gage rolls his eyes and shrugs. "Doesn't really matter now. Anyways, I had to see what you were up to. A reasonable response to your actions, I think."

"Reasonable. It was reasonable to have me followed?"

"Well, yeah. My fiancé sets up a secret bank account—and I'm just going to pretend I don't notice?"

"Couldn't you have just asked me, like a normal human? How did you know it wasn't some kind of surprise?"

Gage laughs a deep laugh. "Oh come on, Remy. We both know you'd never surprise me that way. You'd actually have to like me to do something like that."

"So, you finally pulled your head out of your ass long enough to figure out that I don't like you? Surprising."

Gage smiles. "This is fun. But look, I'm famished—and I think Oliver knows the rest of the story better than I do. He can start with New York. I'm sorry if I put a damper on your evening. Looks like you were having a really good time. I'll leave you two to talk now." Gage turns his eyes on me. "Goodbye, Remy." He smirks and starts to walk down the stairs, before turning. "Oh, and I plan to get my hands on your trust fund. I'm owed that much." He waves and continues down the stairs before I can respond, whistling to himself.

I can't feel my body except for the heavy beat of my heart as it pulses through me, pounding in my eyes. I can't bring myself to move, to turn and face what's next. I don't know if I can survive what comes next. I see movement out of the corner of my eye and see Oliver moving to stand in front of me. He's trying to catch my eye, but I just stare blankly ahead, his suit blurring as tears begin pooling in my eyes. I can see his lips moving, but I can't hear the words coming out of his mouth.

He reaches a hand out, placing it on my shoulder. "Remy?" Oliver whispers, his voice tentative.

I shrug his hand away and look up at him, letting the tears spill down my cheeks. When I start to speak my voice is quiet, barely above a whisper. "Twenty questions, Oliver. Except it's the final question." I swallow, my hands squeezing into fists at my side. Slowly and quietly, through clenched teeth, I ask, "Who the hell are you?"

Oliver puts his hand out as if to calm a frightened animal. "My name is Oliver Adley."

I shake my head an incremental amount, my eyes flashing, daring him to push me. "Who are you?" I explode, unable to contain my anger any longer. I shove against his chest over and over, each word accented by a blow. "Who. The. Hell. Are. You?"

Oliver keeps his hands raised by his head, letting me pound my fists against his chest, pushing him backwards until his back hits the statue. Finally, my hands still, and I drop my head against his chest, my breathing ragged and tears staining my cheeks. Everything in me aches as I push away from him and look at him once more.

"I'm going to ask you one more time, Oliver," I say, holding his gaze. "Who are you?" I take a few steps away from him, needing the distance between us.

Oliver closes his eyes, pressing his lips into a tight line. His voice whisper quiet, I barely hear the words leave his lips. "I've been trying to tell you." He takes a couple of deep breaths before turning his pained gaze on me. "I'm Oliver Adley, and I'm from London."

"I know all of that."

"A couple of months ago, my mum called me. She asked me to come visit her. She really wanted..." He stops. "No—she needed to see me. You know we've been working to rebuild our relationship, and it's been going pretty good."

"Ok, so what? You thought you'd stay entertained by being a professional stalker along the way?" I spit the words at him.

Oliver runs frustrated hands through his hair and turns away from me. I hear him blow out a breath before turning back to me. Tears gleam in his eyes, and his chin trembles. "She's..." He stops, his voice shaking. "She's dying, Remy." He tries to choke back the tears, but they come anyway.

I close my eyes as my stomach rolls again, and my heart sinks a little. I feel myself sway on the spot.

Oliver starts talking again, but still I don't open my eyes. "She's really sick, Remy."

I think back to our dinner with them: Eliza's thinness as I hugged her, her shaking hands as she set the table, her getting sick after dinner. The signs were there.

"I needed the money to help her. I placed an ad for work—anything legal that paid high."

"No." I shake my head. "You didn't—" My hand flies to my mouth as a sob escapes me. I turn and walk away a few paces. I can feel the stares of the people passing by us.

Oliver continues, speaking a little louder so I can hear him over the jazz band that just started playing below us. "I honestly thought I'd end up on the arm of some older woman at an event. But...but that's not what happened." He stops talking, and I turn back to him, my hands on my hips, waiting for him to continue. "I was contacted by Gage Donovan."

"No, no, no, no." I look up trying to blink back tears, but it's useless at this point.

Oliver rushes towards me, taking my hand. "You have to believe me, Remy, when I say I had no idea any of this would happen. I didn't realize we'd..." His voice trails off. "You have to understand the position I was in."

I pull my hand back and turn away. I can't hear anymore. I need a minute to process. I walk around the statue, my fingers toying with my necklace as I look at the cathedral. How could I have been so blind? How did I not notice? I think back to every moment of the trip. Gage knew where I was the whole time. Gage. I shake my head. Of course this is all tied to him. Had all of this—everything between Oliver and me—an act? I close my eyes and can feel his hands as he held me in front of the fireplace. I can see the pain in his eyes as he held me while I cried into his shirt in the car. I can feel his lips on mine as we kissed for the first time. It can't all be a lie.

I circle back around the statue to where Oliver leans slumping against it, his hands in his pockets, head bowed, staring at the ground. When he hears me, he looks up, his eyes red and his cheeks damp. My heart aches for him, but it also aches because of him.

"The phone call, after we...when I woke up. That was Gage, wasn't it?"

A look of shame settles on Oliver's face, and I get the urge to be sick. "You called him after we had sex? Did I—" I stop, trying to swallow the lump in my throat. "Did I mean so little to you?"

Hurt springs to Oliver's eyes. "Do you really think that? Do you think so low of me?"

"Oh, I don't know, Oliver. Let's see. You've been lying to me this entire time, and working for my ex-fiancé—tracking me like some kind of wild animal. Yeah, right now, my opinion of you is pretty low."

Oliver shakes his head as though he can shake my words away. "He called me, Remy. I told him, like I'd told him all of the other times he'd called me, that I didn't want any part in it anymore."

"I trusted you. You asked me to trust you—and I did. How could you do this?"

Oliver pushes off the statue, walks to the railing, and watches the traffic in the street below. He's either unwilling or unable to answer me. My head spins as more questions fill it, unable to iron out all of the details.

"Dammit, Oliver, answer me!"

"What can I say to you, Remy? I had my mum dying, and if I could just get you back to him, I would have the money she needed to possibly keep living. Fuck, Remy. What was I supposed to do?" His eyes plead with me, begging me to tell him what he was supposed to do. "I was desperate when I agreed to this. I had no idea who either of you were or what kind of situation I was getting into. I definitely didn't know how big of a dick Gage was." Another tear falls and slips down Oliver's cheek as he squeezes the bridge of his nose.

My emotions are being tugged in every different direction. Hurt, anger, guilt, and even sympathy flood through me. I'm pissed that my mother has spent my whole life lying to me. That Gage held the secrets over my head so he could get what he wanted. I feel guilt that I left my dad to discover the truth on his own and in the way that he did. I hurt for Oliver and his mom and their impossible situation. Mostly, though, I just hurt. Deeply. Had I been so wrong about him? I thought Oliver was genuine and real. I thought what had been growing between us was pure and simple.

"So, all of the kismet crap? That was just a bunch of bullshit? Some sort of ploy to get me to like you? To trust you?"

"No—"

"I let my guard down for you, Oliver. I trusted you—and you let me crash blindly into this mess."

"I tried—"

I hold up my hand, cutting him off, not able to stomach anymore. "I'm really, truly sorry about Eliza. She is a wonderful woman who doesn't deserve the cards she's been dealt." I turn towards the stairs, ready to get my stuff and get the hell out of here.

"Remy, please." Oliver's voice breaks.

I stop, feeling all of his agony with those two words, ricochet around my heart. I turn around to see tears flowing freely down his face. He doesn't try to wipe them away.

I close my eyes, more tears sliding down my cheeks, unable to look at him. "Goodbye, Oliver."

I descend down the stairs, not allowing myself to look back. There's an ache in my heart, and I feel it crack as my thoughts rage like fire, burning memories to the ground.

Chapter Twenty-Eight

Three Months Later

When I'd arrived in Savannah, Georgia three months ago, I'd had no idea what I was doing. Nursing a lot of hurt and needing a place to help me heal from it all, I'd landed here hoping it would be my saving grace. I'd seen the city on the lists I'd looked at; it had made the list for its beauty and the history that engulfs it.

Savannah has turned out to be more than I could have ever dreamed of. Here, I've found peace, beauty, and the kind of home I've always wanted.

I look out at the river, at a boat hauling shipping containers slowly trudging through the water, heading for port. A few people sit along the water's edge like me, but most are tourists, swarming the shops behind me along the cobblestone street. I look back down at my phone and read another comment to the video I'd made explaining my absence from my social accounts.

Books'O'Clock

This sounds like the plot of a movie. Or a really good book...

Unfogging_The_Books

Have you ever thought of writing a book @Remyis-
LIT…erary?

freetheBooks

I detect a best seller in our hands….

I roll my eyes, smiling. My phone rings, and my smile grows. I answer it, but before I can get a word in, Celia explodes on the other end.

"I'm in love! I'm so freaking in love it's not even funny!"

"Hello to you, too," I say, laughing. "I assume you're talking about your stalking victim?"

"She has a name!" Celia huffs.

"I'm sorry, you're right. I assume you're talking about Tahna?"

"Yes! She's just the fucking best!" Celia squeals.

I can picture her lying on her couch, kicking her heels in the air. "Have you told her how you feel?"

"Are you kidding me? It's only been three months. Too soon, right?"

"You're asking the wrong person, Celia." I squint out at the river, the sun glaring off the water.

"Still on the struggle bus?" she asks.

"A little bit," I say, trying to swallow down my feelings.

"I thought things were better, that Savannah was healing you?"

"It is—but it's not going to happen overnight."

"How's the bookstore? Robynn take my place as best friend yet?"

I shake my head, smiling. I'd spent my first day here wandering the streets and squares, taking in all the richness the city had to offer. Tucked into the corner of one of the squares was this bookstore, Bookology. It had been busy with people shoulder to shoulder inside. Despite how busy it was, the owner, Robynn, was as sweet as could be. True southern hospitality. She mentioned she was looking for help, and I jumped at the chance to take the job. Robynn happened to have heard of my social media accounts and that had been enough to convince her to take me on despite my lack of work experience. Most days the bookstore is packed to the brim with tourists wanting to get lost in the twists and turns and corners. You can look out the window onto the square with its enormous southern oak trees.

"Nobody can ever replace you as my best friend. Got it?" I say, authority in my voice.

"Out of sight, out of mind. But ok," Celia teases.

"But it's going great. Robynn is cool and her twin sister Kelly is so bubbly it's hard to not be in a good mood around her. We have dinner at least once a week—per Robynn's orders."

"Have you heard from anyone? Like—?"

"No," I cut her off. "Just Charles."

Celia doesn't say anything for a minute and then asks, "Have you given any more thought to my suggestion?"

"Which one? You make so many."

"Remy, you've had so much happen to you. There have been so many changes in your life—and so quickly. I think talking to someone could help."

I sigh. "I told you, I *am* getting therapy." My free time is spent exploring the city and all its hidden secrets. Most evenings are spent either by the river or in one of the squares with a book. I make weekly trips to Tybee Island for ocean therapy. It's cheaper than the real stuff and more effective for me. "It's just not the kind of therapy you want for me."

"I just want to make sure you're ok. And happy."

"I know. But we've talked about me enough. Back to you and Tahna. I'm so happy for you, Celia. I love that you're so happy."

"It's scary, but I love every second of it. We were talking about taking our first trip together."

"Yeah? Where to?"

"Oh, I know of this cool place, full of history and shit. Someone I know highly recommends it."

"No way! Are you coming to see me?" I ask, giddy.

"We're talking about it. Don't want to rush things, but it was her idea."

"Oh my unicorns! I would love to see you!" My phone pings, and I pull it away to look at it. "Shit, Celia, I have to go. I have to get to work."

"Fine, go be with your new best friend," she teases, her smile coming through the phone. "I miss you, friend."

"I miss you, too. I hope you guys do come down. I'd love to show you around."

"Hugs!"

"Kisses," I say and end the call.

Chapter Twenty-Nine

I pass over River Street and head up Factors Walk towards Bay Street. From here it's about twelve blocks to the bookstore. I look up at the many businesses that line Factors Walk in the old historic cotton district's 18th century warehouse buildings. Each business, rammed haphazardly against its neighbor, occupying its own business space in the joined row-buildings that have been subdivided and let out to different shopkeepers, warehouses, restaurants, and knick-nack shops.

Gazing down the row, I see a woman standing outside what appears to be an empty space. Brochures are clutched in her hand and she scrolls through her phone with the other. I spot a sign next to her that says 'Open House 10am-2pm'. Something pulls me towards this woman and her sign. Curiosity maybe? Or something else? Fate? I push the word out of my head as quickly as it had appeared. I climb the metal stairs and stop in front of her. She's so engrossed in her phone it takes her a moment to realize I'm standing there.

"Hi, are you here to see the listing?" she asks, not looking up from her phone.

"Um, what exactly is the listing?" I have absolutely no idea what kind of space I'm looking at. It could be a former restaurant, it could be a storefront, or it could be an apartment. I figure there's no harm looking. She hands me one of the pamphlets in her hand.

I look at it and realize it's a retail space. They're looking for buyers or longtime leasers.

"This," the woman says, "is a quaint little space. Once a former clothing boutique, then a jewelry store, and now just waiting for someone to come along and make it their own. Feel free to go in and have a look around. I'll be with you shortly."

I open the heavy door, which has probably been there since the building was first built. I take a step inside, and something clicks inside me as I take it all in. Despite the place being under a thousand square feet, there seems to be plenty of potential. The ceilings are tall, and the floors appear to be the original hardwood. At the very back wall, windows overlook what I can only assume is the river. I walk to the middle of the room and turn in a slow circle, taking it all in. My mind starts churning, ideas forming faster than I can keep up: I see bookshelves there against that wall, a seat by the window to watch the river, a display in the window seat, and a sign written in elegant script hanging on an emerald green wall.

"What do we think?"

The woman is right behind me, and I startle at her presence. "Oh, um, I really...it's just so..." What is wrong with my brain right now?

"Perfect, right? Like I said, perfect space for the right person. I've had some interest, since it's a prime location. You know what they say: location, location, location!"

"Right," I say, unsure what else to say. "Can I contact you if I want more information?"

"Of course. My info is there on that paper, and here"—she digs in her purse—"here is a business card. Hope to hear from you soon."

»» ·•·•·•· ««

A group of tourists blocks my way into Bookology. I wait until they've all entered the shop before I follow in behind them. Clearly we're in for a very busy day. Kelly is at the counter with a line of about ten people waiting to pay. The only way I can tell her apart from Robynn is the mossy oak tree tattoo that covers her arm from her shoulder to her wrist.

"Hey, Kelly, I need to talk to Robynn really quick, and then I'll be back out to help," I say, darting around customers.

"Oh sure, leave me here to fend for myself." She winks and nods her head towards the backroom and Robynn's office.

I finally make it through the crowd of people and into the backroom where I can hear Disney music coming from the office. Excellent, she's in a good mood. I knock on the door. "Robynn? You there?"

"Yeah, I'm here. Come on in."

I poke my head in the door to find Robynn taking a bite out of a donut and staring at the newest book release list. She looks up and smiles, that same smile Kelly just gave me.

"Hey, Remy, how's it going?" She peers at the security camera monitors. "Busy out there. Kelly doing ok?"

"I should probably be getting out there soon, but there's something I wanted to talk to you about first."

"Oook?" Robynn puts her donut down and sits forward, leaning on the desk. "Are you quitting on me?"

"What? No! I mean..." I pause, taking a seat across from her, not sure how to address the topic. "Have you ever thought about branching out?" I ask, suddenly very nervous.

"Branching out? In what way?"

"The business—have you ever thought about expanding it?"

Robynn seems surprised by my question. "Um, I entertained the idea a while back but never pursued it."

"Can I ask why?" I ask, fidgeting with the strap of my bag.

She shrugs. "Just too much work. Didn't seem worth it. What's this about?"

I take a deep breath, and the words come tumbling out. "I want to open a bookstore."

Robynn stares at me. "So, you are quitting? To be a competitor?"

"No! Not at all. I'd never do that to you."

"Then what are you talking about?"

"I found this retail space today—on my way here—freak accident. They're looking for a buyer or a long-term lease. It's the perfect spot for an extension of this bookstore."

"You want to open another location of this store?"

"Sort of. But I want to take a huge risk with it and narrow the market. I want it to be a romance bookstore. Filled with romance and smut and romantasy and everything in between to do with the topic."

Robynn sits back and looks at me, eyes narrowing. "That's a pretty narrow market, but on this year's top one hundred, they're pretty much all that—romance of some nature."

"That's what I've noticed too. And I think it's a great trend to jump on."

"But trends change. What do you plan to do when the trends change and people don't want romance anymore?"

I look at her like she can't be serious. "Robynn, people have always wanted romance books in one capacity or another. Besides, were the trends to somehow change, we could tailor the shop to it." I sit forward. "Look, I want to partner with you. I've been thinking about this for a while. I want to be your partner in this store—and I have the means to do so. But I think I want to do it by opening a secondary location that is themed." My stomach is flipping with nerves, having never done anything quite this bold before. Minutes pass as Robynn clicks around on her computer, not saying anything, and I take that as a sign that she's very much not interested. "Right, look, I'm sorry. That was out of the blue and so forward of me. Just forget it." I stand to leave when she stops me.

"Remy, wait." She gestures for me to sit back down. "I was just looking at the numbers from my accountant for the midyear review. They look good. Really good, actually. There's a lot of red tape and a lot of details to go over but..."—she pauses, smiling—"I really like the idea of partnering with you too. You've not been here long—but I can tell you're a good person and this is where you're supposed to be."

I smile, and apparently I'm crying—because why not? "Sorry," I say, wiping away the tears. "I've cried so much recently. These are at least happy tears. Robynn, this is so good to hear. I know we have so much to work out, but I'm just honored that you want to do this."

"We'll need to draw up a business plan, I'll need to get paperwork drawn up with my lawyers, and we have a lot to iron out—this isn't going to happen overnight, but I think this will be good.

I nod. "Me, too. In this short amount of time, you've become like family. And I know it won't happen overnight. Great things take time."

Kelly pops her head in the door. "Look, I don't want to interrupt or anything, but it's a zoo out here, and I could really use some backup. Remy, can you help, please? Oh, and some guy stopped by looking for you earlier."

My heart stutters. "Who? Who stopped by?"

Kelly shrugs. "Dunno, he just asked if you were working, and when I said 'no' he thanked me and left."

My head spins. Who the hell would be looking for me here?

"Remy? The help? Can I get some?"

"Yeah, of course, sorry." I jump up and turn for the door.

"Kelly, Remy—I think we should celebrate tonight," Robynn says, standing to follow us out.

"Celebrate what?" Kelly asks, confusion on her face.

"Remy joining the family."

"Pick up the shot glass—you're doing the damn shot!"

Robynn slams her hand on the table, giving me a stern look. After the closed sign had been flipped for the day, she'd sent us home to change and to meet at her favorite bar to celebrate. The music is loud, the people are plenty, and the drinks are strong.

"I've already done two!" I say, shouting over the music and voices. Thirsty Thursday plus Throwback Thursday has really drawn in a crowd.

"So? We all have. Do the shot." Robynn nudges the shot glass towards me, spilling some on the table.

"Shots! Shots! Shots!" Kelly shouts, her bubbly voice full of enthusiasm.

It pulls a laugh from me. "Fine!" I pick up the shot glass and toss it back, the spiced rum going down smooth. My head is a little fuzzy from the first two shots and my vodka cranberry.

"Ok, dancing time," Kelly yells as a Spice Girls song comes on.

Kelly grabs my hand as she pulls both of us towards the dance floor. Sweaty bodies push and pull to the rhythm of the music, moving around the dance floor in a whir of color and emotion.

I let the music consume me as we dance, all of us screaming out the lyrics. Kelly finds a dance partner, grinding up against the front of a guy who buries his face in her hair. Robynn keeps stepping on the foot of the girl behind her, and I can't hide my laughter as the girl keeps shooting dirty looks her way. I don't know how much time passes on the dance floor, but by the time we're stumbling back to the bar, my shirt is sticking to my skin and a sheen of sweat covers my face and neck.

"Shots!" Kelly shouts again, motioning to the bartender.

"You act like we're at sorority night," I laugh, as Kelly starts passing out the shots.

"Excuse me if it's been a long ass week and I need to let loose," Kelly says, downing her shot. "Besides, we're celebrating, right? Drink!"

Robynn and I shrug and toss back our shots, but before we even set our glasses down, Kelly is pushing another shot glass into our hands. I give her a look, and she laughs.

"Last one, promise." She winks, and we take the supposed last shot.

I'm really feeling the alcohol buzzing through my veins. I order a water and stumble over to an open table, perching on the barstool. My head drops into my hands, and I feel Robynn come up behind me, putting a hand on my back.

"You ok?"

I try to nod, but my head moves in a circle instead. Robynn chuckles and takes the seat next to me. I look up at her, and she doesn't look nearly as wasted as I feel. "Why aren't you more drunk?" I narrow my eyes at her, my words coming out a little slurred.

"For one, I can apparently handle my alcohol better than you, and for two, someone has to be the responsible adult."

"This was your idea!" I yell, throwing up my hands.

"You needed this, Remy."

"Yeah you did!" Kelly pipes up. "You needed to get out of your head and stop thinking about that guy."

Robynn shoots Kelly a look. "Bringing him up doesn't get him out of her head, Kelly."

"Right, sorry." Kelly pats my arm.

"It's fine, Kelly." I wave her off. "Talk about him, don't talk about him, I don't care. Who needs him?"

"Exactly!" Kelly shouts. "Although, I could definitely go for a hot British guy right about now," she says, looking around the bar as though one might materialize right in front of her.

"Kelly!" Robynn shoves her sister. "What the hell is wrong with you?"

"Joke! Damn, Robynn, calm down."

I pull my phone out and open my photos. I scroll backwards, time reversing to three months ago. I stop when I see the photo and tap it so it fills my screen. Oliver is standing on the balcony of Muriel's in New Orleans, his arms resting on the railing as he takes in the sights below. It's dusk in the photo, the lights are just starting to kick on, and he's illuminated in a way that makes his eyes shine bright, even in the fading light. I remember how at ease I was, how happy I felt, and how, when I watched him, my stomach dipped and my heart felt full. I feel arms wrap around my shoulders and a chin rests on my shoulder.

"Girl, you've got it bad...still," Robynn whispers in my ear. "Why are you fighting it?"

"He hurt me, Robynn. He broke the trust between us."

"So, find some damn super glue and fix it. You're all the time reading romance novels, and they all have their happily ever afters. Don't you think you deserve one?"

I just shrug and watch my phone go dark on the table. "There's a difference, Robynn. Those are fiction. They're not real. Things like that don't happen in real life."

"But things like that did happen to you, Remy. You had this gorgeous man dropped into your life. I know you're hurt, and I know you're scared, but I'm a firm believer in second chances. What do you have to lose? If he turns out to be the asshole you're scared he is, then, sure, you've wasted a little bit of time—but what have you gained? The ability to let him go, and the chance to finally truly heal. And if he turns out to not be the asshole you think he is, then you get your happily ever after." Robynn comes around to look me in the eyes. "Really, I just see a win-win situation for you here."

I sigh and stare at my phone on the table. The music swells, and the crowd around us gets louder. I look over to see Kelly bopping along to the music, a twisty straw to some fancy drink pressed between her lips. She looks at me and winks.

"I'm gonna go to the bathroom!" I shout over the music and stumble off my stool.

Robynn catches me and steadies me, sending me off in the right direction. Of course there's a line—because there's always a line for the bathroom at bars. I open my phone, and the picture is still on the screen. In a moment of bad drunken judgment, I find his number and send a text.

Remy

y did you half to turn out to b just like evry other mail guy

The music in the bar, while still loud, is muted by the walls of the z-shaped hallway. Instead of a text my phone starts ringing. "Shit," I say, staring down at it as it continues to ring. It stops but then starts up again. Sighing, I hit the answer button.

"Remy?" Oliver's tone is anxious, worried.

I don't say anything, feeling stupid for drunk texting him.

"Remy, are you there?" Concern colors his voice. "Remy? Is everything alright? Where are you? It's loud."

"Hi," I manage, still not sure what I was planning to say. My head is swimming with alcohol and memories as my eyes try to focus on the wall across from me.

"Are you ok? Your text—it didn't seem like you."

"Yeah, everything is fine." I stop and replay that sentence in my head, and suddenly I'm filled with anger. "You know what, Oliver? No, everything is not ok."

"What's wrong?" he asks.

"What's wrong? You're joking, right?" I spit the words out. As quickly as the anger arrived, it disappears, and I sigh into the phone. I lean my head back against the wall and close my eyes. "Oliver, do you remember that night in Nashville? After we'd gone up to bed, after I'd told you everything? Do you remember that night?"

Oliver clears his throat. "I remember," he says, so quietly I can barely hear him over the music.

"Do you remember how bad I felt that you were going to sleep on the couch? And I ended up letting you sleep in the bed?"

A soft laugh comes through the phone. "You were worried about me being cramped on the sofa."

I don't react to his words but push forward. "Do you remember lying there in the dark, there was an electricity in the air between us? And do you remember how you reached over and laced your fingers through mine?" I flex my fingers. "I still remember the feeling like you were just doing it five minutes ago. The way you tangled and untangled our fingers, our skin brushing against each other...it tickled and sent shivers through me. Do you remember that, Oliver?"

"I do," he says, quietly.

"In that one touch from you—after everything that had happened—I felt safe. I felt cared for." There's silence on the other end, so I go on. "I was just looking at a picture I took of you at Muriel's. You were leaning against the railing. Do you want to know what I remember about that moment?"

"Tell me, Remy," Oliver says gently.

"I remember feeling so full: full of happiness, full of butterflies, full of pure adoration for you in that moment, full of..." I trail off, not able to finish the sentence. People go around me as the line to the bathroom moves forward. I sink to the floor and sit there, waiting—for what, I'm not sure.

"Full of what, Remy?"

Instead of answering his question, I ask one of my own. "Why, Oliver? Why did this have to happen to us? Why did you do this to us?" I stop, another question coming to mind. "Do you still believe in fate?"

"I will always believe in fate. And I believe that fate did bring us together, that you were supposed to come into my life."

I can tell he's sincere, but I somehow can't bring myself to care. "In a pretty twisted way, if you ask me," I spit out.

"So, you believe fate brought us together, too?" Oliver asks, and I hear that hint of hope in his voice.

"I don't know what I believe, Oliver. Honestly, I'm drunk right now, sitting on the dirty floor of a bar in line for the bathroom."

"I gathered you may have been sloshed from your text."

"Thank you, Captain Obvious," I say.

"Why did you text me, Remy?"

Because I'm in love with you, I think to myself, and my throat tightens. *Because I wish you weren't all the way in England right now. Because I need to feel your arms wrapped around me again. Because I need to feel the kind of stillness I've only ever felt when I'm with you.*

But I don't say any of those things out loud. "Chalk it up to drunkenness," I say. "Sorry I bothered you."

"You aren't—"

"Bye, Oliver," I cut in and hang up before he can respond.

Chapter Thirty

Robynn sets another box down next to me on the floor. "Did you have to set that down so loudly?" I ask, holding my head in my hands.

"Hung over much?" Robynn asks, laughing.

I groan and nod. "It's not fair...you had just as much as I did, and you're fine."

"You just think I had as much as you did. Someone had to be the responsible one in the group—and it wasn't going to be my sister. The bartender is a friend. They know if I come in with Kelly, that after the first shot to just give me water." Robynn walks away and comes back a minute later. She nudges me with her shoe. "Here, take these and drink this." She hands me two Tylenol and a bottle of water.

"Thanks. Also, that's dirty, pretending to take shots." I sound like a whiny child who was just tucked back into bed by their mom after being sick.

"This"—Robynn kicks the box next to me—"is the last of the new James Patterson books. Can you get them out on display in the front left window for me? I'm going to take my lunch break."

"Yeah, sure. I just need to finish stocking these Colleen Hoover books. How is that man still writing? He has like a billion books out by now, right?"

"Something like that," Robynn says. "I'll be back in about an hour."

I nod again, resting my head in my hand.

"Just make sure you pull yourself together if you hear the bell chime. You got lucky with a slow day today." Robynn starts to walk away.

"You only have yourself to blame for this," I call after her. "It was your idea."

She laughs and vanishes through the storeroom door. I take the Tylenol and chase it down with the water, giving myself a few more minutes on the floor before I pull myself up, my stiff legs protesting from sitting in the same spot for too long. Just as I get stretched out, I hear the bell above the door chime and inwardly groan.

"Welcome to Bookology, I'll be right there," I call out in the most cheerful voice I can muster. I weave my way through the store dodging cushy armchairs and squat coffee tables. "Sorry to make you wait," I call out, almost to the counter.

As I come into the front of the store, I see the backside of a man standing at the counter, and as he hears my approaching footsteps, he turns—and I freeze. I stare blankly as Oliver's mouth crawls into a sheepish half-smile. The shrug of his shoulders and expression says 'what can I say?'.

"Oliver? What are you doing here?" I must have forgotten how to breathe because the words come out barely a whisper as I force myself to take a breath in.

He shrugs again, shaking his head. Maybe he's having as much trouble speaking as I am. I take him in. He's the same and yet different. His eyes are still impossibly blue and the dimples are still there, just hidden under a thin layer of beard where he was once clean-shaven. My eyes roam over his body, and I swallow—my body still well aware of exactly what is underneath those clothes.

I have the urge to curl into his arms and smack him all at the same time. My eyes find their way back up to his face and there's something there that wasn't before. Something I can't quite put my finger on.

Oliver finally finds his words. "I needed to see you. I needed to talk to you. After the phone call last night—"

"Wait, phone call?" I ask, confused.

"You called me last night, don't you remember?"

Dammit. I drop my head. The bar. The drinks. I must have been *that* girl and drunk dialed him. "Right, I called you. Last night. Right."

"You don't remember, do you?" Oliver asks, shaking his head. "You told me you were at a bar drinking. Blimey, did you—did you drunk dial me?"

"It would appear so," I say, running a hand through my hair. What was I thinking? What was Robynn thinking not taking my phone away from me?

"Anyways, after the phone call last night and the way we left things, it's tearing me up inside." He actually puts a hand to his heart.

"Funny, I thought we'd said all there was to say in New Orleans." The words come out cold. "Did you ever stop to think about what I need, Oliver?" I turn away from him, making my way back through the store. I hear his footsteps on the wood floors behind me. "Duck," I say, stepping through a doorway into the next area.

"Huh?" Oliver's confusion is followed by a loud thunk. "Ow! Bloody hell!"

I turn to see him rubbing his forehead, staring up at the door jam. "I told you to duck." I turn and grab the box of James Patterson books, moving towards the display in the front window.

"Remy, please just stop and talk to me. You seemed pretty chatty last night."

I throw a glare over my shoulder at him.

"Or let me talk. Blimey, let me explain."

I laugh and shake my head. I pull books from the box and place them in book stands, neatly arranging them so they're all visible. "I think I heard plenty of your explanation in New Orleans. As for last night, that was a mistake."

"Remy, please?"

"I'd ask how you knew where to find me, but you probably just asked Gage when you picked up your check."

Oliver winces but not from the pain of hitting his head. My words are like a slap across his face. Shame washes over him—but something else too. "Actually, you told me where you were."

"Of course I did," I mutter to myself. "Because I'm one Chatty Kathy when the alcohol is flowing." I look at him and still see something else he's not saying. "What?"

"I didn't pick up the check," he whispers, staring at the floor.

"What do you mean?" I look around the shop, searching for an explanation. "Was it direct deposit? Venmo? Paypal?" He shakes his head. "Wait, did that asshole back out because he didn't get me?" I laugh bitterly. "Sounds about right." I turn back to the display. "Look, I'll make sure you get your money."

When no reply comes, I turn to make sure he's still there. Oliver is running his hands through his hair and down his face, shaking his head. He clasps his hands behind his head, closing his eyes.

"Oliver?"

"I don't need the money, Remy."

I watch as his face seems to age as the grief tries to take over, and that's when I realize what I'd been seeing in his face before, hiding just beneath the surface. "Oh, Oliver, I'm—"

"Don't," he cuts me off, holding up both of his hands. "If you tell me you're sorry, I'm not sure I'll keep my shit together—and I really just want to get out what I came here to say." Oliver takes a deep breath through his nose, holds it, and slowly releases it. He opens his eyes and looks at me, and I see the pain. "Remy, don't you understand I don't give a damn about the money? Even if she..." he trails off, his jaw clenching and unclenching. He looks out the window before beginning again. "It hasn't been about the money since I got on that train to Chicago."

"You earned it, though." As the words leave my mouth, I hate that I say them.

"Do you really believe that?" Oliver asks. "Do you really believe that I earned it? I was hired to make sure Gage got you back. Pretty sure I failed at that. Would you say you earned your paycheck if you managed to send a highly anticipated batch of novels to another city?"

I raise an eyebrow. "I'm sorry, but did you just compare me to a shipment of books?"

Oliver pauses. "S'pose I did, yeah. But a highly anticipated shipment. I sort of managed to send you to another city and then another and another."

"Weird comparison," I say, shaking it off.

Oliver huffs. "You get my meaning, yeah?"

I ignore his question and ask my own. "Why did you help me? Why did you let me leave Chicago?"

The truth blazes from Oliver's eyes without him having to say a word. I look away not sure what to say next.

"Can I continue?" Oliver pleads, sidestepping to try and look me in the eyes.

I sit in the window, my arms crossed, and nod.

Oliver takes another deep breath, as though steadying himself. "You know why I agreed to take the job—if that's what you want to call it."

"You wanted—"

Oliver holds a hand up. "Please?"

I close my mouth and zip it closed, handing him the key.

"I was in a panic and desperate," Oliver continues. "I was willing to do anything at that point. I wanted to be able to show up to my mum's and tell her everything was going to be ok. I didn't know what I was getting myself into when I agreed to this. I knew the idea of following around some woman I didn't know felt creepy, invasive, and wrong. But, again, I was so desperate, and I had no other options. But when I first saw you..." Oliver stops, a smile spreading across his face, a chuckle shaking his shoulders.

I straighten up, suddenly self-conscious, and give him a quizzical look. When Oliver continues to just stand there smiling, I push off the window seat and move closer to him, my eyes narrowing. I point to my lips, reminding him that I've sealed them, and then raise my eyebrows in question again.

"It was about"—Oliver ponders it, looking up at the ceiling—"well, four months ago now, on a Saturday. I can still remember it like it was yesterday. It was a really pretty spring day, the kind that you can't just stay inside for. Gage mentioned you were supposed to be meeting your dad for coffee that day and that your favorite spot was in the park. He thought it might be weird having me stand outside your building."

I grab for the invisible key in his hand and unzip my lips. "Well, we wouldn't want it to be weird." I roll my eyes but rezip my lips, handing him back the key.

He smiles, shaking his head. "Anyways, when I first saw you, you were standing at a hotdog cart. Your hair was in this messy knot on top of your head, and you were in a sweatshirt and pants like those." He points to my workout pants. "I think the only makeup you had one was whatever was leftover from the day before. It didn't look bad, just worn," he rushes to say. "So then the vendor asked what you wanted on your hotdog, and you stood there, contemplating, and you bit your lip and got this cute little crease, right here." Oliver reaches out and touches the spot between my eyebrows. "I never thought choosing hotdog toppings could be such a difficult process—but it was for you. You finally settled on ketchup, mustard, and just a hint of relish. You sometimes didn't like relish, you told the guy, but thought you might be in the mood for it. Bloke didn't seem remotely interested in what you had to say."

I narrow my eyes, trying to remember the day he's talking about. I pull a memory from my mind.

"So, you got your hotdog and found a bench to sit on, and you started eatin' it. Everyone who passed by, you gave them this, I dunno, encouraging smile. Like you were giving them the silent words of encouragement they each needed to hear. Then..."—Oliver stops and chuckles again—"this stinkin' squirrel came down out of the tree behind you and sat on the arm of the bench. You looked over at it, and you started having a conversation with it. I thought, 'This girl must be bonkers'. But the squirrel just sat there and seemed to listen. You tore tiny pieces of your bread off and set them on the bench while carrying on talking to the squirrel. You told him how simple his life must be. I stood there watching you be totally and completely what I've come to realize is the real you. So adorable and just authentic. That's when I knew..." Oliver stops and shakes his head, turning and walking back through the store to the counter.

I think back on that day. Where had he been? Another memory tugs at my mind. His Instagram had a picture of a squirrel. I follow him to the front of the store and hold out my hand for the key. He hands it over, and I unzip my lips. "That's when you knew what? That you were in for a boring time following around some lunatic that talks to squirrels on park benches?"

Oliver spins around and walks back to me, coming inches from my face. My breath hitches.

"That's when I realized I wanted to know you, like really know you. All it took was twenty minutes in a park to realize something Gage had never realized in all those years."

"And what's that?" I whisper.

He looks at me, questioningly, like 'How can you really not know?'. "Just how special you are," he says.

I look away, and when I bring my eyes back to Oliver, he's staring at me with such intensity. "In the train station," he continues, "I knew. I made up my mind on the train. I saw you sleeping—and the way the sun hit your face illuminating your beauty, I just knew. I could never take Gage's money, but I didn't want to lose you. The candy shop, that truly was coincidence. Fate maybe? After you left the coffee shop, I was just going to let you go. But then...then I found you in that tiny candy store, and I knew I had to tell you the truth and hold on to you for dear life. I tried to tell you in Indianapolis and in Nashville. I didn't want to lie to you anymore. Hell, I didn't want to lie to you after that first day in the park. I knew you deserved better. You have to believe me when I say that hurting you was never my intention."

"And yet...here we are," I say, forcing myself not to cry.

He's close enough that I can hear his heart beating, fast and hard. His eyes search mine, desperate. I want so badly to tell him that I understand and that I forgive him. I want to lift up onto my toes and touch my lips to his and feel his arms wrap around me. I want to hear the words I know must be on the tip of his tongue. But something stops me. Because he hadn't told me. He'd known I deserved better, but he still hadn't found the time or made the way to tell me. He'd just gone ahead and betrayed me and lied to me! So how can I ever completely trust him now? How can I ever? Do I really want a relationship that is built on lies? Just look at my parents!

"Remy, I—"

"Don't." I stop him before the words can fall from his mouth. I close my eyes and step backwards. "Look, I understand that you did it because you were desperate. If I had been in that situation, I'm honestly not sure what I would have done. But, Oliver"—I shake my head—"I can't do this with you. I—we...can't be a thing. I can't follow in the footsteps of my parents, you have to understand that."

"Remy, you put your trust in a total stranger in the train station, but you won't trust me now? You know me."

"Do I though? I thought I knew you—but you hurt me, Oliver. I've spent my whole life wrapped up in lies and bullshit. It's time I live my life for me."

Oliver's eyes plead with me to believe that the words coming from his mouth are true. I shake my head, trying to keep the tears from coming. I've cried so much in the last few months that I don't know how I have any tears left. Oliver's eyes fall closed and his shoulders sag as he slowly nods. He steps back, opening his eyes and giving me a sad smile. He looks out the window, to the square, to the people milling about.

"Did you find it, Remy?"

"Find what?"

"The place where beauty never fades?"

I follow his gaze, looking out at the city I've come to call home. The one that welcomed me with open arms and gave me a soft landing after such a bumpy ride. The sun filters down through the mossy oaks, the moss blowing in the breeze. "Yeah, I think I have," I say, softly.

Oliver just nods, swallowing hard. He opens his mouth a couple more times to speak, but closes it again, and nods. He turns and walks out of the shop, and I feel my already cracked heart shatter.

To be Continued...

Book Two

Preview

Chapter One

Chapter One

"Can you go any faster, Mate?" I tap the front seat of the Uber as it seems to crawl through traffic.

The driver shoots me an annoyed look. "Would you like to try and drive then?" he asks, honking at a car that just cut him off. When I don't answer, he nods. "Right then, that's what I thought. You know you're all the same. 'Go faster. Can't we go any quicker?' I'm doing my bloody best."

"Right, sorry. I wasn't trying to be a wanker." I lean back and try to settle my nerves, but my knee starts to bounce. I blow out a breath and try to focus on the people outside my window, but then my phone rings. I fumble trying to get it out of my pocket, and it falls onto the floor behind the driver's seat, still ringing.

"You going to get that or just let us all be lulled to sleep by it?"

I finally snatch it up and slide to answer without even looking at it. "Hello?"

"Oliver? Where are you?"

I pull the phone away from my ear to look at the caller ID and roll my eyes. "I'm in the Uber, Sophie. What do you want?"

"Why are you in an Uber? Why didn't you take the tube?"

I sigh. "If you'd bothered to look, there was a delay on the tube, and I'd be running even more behind had I taken it."

"You're not at the airport? What time did the plane land?"

I look at my watch and wince. "It landed five minutes ago."

Sophie scoffs at the other end. "How far out are you?"

I glance at the driver, debating if he'll kick me to the curb right here if I criticize his driving again. "Traffic sucks," I say to Sophie, "We're probably ten to fifteen minutes out."

"You need to let her know you're still coming to pick her up. She'll think you chickened out or something."

I sigh and run a hand through my hair, my stomach already a twist of knotted nerves.

"Oliver? Did you hear me?"

"I heard you, Sophie. I've got it handled. Don't you have a wedding to worry about?"

"Probably. But I have an older brother to worry about too."

I smile and shake my head. "It's my job to be worrying about you. Go fluff your dress or something," I tease.

"You suck. I hope she doesn't show," she teases back.

"Bye, Sophie."

"Text her!" she yells before I end the call.

I tap my phone against my knee, wondering if she's right. Should I send her a text just to let her know I'm running late? I look at the app and see we're still ten minutes out. I open my messages and find her name.

Oliver

On my way, traffic is horrid. Meet you where we agreed.

I wait for a reply, but nothing comes through. Maybe she doesn't have her phone on yet, or maybe her phone is buried in her bag and she didn't feel it go off, or maybe it's dead. Maybe she never got on the plane. What if she decided this whole thing was a bad idea? My stomach clenches as a new wave of nerves rolls through me. I have to blow out another breath to try and calm myself down, but just like the first one, it does no good.

The Uber driver finally merges into the lane that leads to the pick-up area of the airport. We follow a line of cars that are slowly creeping towards the designated area. Finally, when we're close enough, I jump out of the car. I hear the window sliding down behind me.

"So, five stars then, mate?"

"Right, sure, whatever." I look down at the app and hit five stars and wave at him before jogging towards the doors of the airport.

My heart is pounding, and I feel sweat prickling on the back of my neck. I duck into the loo and grab a paper towel, wetting it with cold water, and press it into the back of my neck. I take a deep breath in through my nose, and then let it out through my mouth. I grab another paper towel and dry off the back of my neck. I lean against the sink and look at my reflection in the mirror. The nerves shine through, and I close my eyes, trying to will the nerves away.

"Buck up, Oliver. It's going to be fine. She wouldn't be coming if she didn't want to see you." I stop talking when I realize the man next to me has stopped washing his hands to stare at me. "Sorry," I mutter and leave.

I follow the signage that leads me to where the passengers should be coming from their flights. I can see the giant boards ahead that display the incoming and outgoing flights. As I get closer, I start searching for her flight. I stop in front of the board, my eyes roaming over it, trying to find the one I need. Maybe her plane hasn't landed yet. Maybe it was delayed. I peer around and don't spot the flash of red hair. She isn't coming. I just know it. She bailed on me.

"Excuse me."

I freeze at the voice behind me. My heart literally skips a beat—and I think it might have forgotten how to function.

"I think I've gone and missed my flight," the voice says.

An uncontrollable smile spreads across my face as memories float through my mind. I close my eyes, breathe out, and slowly turn around, opening my eyes. There standing in front of me, her red hair a tangled mess from the flight, a sheepish smile on her face, is...

"Remy," I breathe out, truly feeling like, for the first time in a year, I can really breathe.

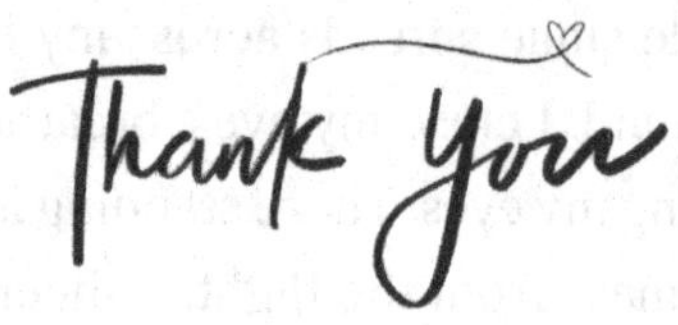

If anyone ever tells you that writing a book is easy...they are lying. A book takes a lot of hard work, time, dedication, and most importantly, a support team that is there cheering you on each step of the way. Seven years ago, when I started this book, all I really had to go on was some girl named Remy yelling in my head about needing to escape the life she was imprisoned in. I needed to know more, so, I let Remy tell me her story.

I want to thank my husband for being there every step of the way; for "putting up" with road trips and vacations for research, for enduring bizarre questions and 'hey can you Google...' requests, meltdowns, and happy dances and everything in between. You have truly been my number one supporter of this book and in all that I do. I love you, like a mad weasel.

To my mom I want to say thank you. Thank you for always supporting me to do my best, be my best, and to always go after what I want. You were there, reading my work, when I was just a child aspiring to be an author. I promise Mom, I've gotten better.

One person has been my biggest fan throughout this entire process: Heidi, thank you. First drafts are never pretty, nor are second and third ones, but you read them. You answered my random questions of 'what if...' and 'do you think...'. You have always begged for more of the book, always wanting to know what was going to happen next.

Another big thank you to my editors for all their hard work. You both seemed to think I was going to murder you for pointing out how terrible I am with punctuation. But, as I said before, I shouldn't be allowed to write without adult supervision. Thanks for all the commas.

To all my other readers out there, who read the early drafts and gave your feedback, I can't thank you enough. Having that unbiased opinion on my work truly has made me a stronger writer.

Thank you to the coffee shops that helped make this happen. Main Street Coffee and Hopscotch Coffee supplied me with copious amounts of coffee and provided me with the perfect atmosphere for writing.

Finally, to all of the readers who go on this adventure with Remy, thank you for letting her share her story with you.

Remember, there will always be a place where beauty never fades, you just have to find it.

ABOUT THE AUTHOR

Nikota is an emerging author whose debut novel marks the beginning of an exciting literary journey. Fueled by a lifelong passion for storytelling, she's the kind of writer who'd jot down plot ideas on napkins if inspiration struck mid-adventure. When she's not working at her day job as a librarian or writing, you'll find her traveling, snapping photos, or surrounded by her husband and a small menagerie of pets—all of whom think she's writing about them. (Spoiler: She's not.) And she firmly believes a really good pizza will solve just about anything.